Readers love
KATE MCMURRAY

The Boy Next Door

"The story was unique and not something I've read over and over, which is refreshing!"

—Alpha Book Club

"I was completely captivated by this book."

—Inked Rainbow Reads

Out in the Field

"I loved it all over again and it remains firmly on my absolute favorites shelf. Baseball romance perfection."

—Gay Book Reviews

"…you'll be able to appreciate this as a wonderful romance between two sexy, sweet men who just want to be able to love who they want on their own terms and are willing to fight for it."

—The Novel Approach

By KATE MCMURRAY

Blind Items
Devin December
Four Corners
Kindling Fire with Snow
Out in the Field
Playing Ball (Multiple Author Anthology)
The Stars That Tremble • The Silence of the Stars
There Has to Be a Reason
A Walk in the Dark
What There Is
When the Planets Align

DREAMSPUN DESIRES
#14 – The Greek Tycoon's Green Card Groom

THE RAINBOW LEAGUE
The Windup
Thrown a Curve
The Long Slide Home

Published by DREAMSPINNER PRESS
www.dreamspinnerpress.com

THERE HAS TO BE A REASON

KATE McMURRAY

Published by

DREAMSPINNER PRESS

5032 Capital Circle SW, Suite 2, PMB# 279, Tallahassee, FL 32305-7886 USA
www.dreamspinnerpress.com

There Has to Be a Reason
© 2017 Kate McMurray.

Cover Art
© 2017 Aaron Anderson.
aaronbydesign55@gmail.com
Cover content is for illustrative purposes only and any person depicted on the cover is a model.

ISBN: 978-1-63533-211-7
Digital ISBN: 978-1-63533-212-4
Library of Congress Control Number: 2016915170
Published January 2017
v. 1.0

Printed in the United States of America
(∞)
This paper meets the requirements of
ANSI/NISO Z39.48-1992 (Permanence of Paper).

CHAPTER 1

THE FIRST genuine spring day inspired everyone to congregate on the North Quad. It wasn't even that warm, but girls in bikinis were sunbathing in clusters. Peppered around them were kids sitting with books open in their laps as they studied. A lively game of ultimate Frisbee kept threatening to take out one of those lounging students with a flying disk to the head.

Joe and I had gotten a halfhearted game of touch football going, but we didn't have enough space to do more than toss a ball around. There were too many other kids taking up the grassy parts of the quad to score actual touchdowns.

Kareem called a time-out and ran over to me, panting and clasping his stomach.

"You all right, man?" I asked.

Kareem nodded. "Yeah. Shouldn't have eaten all those fries at lunch."

Joe approached, looking annoyed. "Where the hell did all these people come from?" he asked in his Southie accent. "I mean, did you see that pass? Mike would have caught it if he hadn't gotten tripped by the girl over there."

Joe pointed. Kareem and I followed his finger. There was, indeed, a girl. She wore a tight tank top and very short shorts sitting on a My Little Pony blanket and grinning up at Mike. He grinned right back. I suspected he hadn't tripped so much as gotten distracted by the girl's ample cleavage.

"I think the game's over, guys," said Kareem.

"I should get to class anyway," I said, pulling my shirt from the belt loop I'd shoved it in earlier and putting it back on.

"Psshh, class," said Joe. He waved his hand as if class were a trifle and not most of the reason we were all encamped at Western Massachusetts University. "You want to get dinner later, Dave?"

"Sorry, bro," I said, scanning the grass for my ball cap, which had flown off my head when I'd made a beautiful running catch. "Going out with Britney tonight."

Joe and Kareem both nodded appreciatively. It was generally agreed Britney had… assets. I'd been dating her for about three weeks, and though we hadn't slept together yet, I felt good about that night. Really, "going out" meant we'd probably eat cheeseburgers at the Mac and then go back to her room to "watch a movie."

I retrieved my hat and told Joe and Kareem I'd meet them later. Kareem patted my back and wished me luck while Joe informed me he'd be cutting his chem class because the weather was too beautiful to be inside. I waved and loped off across the quad so I could stop by my dorm room to get my books.

Class was… class. I always found it hard to concentrate once the weather finally turned warm. The winter had been particularly terrible, even by New England standards; a series of blizzards had dumped several feet of snow, and the constant brutal cold between January and mid-March meant it took forever to melt. Then a surprise storm on April 3 had dropped two more feet of the white stuff on us, and I was quite done with winter, thank you. We'd had a few spring teaser days, but this day was truly gorgeous, sunny, and warm enough to wear shorts.

Not to mention all the eye candy sunbathing on every available bit of grass across campus.

But I needed an A in this class to maintain my GPA—I had to have at least a 3.5 to keep one of my scholarships—so I listened to the professor drone on about… something. The class was a seminar on literary autobiographies, and the one we'd just read—about an Irish immigrant woman who had moved to the States in the late nineteenth century—was so boring it could induce narcolepsy, so I had a hard time getting invested. I wrote down whatever words from the professor filtered through my hazy brain so it would look like I was diligently taking notes. I was overjoyed when class finally ended.

Britney texted me as I walked out of the class, instructing me to meet her at the Mac at five. I glanced at my watch. I had just shy of thirty minutes to get there. That gave me only enough time to go to my dorm, put on clothes that didn't smell like sweat and football, and meet her.

But first I had to pee.

I slipped into the restroom at the end of the corridor on the third floor of Dickenson Hall and took care of business. As I zipped up, I heard a strange mewling sound. At first I thought it might have been a cat. I quickly realized how silly that was, so I called out, "Hey, man, are you okay?"

A distinctive sniffing sound filtered out through a stall door. Then: "Uh, yeah. Fine."

"'Kay." I didn't want to just leave a guy there if he was genuinely hurt or whatever, so I added, "Uh, if you need something…."

One of the stall doors opened and out came a tall blond guy with a tearstained face. He walked to one of the sinks and washed his hands.

Now, I'd been a dude my whole life, so I knew better than to ask another dude what he'd been crying about. I decided to ignore him as I washed my hands and threw my bag back over my shoulder. I stepped toward the door, but something in his body language held me back. He seemed… wrecked.

I glanced at his reflection in the mirror. His hair was so blond it was nearly white, and it was kind of wispy, cut short on the sides but long on top, falling in a soft swoop over his forehead. He was really pale, too, with pinkish skin and red-rimmed blue eyes. He was thin but not skinny, like he probably ate plenty but had a zippy metabolism.

The thought popped into my head: *God, he's pretty.*

Of all the inappropriate things. I shook my head and moved to leave again, but he looked devastated, so I stopped and said, "You all right?"

He sniffed and nodded. "Fine."

"Okay. I mean, I don't want to pry, but you don't really look okay. Tell me to fuck off if you want, but if you need help with something…."

He turned and looked at me. It struck me again just how pretty he was. Beautiful, even. Definitely a dude; he had a long nose and a square jaw and a defined chest. His body was like an extended straight line. He had long arms and prominent elbows, kind of like someone had taken a smaller guy and stretched him out. He stood taller than me, but he seemed smaller, somehow. But, yeah, definitely a guy, nothing especially feminine about him, unless you counted the pouty lips and the….

What the hell was I doing looking at a guy's lips?

Britney. I had a date in less than half an hour with Britney, and we were finally going to get naked together, something I'd wanted all semester.

Right?

The blond guy rubbed his eyes. "It's… yeah. Thanks. Just a shitty day."

"We've all had those." I sighed. The words sounded stupid and meaningless coming out of my mouth. "Ah, well. Anyway. I should go. I've got a… thing." I pointed at the door.

He nodded and smiled faintly. "Thank you."

I had done exactly nothing except be a nosy asshole, so I shrugged. Then, and I didn't even know why, I said, "I'm Dave, by the way."

"I'm Noel."

"Well. Maybe next time we run into each other it'll be… uh, better circumstances."

And then I left because I'd already wasted enough time.

THE MAC was basically the heart of the WMU campus. Once upon a time, it was MacGregor Hall, the university's first classroom building, but by the time I got there, it had been renovated so many times only parts of the original husk remained. It had become kind of an all-purpose student center, with meeting rooms, a huge auditorium, and a couple of little shops. A restaurant, also called the Mac, took up most of the first floor. I was pretty sure every WMU student breezed through the building at least once a day.

Britney already had a table because talking to Noel had made me ten minutes late. We awkwardly negotiated who would monitor the table and who would get dinner from the counter, but eventually we sat down together and she smiled at me.

Britney was on the petite side. She had long, shiny brown hair that I knew from experience was even softer than it looked, and a tight body she maintained by teaching aerobics to undergrads two nights a week. She was pretty, if not conventionally so, with a wide face and a lot of freckles. That evening she wore a WMU T-shirt and a very tight pair of jeans, pretty much how she always dressed. It was one of the things I liked about her; she wasn't super girly, didn't seem to go for a lot of pink frills or fashion or hair products or any of that. Not that there's anything wrong with any of those things; she was just so naturally pretty she didn't need a lot of flash covering it up. I had never seen her wearing makeup or a dress, and she kept her hair simple, the ponytail she currently sported being the most involved her style ever got. But she was objectively hot if you were into boobs and hips; Joe greatly admired her ass, for example, and probably would have asked her out himself if he hadn't had a girlfriend.

No, it had been me who got a little too blitzed on cheap light beer at a frat party and wound up making out with her on a grody sofa, serenaded by the dulcet tones of the bland but loud hip-hop that frat party DJs seemed to prefer. Britney had a lovely heart-shaped face too, and really long eyelashes. Easy on the eyes all around, in other words. So I got drunk that night and thought, *Hey, why not?*

Three weeks of casual dates like this, plus a couple of make-out sessions on the couch in the lounge down the hall from my dorm room, had given me enough evidence to prove I liked her. At least as a person. I was still working out if my goal for this date was driven by a desire to have sex with Britney or a desire to have sex generally. As I looked at her across the table, I was charmed, but she didn't quite light my loins on fire, and I worried it was more general horniness than anything else motivating my actions. That made me feel like a jerk.

Or, what really made me feel like a jerk was that my thoughts kept straying to poor Noel. What had he been crying about? Why had I found his appearance so stunning?

I managed to stay engaged enough in conversation that Britney didn't seem to notice she didn't have my undivided attention. We ate burgers and drank milk shakes, and then she not at all subtly said, "My roommate's gone for the night," and then we were walking back to her dorm.

I was into it, though. She held my hand as we walked, and I liked the way her small hand fit into my larger one. She really did have a very nice ass, well displayed by her jeans; I made a point to look. I made a joke involving a movie reference she didn't get—somehow she'd never seen *Beetlejuice*—but she said, "No, that's a funny line," and giggled anyway. We chatted about people we knew and how much she hated her psych class that I'd taken the previous semester, and she was funny and smart and all those good things. Once we got back to her room, I was happy to watch her take her clothes off.

A half hour later, I was on the receiving end of a pretty good blow job, but I wasn't quite getting there. I could tell she was getting a little frustrated. I leaned back on the bed and closed my eyes and…

Noel.

I thought about how his shirt had hung from his shoulders, about how flat his chest was, about what might have been lurking beneath his jeans. I thought about his blue eyes and pink skin and how soft his blond hair probably was. I thought about what it might be like to touch him, how his skin would be warm and soft, his lips pillowy, what it might be like to kiss him—

And pow, just like that, I was coming in Britney's mouth.

Afterward she leaned back and grinned at me. "Stay the night?"

Normally I would've been on board to accept her invitation for more, but Noel entering my mind during the blow job had freaked me right out. Thinking about a guy during sex wasn't something I did… well, ever, really. And this was not just a stray thought; I had mentally stripped him and that finally pushed me over the edge. What the hell did this mean?

I hopped out of bed and started pulling my clothes back on.

"What the hell?" Britney said. "Did I do something?"

"No! No, I just… I have a thing… um, test. Tomorrow. Just remembered. Gotta go study." I didn't think it would be fair to Britney to stick around if I had the nervous breakdown I could feel coming. Suddenly my need to get out of Britney's room—which was uncharacteristically feminine, with the kitten posters on the wall and the pink bedspread and the faint smell of flowers—was urgent.

I was fucking this up so hard, and I knew it, and Britney was never going to talk to me again.

"What class is the test in?" she asked.

"Uh. Film studies."

"Oh, with Carlucci, right? Italian Cinema? I took that class last semester. Maybe I can help you study."

She rose to her knees on the bed. She had made the bold choice not to put her clothes back on, and her breasts were perky and exposed and *right there*. I walked over to her and, as if compelled by some force beyond my control, I put my hands on her waist. She put her hands behind my neck and pressed her body against mine.

She was so… naked.

"Uh, yeah, that's the class." Wait… *did* I have an exam? This was all very confusing. I tried to think fast. "I'd love your help, but if I stay here, we're just going to make out, and then I won't study because no guy can resist a naked girl, and then I'll flunk the test, and then I'll lose my scholarship, and you don't really want to be responsible for that, do you?" I kissed her as if to emphasize my point. She still kind of tasted like french fries. Well, and like me. Not the most pleasant kiss I'd ever had.

"You sure you can't stay a little while longer?"

"You *are* naked," I said, "which is a compelling argument, but I really gotta go. I'm so sorry, Brit."

A few kisses and several minutes later, I managed to escape. I didn't think Britney was too angry, and I hoped whatever madness had overtaken me was temporary, hormones and fatigue mixing together in lethal ways or something.

When I got back to my room, Joe was there. He sat on the bed with his organic chemistry book open in his lap, but the baseball game on the television had snared his attention.

"Sox are up three in the eighth," he said as I walked in. "I take it your night was not a home run?"

It was going to be hard to have a nervous breakdown with Joe in the room. "Ah, it went pretty well, actually. There was nudity."

Joe nodded but didn't look away from the TV. "What are you doing back here, then?"

"Oh, you know. We're taking things slow."

Joe seemed to understand that. He nodded again.

I sat on my bed and looked at the TV. I quietly freaked out.

CHAPTER 2

SO THAT happened. April continued to bring us lovely, distracting weather. I continued to go out with Britney, but we didn't have many opportunities to be alone together, for which I felt strangely relieved. One afternoon we did end up alone and making out on my bed, but some circuits had clearly gotten crossed in my brain, because now making out with Britney made me think of Noel and the strange afternoon when I'd found him crying, and that was fucking weird.

So things weren't going well, and the humane thing probably would have been to break up with her, at least until I got my head screwed on straight, but what was I going to say? "Sorry, but every time we make out, I keep thinking about this guy I met one time"?

It was stupid. First of all, I was straight. I liked women. I'd been with quite a few in the nearly three years I'd been in college. I liked Britney, was attracted to her, but this… this was not working.

Probably the Noel thing was an escape hatch. I hadn't really been feeling Britney for whatever reason—lack of chemistry, too much peer pressure from my friends who thought we should go out together, I was just not that into her, whatever—so I looked for a convenient exit. On paper we should have worked, though, so I wasn't quite ready to call it quits yet, hoping whatever was wrong with me would pass. Temporary insanity. I'd get over myself.

Then something very strange happened in my English class.

Well, not strange. Exactly what should have happened in English class. We were assigned a book to read. It was just strange for me.

Professor Strong strolled into class one afternoon and smiled at us all. "I have good news."

The room filled with the din of suppressed groans. Good news for Professor Strong was probably bad news for us, like an extra homework assignment or something. We were wrapping up our discussion of *Maus* and were next scheduled to read a book called *In the Wind* by some guy named Jerry Grossworth. I had no idea what the book was about.

"I just confirmed this afternoon," Professor Strong said in her sultry New York–accented voice, "Jerry Grossworth is coming to campus in three weeks. I've arranged for him to do a special presentation just for this class. Isn't that great?" she gushed.

My classmates gave a tepid response.

Professor Strong clucked her tongue and waved her hand. "You'll be excited after you read the book."

When I got back to my room a little while later, I pulled the book off my shelf, where it sat with a handful of other slightly used paperbacks I'd purchased from the campus bookstore at the beginning of the semester. According to the text on the back, *In the Wind* was a coming-of-age story about a boy who grew up in an ultraconservative household and had to overcome a lot of the preconceived notions he was raised with in order to cope with the real world. In other words, according to the cover copy, he had to let go of his past and let it float away "in the wind." One of the critics blurbed on the cover called it one of the most important LGBT books of the decade, so I supposed this guy had grown up conservative and then discovered he was gay or something.

Not a new story, exactly, but something about it piqued my interest.

Without consciously setting out to do so, I opened the book and started to read.

I wasn't any closer to discovering Mr. Grossworth's personal revelation, the big one that caused him to question his upbringing, when Joe came home. I'd been reading about what it was like to grow up with a preacher father in the Deep South, which was fascinating to me as a kid who had grown up in the Boston suburbs with hippie parents. Jerry Grossworth and I had grown up on different planets. The book had sucked me in. So the interruption of Joe's triumphant return to the room irked me.

Joe dropped his backpack on his bed and looked at me. "Earth to Dave."

"What?" I asked.

"I've never seen you so riveted to a book before. Are there naked women on those pages?"

"No. What?"

Joe raised his eyebrows and shook his head. "I've got an exam in the morning. Come with me to the Mac for some protein before I have to study."

Part of me wanted to stay behind and read more of the book, but I got up and grabbed my wallet.

Joe and I got burgers and found a table in the corner. I thought he might babble about class or the test he needed to study for—I helped him study periodically—but he seemed to want to talk mostly about his girlfriend, Vanessa.

"So, okay, she's got this apartment off campus lined up for next year. She's decided I should move in there with her because rent would be super cheap divided in two. But it's a bad idea, right?"

I agreed but decided to play along. "Why do you think so?"

Joe stared at his plate. "It's a big step?" He raised his shoulders, sort of a half shrug that indicated he didn't know the answer. "I mean, moving in together."

"Yeah, it is."

"I just keep thinking, does she want to get married? I'm only twenty-one years old. I don't want to get married. I love her and all, but moving in together feels like a step toward marriage."

"Have you talked to her about that?" I asked.

He shrugged.

"So what are you going to do?"

Joe ate a fry. Leave it to him to rely on food for comfort. "Probably stay in the dorms. Or, I don't know. *We* could get a place off campus." He pointed to me and then sat up a little straighter and smiled. "There's a vacancy in the apartment complex where Vanessa's gonna live. Maybe you and me could take it."

I had about three weeks left to make a housing decision. Living off campus with Joe didn't seem like a *terrible* idea. "Maybe."

"Well. Just saying. We know we can live together without killing each other. And believe me, I would have killed that asshole Jared if I'd had to live with him for another semester." Jared had been Joe's roommate freshman year, and he'd been an annoying kid with a nasal voice and a questionable relationship with personal hygiene. Joe only ever referred to him as "that asshole Jared," which said everything about their relationship.

"I shall consider your proposal," I said.

"I'm not marrying you either, for the record."

I glared at him. "Gross, dude."

"How's Britney?" he asked.

I let out a sigh. "Fine." I considered whether to tell Joe I'd been thinking about breaking up with her for no particular reason, when I spotted a familiar face across the room.

Noel. My heart pounded as I watched him from a safe distance. I'd thought about him so much in the ten days or so since our weird bathroom encounter that I had committed his features to memory. So I recognized him easily, despite the fact that he was now a more natural color—not so ghostly pale as he'd been the day I'd met him—and he smiled brightly. His clothes seemed a little silly, of a different era: gray trousers, a white shirt, suspenders. I wondered if that was how he dressed or if he was in the theater department—that might have explained his appearance in the Dickenson bathroom, since the building was linked to the Fine Arts Building via a strange underground tunnel—and then I noticed there was a dark-haired guy with him, at whom he stared adoringly. The guy kept touching Noel in a way I could only think of as flirtatious, long glides of his fingers down Noel's arm, quick pats on the small of his back.

I didn't like it.

Joe said, "Uh, dude. You have a girlfriend. What are you doing staring at Jenny Howard?"

"What?" I blinked and scanned the room and—oh, right. Behind Noel and his companion stood Jenny Howard. She lived down the hall from me and Joe. I'd always found her kind of plain, but I knew from one of Joe's drunk confessions he thought she was hot. I knew he'd never act—Joe had been faithful to Vanessa since they'd started dating in September, and he loved her like crazy—but it never ceased to amaze me how he treated the female student body at WMU as if it were his own personal art gallery.

"Sorry," I said.

"Dude, don't apologize to *me*."

"Anyway, Britney is not my girlfriend. We're just dating." I put some effort into turning toward Joe, but I was still peripherally aware of Noel. "Wait, what are *you* doing staring at Jenny Howard?"

"I wasn't. Oh, did you hear, the Sox won this afternoon."

I could talk about baseball out of the side of my mouth, so I surreptitiously stole glances at Noel while still participating in a conversation about the Red Sox with Joe. Most of our conversations about sports were the same and could roughly be summed up as "How great is This Guy? Boston teams are the best, man." So I watched Noel and the guy flirt, go up to the counter together, walk away with milk shakes, and gaze at each other as if they were totally head-over-heels. I had no business feeling anything like jealousy, and yet my chest burned with it. What if it had been me on the other end of that adoring gaze?

No, that was crazy. Straight guy, dating a hot girl. I needed that on a T-shirt.

"But Ramirez, man," Joe was saying. "That homer in the seventh sealed the game. Go Sox! Am I right?"

We high-fived.

After we ate, I had to stop at the men's room before we hiked back to the dorms. Joe went into the Mac's little convenience store for munchies while I went to pee, and after I took care of that, who should walk into the men's room but Noel.

"We have to stop running into each other this way," I said.

A shy smile crossed his face. In a way, this happy version of Noel looked completely different from the one I'd seen the other day. He looked even better, if that was possible.

He walked over to the sinks and washed his hands. He said, "That day in Dickenson was not one of my finer moments. I mean, for the record."

"No, I didn't think it was."

"It figures. We have probably passed each other a hundred times this semester, and you never noticed me until, well...." He gestured at his eyes with his hand, kind of a swirling motion. I noticed his fingernails were painted bright blue. His voice, now free of the croak from his tears, had a bit of a lilting, musical quality to it, and it was soft. Not feminine exactly, but not as aggressively masculine as Joe's honking Southie-afflicted voice or my own deeper baritone.

"You never noticed me either," I said.

His face went red. "Well, that's not entirely true. You have a class in Dickenson at 3:05 on Tuesdays and Thursdays. You always wear the same Red Sox cap, right? And usually you have a red backpack." He ducked his head. "Sorry, I'm not, like, stalking you or anything. I have a class at the same time in Hawthorne, but I usually cut through Dickenson to get there, so I see you coming and going. And I, uh, notice people, I guess."

I didn't know what to make of that. He looked so bashful I believed he'd just seen me around—he didn't come across as creepy, in other words—though I still found him so striking I couldn't believe I would have walked past him without a second glance.

Then again, Kareem made fun of me constantly because this one time I blew right past him on campus. I always had metaphorical blinders on when I walked to class. I got into my own head and didn't see anything. "I'm your best friend, Dave!" Kareem had cried after the incident, and then he and Joe got into a scuffle about which of them was really my best friend; it concluded with some wrestling and their deciding to be each other's best friend and not mine anymore, and then I told them to stop being children.

Anyway.

I didn't want to let Noel walk out and for that to be the end. I wanted to see him again. I wanted to get to the bottom of the mystery of why I found him so magnetic or what had upset him to the point of tears that day or probably both, plus some other things. How did you keep someone in your life when you had so little in common?

"So, well," I said, "now that we're old friends, maybe we should, I don't know. Hang out sometime."

He looked at me, his eyes wide. "Are you—?"

"Not, like, a date. Just, I mean, two guys who are friends. I mean, I have a girlfriend. Well, not really, just a girl I see sometimes, but...." I let out a breath. "Sorry, sorry, I just... forget about it."

He smiled. "No, it's.... I can always use more friends."

"Oh. Good." Then, because I had to know, I asked, "That guy you were with in the Mac, is he your boyfriend?" At his startled expression, I backpedaled. "Sorry, none of my business. Maybe you're not even gay, I just.... No, forget I said anything. You don't have to tell me."

He took a step toward me. "He's a guy who I see sometimes." He smiled again. His smile was charming. It went to his eyes, lit up his whole face. He seriously seemed to glow. It was like the slow-motion moment in a movie when the main guy and the main girl set eyes on each other for the first time and the music swells so you know this is a Significant Moment. Me staring at Noel in a grody men's room in the middle of the Mac as he glowed was my Significant Moment. I kind of wanted to touch his lips, but instead I shoved my hands into my pockets, because this wasn't a goddamned movie and also he was a guy and I was not gay.

Still, Noel's implication was clear, so I nodded. "Good to know."

"I should get going," he said.

But we still hadn't made any plans. "Oh, uh, yeah. But, so, there's going to be a party on Friday? Fourth-floor lounge in Emerson. That's North Quad."

"Yup, I know where it is. You're inviting me?"

"Yeah. It's, you know, just a social thing. The RA on my floor throws these parties once a month. We're not supposed to have alcohol, but a couple of the rooms on the floor always do. And my roommate just turned twenty-one, so...."

"Sounds great."

"Oh. Good!" Yikes, he totally flummoxed me. I didn't even get this nervous asking out girls. "Ah, just tell security you're going up to the fourth-floor party. They'll let you up as long as you have a student ID."

"All right. I'll see you Friday, Dave."

"Great!"

When I walked out of the men's room, Joe waited outside, a plastic bag full of junk food in his hand. He was checking his phone.

"Hey, the Celtics are up thirty points," he said.

"That's great, Joe."

He raised an eyebrow at me. "Come on, let's go. I gotta cram."

So I followed him back up to our room.

CHAPTER 3

JOE WENT out Thursday night to celebrate passing his exam, but I begged off, claiming I didn't feel so great. Really, when it became clear Joe had invited just me and Vanessa, I didn't want to be the extra wheel. Plus I figured she'd quiz me about Britney—Vanessa had good intentions but loved gossip like cats love yarn—and I wasn't in the mood. Instead I sat in my room and read more of Jerry Grossworth's book.

Jerry moved to New York City in the late seventies for work. He had a cousin who had moved up to the city a few years before and introduced him to some friends, a crowd of men who enjoyed parties and anonymous sex. It was such a culture shock for a sheltered boy from the South, he found the experience jarring.

Then Jerry had a revelation: some friends dragged him— reluctantly—to a club one night and he witnessed two men kissing each other. In the book he described his stomach becoming a cauldron of shame and excitement, to the point where he knew something significant was happening. A few nights later, he met a man so striking he couldn't keep his gaze away, and when the man asked him to dance, he consented. And so, in a rum-soaked, disco-fueled night, Jerry kissed a man and found what had been missing his whole life.

He described the scene in the club with such luscious detail I could picture it clearly—darkness punctuated by flashes of strobe lights and neon, sweaty bodies pressed against each other, music loud enough to deafen the listeners—and when he wrote about kissing this man, I could see their tongues meeting where their mouths just slightly parted, I could see their fingers grasping each other's arms and shoulders, I could see bad seventies hair and round muscles and sleeveless shirts and tight pants. I could see all of it.

I was unaccountably aroused.

I put the book down and thought about Jerry's revelation, the moment when something he'd never even spared a thought for suddenly became not only a possibility but what he wanted most in the world.

In the book the man Jerry kissed in the club was nameless, an abstract. Jerry wanted men, was drawn to them, and attracted to them, and this man was a symbol of that, but he didn't seem like a real person.

Yet reading the scene, all I could think about was Noel.

I was still rocking a hard-on when I heard Joe's key in the lock. I quickly grabbed a pillow and put it on my lap. I placed the book on it, open, so it would look like I'd just been studying. No big. Totally not getting a boner from reading about dudes kissing. Nope. Not me.

Joe walked in with Vanessa in tow. She smiled at me and said, "Hey, Dave."

"Hi. I thought you were going out?"

"Fucking New England weather. It was so awesome all afternoon, and then suddenly it's all cold and shit." Joe grabbed his jacket from where he'd left it draped over his desk chair.

Vanessa shrugged, looking unfazed. "Well, you know what they say. If you can't stand the weather in New England, wait five minutes." She smiled at me. "How are you, Dave?"

"All right. You?"

"Great. If Joe here ever learns to check the weather before leaving campus, we're going to the movies."

"What are you seeing?"

"Whichever one has a comic book hero," Joe said, shrugging into his jacket.

"*Spider-Man*," Vanessa supplied. She rolled her eyes but still smiled.

I liked Vanessa. She was a good foil for Joe. She was smart and sarcastic and a bit of a geek. She was short and curvy—there was more of her to love, let's say—and also pretty, with fine features and a lot of dark brown hair. They'd been dating less than a year, but if ever there were two people who seemed meant for each other, they were Joe and Vanessa. Joe liked to play it in public like she was the old ball and chain, but when they didn't think anyone was watching, they were sweet with each other. Vanessa got Joe in a way no other woman he'd dated in the three years I'd known him. Also she was probably the nicest person I'd ever met, someone who was just genuinely happy all the time, and not even in an annoying way.

"Oh, hey," Joe said, once he had his jacket on. "We just went to look at that empty apartment in the building Van is moving into."

"So you're not...?" I said, gesturing between them.

Vanessa smiled. "No. Joe was right. It's too soon. I found another roommate. But how fun would it be if we all lived in the same building?"

"You mean like in the dorms?" I said. "Where we all currently live?"

Vanessa laughed and waved her hands at me like she thought I was being silly.

Joe said, "Look, this place is cheap, but it's also clean and close to campus. Two bedrooms, so I'll never have to risk seeing your ass naked again, and we can forego the star system on the whiteboard." The star system was a code we'd invented to indicate one of us was alone with a girl and didn't want the other to come in. Mostly it involved drawing stars on the whiteboard that hung on our door. We thought it more subtle than a sock on the doorknob, but then everyone on the floor had found out about it, so it wasn't really a secret. Also, lately Joe had been drawing other celestial bodies—a half-moon, Saturn—when he was alone with Vanessa, so now it was all very ridiculous. Or else the sex with her was so good it needed more than just stars to illustrate. I didn't know. I never asked what it all meant.

"Okay," I said to Joe.

"It's perfect, basically. Not the biggest apartment you've ever seen—"

"Mine has a much bigger living room," Vanessa said.

"Right," said Joe. "Not the biggest. Pretty small, actually, which is probably why it's still available. It's certainly bigger than this room, though, and if I have to do that dumb senior project next year, it might be good to get away from all this nonsense."

As if to prove Joe's point, our next-door neighbor—we called him Pimpin' Steve because he never slept with the same girl twice—cranked up his music so loud, it was like his subwoofer was in our room. Joe raised his eyebrows.

"Point taken," I shouted.

"Anyway, there's a catch!" shouted Joe.

"Boys," said Vanessa, throwing her arms in the air. She walked out of the room. I heard her bang on Pimpin' Steve's door. Then they exchanged a few muffled words, and the volume went down to a more reasonable level. Vanessa came back and crossed her arms over her chest.

Joe smiled at her. Then he turned back to me. "So there's a catch," he repeated.

"Which is?"

"We have to sign a lease starting June 1."

Considering I'd been planning to go home for the summer, probably to do what I'd done every summer since I was sixteen and wait tables at the restaurant my family owned in Framingham, that was an issue. On the other hand—

"Well, we could spend the summer out here. Probably Hale's will let me keep my job." I was a professional waiter, basically. During the school year, I waited tables and occasionally served as a barback at Hale's, an above-average restaurant in Northampton, about twenty minutes from campus via my shitty car.

Joe's face lit up. "Really? Because there's an opening for a tech at the library, and I figured I'd take it so I don't have to spend the summer fighting with my sister." Joe's sister still lived at home but was getting married in August and had apparently become a textbook Bridezilla. He went on, "I have to be home for the wedding, obviously, but how much fun would we have if it was just us all summer?"

"And me," said Vanessa. "I'm moving into my place as soon as the semester ends."

Joe threw his arm around Vanessa and hugged her tight. "This is going to be wicked awesome, you guys. Oh, we better go if we're gonna get decent seats at the movie."

Joe escorted Vanessa out of the room. My hard-on had gone away, but I was still left sitting alone with my thoughts about Noel and the summer and everything. Not a great place to be just then.

CHAPTER 4

"Is BRITNEY coming to the lounge party?" Joe asked as we changed clothes Friday evening.

"I think so," I said, but suddenly I couldn't remember if I'd invited her. Wow, I was the worst. I probably should have broken up with her just to spare her from me.

I didn't know why we dressed up for these parties, but it was part of the ritual. Joe had two uniforms: he wore jeans and a sports-related T-shirt most of the time, or he wore a blue oxford shirt and khakis when he wanted to look nice. He had the blue oxford shirt outfit on now. He'd even taken off the Sox cap that was otherwise permanently affixed to his head. He wore it all the time to hide the fact he was going prematurely bald—poor guy—but he'd shaved his head recently, so one could barely tell.

I had showered to get rid of my own hat hair. So, okay, I also wore a hat almost all the time, but not because I wanted to hide my hair—which was thick and curly and covered my whole scalp, thank you very much—but more out of habit. I'd put on jeans—it was a damn lounge party; it's not like we were going anywhere with a dress code—but I'd stalled at picking a shirt. I wanted to look sexy. But if you'd asked me if I was trying to look sexy for Britney or for Noel, I wouldn't have been able to tell you.

It wasn't even like I had a wealth of options. Aside from my work uniforms, I only owned two shirts with buttons—in my dorm closet, anyway, and only if you did not count the vintage Ted Williams jersey that was among my most prized possessions—so I mostly had a bunch of T-shirts to choose from.

"Just put a damn shirt on, Dave. You already got with Britney. She was impressed, right?"

This was true. I had finally fucked Britney a few days before, and it had been… fine. She hadn't dumped me afterward. I took that as a good sign.

I was so seriously the worst.

"Why are you dressed up?" I asked.

He shrugged. "It's a party?"

I settled on a black V-neck T-shirt and pulled it on over my head. It was a little bit tight, but in a way I thought wasn't obscene. "On a scale of one to douche, how do I look?"

Joe rolled his eyes. "You look like Dave. Come on, let's go."

Kareem was already at the party when we got there, which was funny because he didn't even live in our dorm. He was chatting up this girl Bev, who lived a few doors down from me and Joe. When he saw us come in, he nodded in our direction but then went back to talking to Bev.

The lounge on my floor of Emerson House was a large room with several big couches and chairs and a couple of round tables intended to be places to study. More often, the lounge was sort of a catchall for students who were not in their room for whatever reason—they wanted social interaction, they'd been sexiled, they'd locked themselves out. Sometimes we were able to commandeer a TV. Our RA, a senior named Fred, had decided at the beginning of the school year that he wanted everyone on his floor to be friends, to live together like one big community, so he threw these regular parties. I couldn't tell how successful Fred's project was—the floor was mostly upperclassmen who had other friends before they moved to Emerson and so generally kept to their own social groups—but the parties were fun.

Joe had purchased a case of beer and a bottle of cheap vodka. We'd done shots right before walking down the hall. The vodka was harsh and acidic, like shooting battery acid. The acrid taste lingered in my mouth, and I could feel the burn in my belly. My first act upon arriving at the party was to snag a cup and pour myself a soda to wash that shit away.

As I poured, hands snaked around me from behind. It startled me enough I jostled the bottle and spilled a little on the floor. I managed to put everything down before further disaster ensued. Then I turned around and saw my attacker was Britney.

"Hi!" she said brightly before giving me a quick kiss.

I glanced at the door to see if Noel had arrived, because that seemed so likely. He wasn't actually there, but suddenly I wanted Britney to go away because I didn't want to be seen with her.

Although why the hell shouldn't I? I wasn't gay. I was dating Britney. I wasn't really trying to get with Noel. I just found him intriguing.

"Hi," I said, putting my hands on her waist. I nudged her away.

"Good party so far?" she asked.

"I just got here."

"Oh, good. Then I didn't miss anything."

Someone turned up the music. Fred usually played DJ, though in here, "DJ" meant "iPod plugged haphazardly into a speaker." Thus we were stuck with the hip-hop Fred preferred, though it was kind of danceable. I danced with Britney for a while—we just kind of bobbed and weaved and rubbed against each other, as neither me nor Britney were particularly skilled dancers—and I saw Vanessa come in with her roommate and beeline for Joe. Jorge showed up too. Jorge was a fifth-year who had become something of a legend around the North Quad as the life of every party. I figured because he usually had weed. I was also pretty sure Jorge was not his real name, given that he was a white guy with Nordic features, but what did I know?

The party was raging, basically. Other kids besides Joe were supplying booze. Fred didn't care as long as we weren't obvious about it, but we all knew what the ubiquitous red plastic cups contained.

Britney and I walked over to the snack table to snag some chips, and that was when Noel walked in.

It surprised me that he actually came. I'd doubted he would. Really, what reason did he have to be my friend? I didn't think we had much in common. I mean, here I was in my best T-shirt and jeans, as fashionable as I ever got, but he walked in with every hair in place, wearing a blue-checked short-sleeve button-front shirt that looked tailored to his body, and well-fitted red high-water pants. He looked adorable, stylish... hot.

What the hell?

I walked over to him, and Britney trailed behind. He smiled at me as I approached.

"You came," I said.

"You invited me."

Clever guy. I smiled.

Britney said, "Who's your friend?"

"Oh, sorry. Britney, this is Noel. Noel this is my... Britney." I still didn't know how to define our relationship. We hadn't really had a conversation about it. We were sleeping together, sure, and we went on dates, but there had been no talk of exclusivity. She could have been fucking the whole football team for all I knew.

Britney smiled and put an arm around my waist. "Nice to meet you," she said. Then she let go and hopped excitedly. "Oh, Kara just got here. Be right back." She ran off to talk to her friend.

"Welcome to the fourth floor of Emerson House," I said.

"That's the girl you see sometimes?" he asked.

"Yeah, she… well." I had no idea what to say.

"It's good to see you again. I hardly recognized you without the baseball hat."

I touched my hair self-consciously. "Yeah. I do take it off sometimes."

He smiled. "I heard about the festivities here. Friend of mine lives on the second floor. He said the fourth floor is legendary for its parties."

"We try." True, we were kind of a party floor, which made moving into an apartment off campus an attractive prospect. I would have stuck it out one more year, but it could be difficult to get work done in a noisy dorm sometimes.

"I gotta say, part of why I said yes was that I was curious," Noel said. "So how does a guy get a drink around here?"

"A drink or a *drink* drink?"

"*Drink* drink."

"I can take care of that for you. Come with me."

He followed me out of the lounge. As we walked down the hall, he said, "So."

"So." I had no idea what to say, so I babbled. "Okay, we don't know really each other, but since fate has thrown us together, I figured maybe we could change that."

"Because we're friends now."

He was being a little sarcastic, but I said, "Yes. So, basically, hi, I'm a junior. I'm from Eastern Mass. Framingham. I'm majoring in English and film studies and really should have dropped one because the double major is slowly killing me. So. You?"

He smiled. "I'm a sophomore. Grew up in North Carolina."

"Ooh, really. I went there on vacation with my parents once. It's nice there?"

He laughed. "Yeah, I guess so. It's all right. You probably went to the beaches."

"Outer Banks."

"Yeah, I'm from outside Charlotte. Anyway, I'm a psych major. Only one major for me."

"Psych? Really? I had you pegged as theater or art or something."

He balked. "Because I'm gay?"

"No, because you dress… creatively."

He looked down at his clothes. "Oh. Well, no. I mean, I've got a part in the Theater Club production of *Guys and Dolls* we're doing this semester." That explained his outfit earlier in the week. "But it's just for fun. I like to sing. I don't want to do it professionally."

"Ah, okay. That's cool."

We arrived at my room. I pushed inside and walked straight to the minifridge, where the cheap vodka resided. "Basically, we've got beer and we've got vodka. To mix with the vodka, we've got cranberry juice and, ah, seltzer, I think."

"Cranberry is fine."

"Okay. I'm gonna pour the juice generously. This vodka is nasty, but it gets the job done."

He laughed. "I thought you said your roommate was twenty-one. So you don't have to rely on other people buying your booze."

"He is twenty-one. He's also wicked cheap."

I poured us each a cocktail and handed him a cup.

"So this is your room," he said, looking around.

I wouldn't say the space was something to be proud of. It was clean, at least. Joe's side of the room had one wall covered floor to ceiling with Red Sox paraphernalia: posters, ticket stubs, baseball cards, magazine covers, and, the prize, a signed, framed David Ortiz jersey, because Big Papi was a god as far as Joe was concerned. My side of the room was way less interesting. I had a couple of movie posters up, mostly to hide how dire and prisonlike the cinder-block walls were, and a bulletin board with all manner of things tacked to it—photos, greeting cards, newspaper clippings. I'd hung a few of my track medals on the wall; I ran cross-country every fall semester. And the bookcase with all of my and Joe's books sat on my side of the room. My desk held only my laptop and a lamp.

"It's not the Ritz," I said.

He smiled. "You and your roommate, you're both sportsy."

"Yeah."

"Hence the Red Sox cap permanently affixed to your head."

I touched my head again. My hair was getting too long, to the point where, when I did have a hat on, it curled around the edges. Now it was just kind of an unruly mess.

"You have nice hair," Noel said.

"Oh. Thanks." I felt heat rise to my face at the compliment. I looked down and examined my feet for a moment. Remnants of a potato chip were stuck to the laces on my left sneaker. Yikes.

When I looked up again, Noel raised an eyebrow. I wondered if he was onto me. Then I realized my desk was not, in fact, completely bare, and that my copy of Jerry Grossworth's *In the Wind* was sitting right there. Not that this really meant anything—it *was* a class assignment—but I felt like the book was a big neon sign pointing at me that said "Sexuality crisis!"

And with that, I wished for a door to open up beneath my feet so I could fall through it.

Joe saved me by stumbling into the room with Vanessa. "Oh, hey," he said to Noel.

I made with the introductions, telling Joe Noel's name but nothing more because I wasn't sure how to define our relationship. We weren't really friends, though I wanted to be. And it wasn't like I could just say, "This is my friend," because then Joe would ask why he'd never met Noel before, and then I'd have to explain something to him that I still couldn't explain to myself. And around I went in a circle without explaining.

"Well," I said. "Now that we have drinks, we should go back to the party."

Joe and Vanessa shot us questioning looks, but Noel and I walked back down the hall.

It turned out Noel had a class with Bev and knew one of the other guys on the floor from the LGBT student organization, so he did pretty well at the party on his own. He circulated, chatting with people and proving to be quite agile at small talk and flirty glances. Britney spent a good chunk of the time hanging on me and making it clear she wanted to spend the night with me. I was really not in the mood, in part because I couldn't stop looking at how Noel's pants hung on his hips just so, but then I realized I was checking out a guy's butt, so I studied Britney's rack instead. She took that as a sign I was lusting after her.

I really had to end things.

But I was a goddamn coward. So as I slowly integrated Noel into my circle of friends and made plans to hang out again soon, I let Britney keep believing she was what I wanted, even though it was becoming increasingly clear that she wasn't.

Chapter 5

WHO DID one even talk to when one was having a crisis on this scale? I didn't think I could just go to Joe and say, "Hey, bro, I think I might be attracted to dudes."

Because it wasn't just the one dude. I really liked Noel, yes, but he'd clearly awoken something dormant in me, because suddenly I noticed male bodies everywhere. The guy in my English class with the great hair and the nice shoulders, the guy with the spectacular ass who worked at the Mac twice a week, the bartender at Hale's who was all tall and lean and Italian, even that guy in the WMU sweatshirt who I walked by on my way to class one afternoon.

But not all guys. Joe came back to the room one afternoon, and as he moved around, getting ready to do his homework, I tried to decide if I found him attractive. The bald thing, not so much—I liked guys with nice hair, clearly—plus Joe was a little on the pudgy side, so while he wasn't unattractive, he didn't really get my motor revving, not the way Noel or the bartender did.

"What the hell are you staring at?" he asked me.

"Nothing. I was just spacing out."

I looked back at my laptop screen. Ostensibly I was writing a paper for my film class. Really I'd just decided Joe and I were bros and I wasn't into him in that way, which was a relief. Also, apparently I had a type.

I said, "I think I have to break up with Britney."

Joe turned and looked at me, all googly-eyed, his patented "Are you crazy?" look. "Why?" he asked.

"I'm just not feeling it, I guess."

"Are you asking for advice? Because that's not really my—"

"No." I let out a breath. "Just telling you. Trying to decide if it's what I really want. Because some moments, I'm convinced it's for the best to end things, but then I worry breaking up with her would be a horrible mistake."

Because breaking up with Britney would tell me something about myself, wouldn't it? All of my friends insisted we were perfect together, so why couldn't I see that as well? Everyone said she was sexy, so if I disagreed, there was something wrong with me. These were the thoughts that swarmed through my head as I focused on my homework and not on Joe. Any red-blooded heterosexual male would give his left nut to be with a girl who looked like Britney. If I didn't want to, well, perhaps I was not so heterosexual.

"She *is* pretty hot," Joe said. "Also, pretty sure you just asked for my advice."

I put my laptop aside and turned to face him. "You ever been with a girl who was totally great in all ways—she's hot and funny and smart and likes baseball, right?—but you just don't… click, I guess?"

Joe considered. "Yeah. That girl Jessica I dated sophomore year."

"With the blonde hair?"

"Yeah. Great girl. Gorgeous, right? Has loved the Sox since Nomar was at shortstop. We could talk about baseball for hours. But that was it, that was all we had in common. Now, I love the Sox. You know that. When I die, I want to be buried in right field at Fenway. But I'm more than just a baseball fan. When I figured out we had nothing else to talk about, it kind of just fizzled."

I nodded. Maybe Britney and I just had nothing in common. Maybe this whole crisis about my sexuality was just a manifestation of my anxiety over not clicking with Britney and listening to my friends too much, and there was no *should* about this should-I-dump-her equation. If it wasn't working, it wasn't working. It would work with another woman. Hell, I'd been with plenty of women before.

None of those relationships had lasted, of course.

"We just don't have much in common, me and Britney," I said.

"Is this why you've been so weird lately?"

"What? How have I been weird?"

Joe looked at me warily. "I don't know, dude. Just weird. Quiet. You never want to go out. You spent more time at the lounge party talking to that gay dude than you did Britney, although if you've been thinking about breaking up with her, I get it, I guess." Joe tilted his head. "What's the deal with that guy, anyway?"

I shrugged. "Dunno. Seems like a cool guy."

I could sense what Joe was thinking, though. Any guy who wore red high-water pants to a lounge party was not of the same species as me and Joe.

"You're not going gay on me, are you, Dave?"

"What? No." Though my heart sped up at the words. It was difficult to hold back my body's reaction because I'd more or less talked myself down by reasoning that I'd overthought the situation with Britney, but now here it was right in front of me again. Cold sweat broke out all over my body. I prayed Joe didn't notice.

"Didn't think so," Joe said.

I couldn't tell what Joe thought about the possibility of my "going gay," so I didn't say anything more. I didn't want to think too hard about the possibilities.

Maybe I just needed to see the man himself to confirm things. I told Joe I needed something from the store and went outside. I texted Noel once I was out of my room; he replied that he was wrapping up a Theater Club meeting but he could meet me over by Hawthorne.

By the time I got there, he was already waiting outside, leaning against a large tree and talking to some dude with a pierced eyebrow. Noel must have heard me approach, because he looked up and smiled.

My heart stopped for a moment.

"He actually waited at the bus stop after a performance," the dude was saying. "I was so shocked, it actually worked out! We're going out on Friday." He looked at his phone and shook his head. "I gotta go. See you, Noel."

"Good timing," Noel said to me.

The dude gave me a once-over but then waved at Noel and walked away.

"So what's up?" Noel's voice was so cheery. It startled me to realize I still thought of him as the weepy guy in the Dickenson bathroom, but it was becoming increasingly clear that afternoon was the fluke and this smiling guy was more normal.

"Nothing much," I said. I meant, of course, *I'm attracted to you and can't stop thinking about you but have to make sure there's really something here before I do something stupid*, but there's no good way to say that, is there?

"Okay," Noel said. "I have to return a couple of books to the library. You want to walk with me?"

"Okay."

The main WMU library was smack in the middle of campus, across a walkway from the Mac, maybe a five-minute walk from Hawthorne.

That didn't feel like enough time, but I figured I could use the walk to work up to asking him to do… something. Grabbing dinner at the nearest dining hall or a burger at the Mac seemed like a fairly mundane thing to ask. I mean, if I wanted to take him on a *date*, I'd take him somewhere in town.

Why was I even thinking this way?

"Can I ask you a weird question?" I said.

"The weirder the better."

I glanced at him sidelong. He grinned. I had intended to ask when he'd known he was gay, but that seemed like a stupid, cliché, trite thing to ask. Although now I felt pressure to come up with something weird to ask him. And the silence had drawn on too long.

"Something on your mind, Dave?"

"It's dumb. Forget it."

"All right. So, uh, and not that I'm not glad you did, but why did you text me?"

I shrugged, not knowing how to answer. "Just wanted to hang out," I started, but that sounded lame. "And I, well, I was just reading in my dorm room and wanted to get out for a while. And I'd been reading this book that I guess made me think of you? So I figured I'd text you to see if you were around."

"That's kind of sweet." He nudged me with his shoulder, and it felt a little like we were flirting. "A book made you think of me?" He dropped his voice. "Was it sexy?"

"A little, I guess. Maybe."

He grinned. "And you thought of me and not the girl you're seeing? Is that normal straight guy behavior?" He shot me a little half smile.

"I don't know what normal is anymore, honestly. Is it possible to have a midlife crisis at twenty?"

He laughed. "I don't think so."

We got to the library then. I followed Noel inside and just stood there staring like an idiot while he dumped the books he was returning into the bin and then walked over to the counter to see if the books he requested had come in. I stood next to him while he waited.

"Is this for class?" I asked.

"Yeah, I have a paper due for my abnormal psych class next week. I'm writing it on the history of homosexuality being considered a psychosis in the DSM."

"Oh."

"Kind of a heavy topic. Maybe too on the nose considering *I* chose it. But the assignment was to pick a diagnosis that has changed significantly in the last fifty years." He ran his fingers through the fringe of hair on his forehead. "I'll be honest, it's kind of why I wanted to study psych to begin with."

"You wanted to study psych because homosexuality used to be considered a psychosis?"

He smiled briefly and a flush came to his cheeks. "Not exactly. What I mean is, I wanted to study psych because I thought it was interesting that diagnoses can change. Like, being gay used to be considered a disorder, but it's not anymore, at least not by professional psychologists. Or most of them, anyway. In thirty years some of the things we think are weird or deviant now might be considered totally normal. Like, uh, gender identity. You know?" He bit his lip. "Ugh, I don't know. I just thought it was interesting. Diagnoses and so on."

I agreed and he spoke about it with such passion that I didn't want to make him self-conscious. "Is that what you want to do when you graduate? Be a psychologist?"

"Maybe." He nodded. "I think I want to study child psychology eventually. My favorite professor I've had so far is a child psych specialist, and it seems really interesting. I'm taking her child psych class next semester, so we'll see. But I want to help kids."

"Sounds good." Man, I just had no command of the English language. But he fascinated me, and his excitement about the topic came through in his voice.

"What does one do with English and film studies?" he asked me.

"No idea. I picked them because I liked the topics. Well, and I think it would be fun to be a film critic."

"Probably it would be. To watch movies for a living." Noel smiled.

"There's a little more to it than that," I said.

The librarian handed Noel his books, so I waited while he checked them out. As the librarian scanned them, I got a text from Britney that said, *I want 2 c u tonite!*

Hmm.

The fact that I was reluctant to leave Noel probably gave me all the info I needed. I watched him smile at the librarian, a mousy woman in a heavy gray cardigan. He grinned as he stowed his books in his bag, as if the very act of checking books out of the library made him happy. As someone who had spent a lot of time in the local public library as a kid, I could relate.

Noel turned toward me as I was trying to figure out how to text Britney back. "Something going on?" he asked.

I just... I liked this guy. I liked how he looked. I liked the timbre of his voice. I liked the sunny disposition he seemed to possess when he was not losing his shit in a men's room. I was crazy attracted to him and kept picturing what it would be like if we made out on one of the old overstuffed sofas in the reading room near the circulation desk.

"My... Britney. I think she wants to hook up tonight."

He smiled and punched my arm softly. "Go get 'em, tiger."

I shook my head. "No, I... I think I'm going to break up with her."

"Really?"

"Yeah. Um. It's kind of a long story."

Britney texted me again, telling me to come to her room. I must have grunted or made some sort of noise in response, because Noel put his hand on my shoulder. It was warm and comforting. I looked up at him and our eyes met. I thought for a moment that everything between us was understood, that we had clarity, that he knew I was breaking up with Britney because of him. I imagined he felt whatever it was between us as surely as I did. But, of course, that was all foolish fantasy. He blinked and tilted his head questioningly. So I had imagined any mutual attraction. I looked back at my phone.

"I think I need to meet her somewhere neutral. A public place, not her room."

"You were serious. You're breaking up with her."

"Yeah, I... yeah. I've been wanting to for weeks. I should stop putting it off."

He dropped his hand and nodded. "Well, listen, you go do what you need to. I'm gonna run upstairs and see if I can find another book I need. I'll see you around, okay? You want to talk about it later, you can text me. Text me anytime."

"Yeah, sure."

He smiled. "I mean, we're totally BFFs now, yeah?" He affected a light, lispy voice like a teenage girl and then laughed.

"Totally," I said.

He gave me a soft, loose-armed hug and then sauntered off toward the elevators. I walked out of the library and texted Britney: *Meet me at the Mac.*

I'll be there in five, she texted back.

I fretted the whole walk there, worrying I was making a big mistake because Britney was awesome. I thought about things too much and was reading too much into the situation. Or I'd upset her and she'd never speak to me again, which would also suck because she really was a great girl and I thought we could be friends or something. I must have walked fast in my frenzy, because Britney wasn't there when I arrived. I got a milk shake from the counter. She arrived just as I snagged a table.

I was going to vomit on the table, my stomach churned so much. Why on earth did had I thought a milk shake was a good idea? I set it aside and looked at Britney.

"Hey, babe," she said. "Are we going to get food?"

"Ah, well. Can I talk to you about something first?"

"Okay."

I didn't have a lot of experience being the dumper in a breakup situation. My previous relationships had almost all been ended by the girl after we'd been going together for a month or two and she wanted more commitment than I wanted to give. I imagined by now there must be a poster in Wheatley House (the all-girls dorm) with my picture on it and the headline "Don't Date This Dude!" and the subtitle "Pathological Fear of Commitment." Britney clearly hadn't gotten the memo.

"I like you, Britney. You're great."

"Oh boy," she said. "I kind of saw this coming. You're breaking up with me, aren't you?"

I let out the breath I'd been holding. "God, I'm so sorry. I mean, yes, but… I'm just not… I'm going through some things and…."

"Joe said you were being weird."

That pulled me up short. She'd talked to Joe about me? "I know, and I can't really explain why. I feel weird. Too much stress, I don't know." I sighed. "I feel like I'm losing my mind, because you're awesome. I swear I'm not just saying that. You're sexy and you're fun to talk to, but I just can't…."

"Dave, it's okay."

Wait, was she letting me off the hook? "It's really not."

"We've only been going out, what, a month? Six weeks? I kinda thought the vibe between us wasn't quite right, but I was willing to see where it went." She laughed a little bit. "You are so cute, Dave. You really are. And you're funny. And I think you're sexy, too. Just...." She shrugged.

"This is a cliché, but do you think we can be friends? I mean that honestly."

She smiled. "Sure. Give me a week or two to badmouth you to my friends. And then maybe introduce me to your friend Mike, because *that* guy is hot. Then we can be friends."

I laughed. "Deal."

The fluttering in my stomach started to die down. It seemed safe to take a sip of my milk shake.

"So you're going through some things? What are they? I mean, if you want to tell me, since we're friends now."

I shook my head. "It's hard to say exactly. Thinking about what I'm going to do after graduation, I guess."

It wasn't really a lie. Joe and I had been talking a lot about our apartment off campus, which made me think about senior year and the old pickle about what the hell one did with bachelor's degrees in English and film studies. Mostly it was another thing I'd been postponing making a decision about.

"And there's somebody else, too, isn't there?"

"What makes you say that?"

She shrugged. "You're being so vague. I just assumed. And hey, we weren't exclusive. It's not a big deal."

"You're awesome," I said, still not believing how cool she was being. "I'd ask you out again if this weren't such a messy situation."

She laughed.

"Maybe there is someone else, just a dumb crush really, but I haven't done anything about it. I don't even know if I will," I said. "I *am* sorry. I've been really unsure about this thing between us, and I didn't want to string you along. That's the whole truth."

She reached over and patted my arm. "I appreciate that. You're a good guy, Dave."

"Jury's still out."

Now that my stomach had settled, I was suddenly starving. "You want to get dinner?"

She shook her head. "Hey, I forgive you for dumping me, but I'm still disappointed. I'm gonna call my roommate and go find a place to wallow. But text me sometime. We'll hang out."

"Wow. Okay. Yeah. I'm sorry some more. You're the best."

She stood up with a grin. "I *am* the best."

I was stunned by how well that had gone. I watched her saunter away and took a sip of my milk shake. I was starting to think about getting a burger to go when a shadow fell over me. I looked up.

Noel.

"Hey!" I said. It was probably too bright, the way I said it, but I was really glad to see him.

"I thought I'd find you here. Anyone sitting in this chair?"

"No. Not anymore."

He sat and looked at me with raised eyebrows. "Not anymore? Did you talk to Britney? Is it over? How did it go?"

I sighed. "Better than expected. But I still feel like shit."

He tilted his head. "That sucks."

"Yeah. I mean, it's for the best. But yeah. Even easy breakups are not fun."

"Did you want to sit alone?"

"No, no. It's nice to have company."

His hair was windblown and uncharacteristically mussed. He ran his fingers through the fringe at the front, I presumed to get it to fall correctly. He looked at me with gorgeous greenish blue eyes. I thought again about how he was so nice to look at: his fair skin was smooth, his hair looked soft, his clothes were crisp and well-fitted, his shoulders and arms and really everything I could see before me was basically perfect.

"Thanks for finding me," I said.

"Not a problem. The Mac is on the way back to my dorm, and I figured you'd be here. Do you want to talk about what happened?"

"No." I shook my milk shake cup to get the ingredients to mix around. "I want a distraction. Let's talk about you. Theater Club, right? That's where you were before I met you earlier?"

"Yeah. *Guys and Dolls* rehearsal."

"Oh yeah. When is the show? Who are you playing?"

"Nicely Nicely," he said. "So not a big part, but I get a few corny one-liners. We're doing five shows in May."

In a few weeks, in other words. "Oh, cool. Soon, then."

"You know the show?"

"I've seen the movie. The one with Frank Sinatra and Marlon Brando."

"Oh, really? I've never seen it. I didn't know Marlon Brando was in it."

I stared at him aghast for a moment. "You've never seen it? Brando plays Sky Masterson. I can't believe you haven't seen it. It's great."

"Maybe it's available streaming."

"I have it on DVD. I'll lend it to you. I think it's one of Brando's more underrated performances. I mean, *Streetcar*, *On the Waterfront*, yes, those performances are brilliant, but here, he's allowed to be a little silly. He's charming in a way that works for the role. He even sings okay. I mean, he's outclassed by Sinatra and the rest of the cast, but he's not terrible."

"And this is why you're a film studies major." Noel smiled. Even his teeth were perfect.

"Yeah, I guess so."

"I've only seen *Streetcar*. And *The Godfather*, obviously. I think that's it for me and Brando movies. But I loved him in *Streetcar*. He was so sexy when he was young."

"I know," I said without thinking. Because, his personal life notwithstanding, Brando had always been one of my favorite actors, and I'd always thought he was dead sexy in his early movie roles.

Not a thought many straight men had probably ever had.

If Noel picked up on my flub, he didn't say so. "I actually was totally unfamiliar with the show before I auditioned," he said instead.

"Yeah? Most of the other film majors think those old movie musicals are cheesy, but I secretly love them. *Guys and Dolls*, *Singin' in the Rain*, *Kiss Me Kate*? So great."

Noel laughed. "Who knew? Sportsy likes musicals."

I shrugged. "I have lots of hidden depths."

He leaned back in his chair and looked me over appraisingly. "I'll bet you do."

That hung in the air for a moment.

Noel broke the silence. "I want one of those milk shakes. You want anything?"

"I just broke up with my sort-of girlfriend. They don't serve booze here, so... something sweet?"

"Okay. Watch my bag. I'll be right back."

I watched him walk up to the counter. He was wearing blue and tan plaid pants that were tailored quite nicely, and again, I found myself looking at and being intrigued by his ass. I wanted to get my hands on it. I imagined squeezing it as he knelt above me. I could picture our bodies coming together and….

Okay, these were definitely not the thoughts of a straight man.

I checked my phone while Noel waited for his milk shake. There were a bunch of texts from Joe.

You're breaking up with her, aren't you?

Come back so I can get you drunk. Don't jump off a bridge.

OK, while you're killing yourself, look at this sofa.

He sent a photo of a plaid sofa. It was red and orange and looked like it had been sent to us from 1975. Ghastly, in other words. Luckily I didn't have to wait long to find out why Joe sent me said photo.

Previous tenants at apt. say we can have it for $50. Good deal, right?

Oh, Joe. *It's ugly*, I texted back.

He lives! Joe texted. Then: *We can put a sheet on it. It's already in the apt. No delivery.*

Fine, I texted.

He didn't respond, so I figured we'd decided and Joe would go on with his day. Noel came back with a milk shake and a couple of cupcakes.

"Perfect," I said.

As we dug into our cupcakes, he said, "Can I ask you a personal question?"

And here it came. "Okay," I said reluctantly.

"On the surface we don't have much in common. I'm starting to see we may be more alike than I first thought, but still, I couldn't understand why you'd even want to be my friend. When you invited me to the party and then texted me this afternoon, I wondered if you were only trying to get to know me because, I don't know. You wanted to know why I was crying in the bathroom. But no. You actually want to be my friend, don't you?"

"Yeah." What could I have said? I did want to know why he'd been crying—I desperately wanted to know; the question had been plaguing me for weeks now—but I didn't feel like it was my place to ask.

"Did you want to be my friend because I'm gay?"

I shook my head as I stalled to come up with an answer. "No," I said eventually, which was the truth. "First of all, I didn't know for sure you were gay when I invited you to the lounge party. You didn't tell me until after."

He tilted his head as if he were considering. "Okay. Just making sure. At the party I felt a little like the token. Britney kept asking me for fashion advice."

"I didn't mean for that to happen. I don't even know how to explain myself. I guess I find you interesting and I wanted to get to know you better. That's all." Man, I felt like an idiot. It was also totally the sort of line I would have used on a girl three months ago.

But Noel smiled. "I'm glad you texted me today, for what it's worth."

"Can I ask you a weird, nosy question too?"

"You want to know why I was crying."

"Well, yeah, I do, but that wasn't what I was going to ask. It's more of an… academic question." I saw this as my opening. Maybe closure with Britney would give me the strength to have the conversation I hadn't felt like I could have earlier that afternoon.

"Okay."

"Are you going to tell me why you were crying?"

He popped the last of his cupcake into his mouth. "Maybe someday."

I filed my question about that away for a later date. "Well, so, okay. I'm reading this book by Jerry Grossworth for my English class."

"Yeah, *In the Wind*? I saw it in your room."

"Have you read it?"

"I have."

I nodded, gathering my thoughts. "I haven't finished it yet, but I will soon. The book is making me think, you know?"

"How so?"

I took a fortifying sip of milk shake. The sound of me sucking the last of it through my straw made me think of a tub of ice cream getting thrown into a fan. Not exactly graceful.

"He talks about how it never even occurred to him that relationships other than traditional heterosexual marriages existed because of his upbringing. I wonder if it's possible to, I don't know, just not ever consider being gay, even if you are. To get to be an adult without realizing the whole truth."

Noel shook his head. "I guess I wouldn't know. I've known since forever."

"So you don't think it's possible to not know you're gay?"

He narrowed his eyes at me. "Do you—"

"I'm not. I've only ever dated women. I was just wondering about the book."

He narrowed his eyes. "Right. Well, I guess it's possible."

"Okay."

"I've known guys who didn't really figure it out until they were older. But there's also a difference between knowing you're gay and coming out."

"Yes. I realize that."

We were both silent for a moment. The air felt a little tighter.

"I got outed to my parents," Noel said after a long silence. "That day we met. A friend of mine tagged me in a post online that was, let's say, unambiguous, and I guess I'd gotten kind of complacent all the way up here, away from my family. But my cousin saw the post and told my parents. They, ah... they told me...." He sniffed and blinked rapidly. "They told me not to come home unless I overcame this phase."

"Oh God."

"My family is super religious. My grandpa was a preacher. So they think I'm... well." He sniffed again. "Like I have some kind of disorder. Or I made a choice to be this way." He stared at his milk shake for a moment before speaking again. "They, uh, cut me off, basically. So I'm living up here this summer. I found an apartment in South Hadley. I'm renting the top floor of a house. It's kind of far from campus, but it's cheap and right on the bus route."

"Oh. That's... good. Not that your parents cut you off. That part blows. A lot." I took a deep breath, not wanting to fuck up this conversation. "It's good you found a place. I'm actually staying up here this summer too. Joe and I just got a place in an apartment complex in North Amherst. Not fancy, but it'll be a fine for a year."

He shook his head. "How weird is it that I met you? Here I thought I wouldn't know anyone staying up here for the summer."

"Now you know me."

"Yeah." He looked dazed. He ran his fingers through his hair again. "Anyway, my parents had called me earlier that day and told me not to come home. I mean, I guess I could lie and tell them... but... no. I'm done lying. I'd gone to my class, but all I could think about through the lecture was what my parents said. So I bailed out of class early and went to... I don't know. Lose my mind. Just when I finally calmed down, you walked in."

"I felt like a shitheel for barging in on that moment, but maybe it was fate," I said.

He smiled.

As he finished his milk shake, he got a text message. He looked at it and said, "Oh crap. I gotta go. Totally lost track of time."

"You got a hot date?" I asked, only half joking.

He smirked. "Kinda. That guy I told you I was seeing? I'm supposed to see him again tonight."

I felt like he'd reached into my chest and squeezed my heart, which was fucking stupid, because I had just reiterated my heterosexuality while explaining my breakup. I broke up with Britney *because* of Noel but not *for* him. I had no right to any expectations. There was no reason for him to end his relationship and come running to me. Even if it killed me when I realized "see" probably meant "fuck" in this context. That was really a kick in the teeth.

But I said, "Good luck?"

"Thanks."

Somehow I still couldn't bear to let him go. If nothing else, I wanted him to be my friend. This man was someone I needed in my life. As he stood, I said, "Hey, you know, Spring Fest is this weekend at the North Quad. You should come."

"Spring Fest?"

"You know, the big annual festival. Food and music and drunk kids. It's a lot of fun. You should come and hang out with me there. It's all day Saturday and Sunday in the quad."

"I… yeah. Okay. I'll text you so I can find you there."

We exchanged quick good-byes before he ran off.

I decided to get that burger to go after all. I carried it back to my dorm. On the way there, I thought about Noel getting disowned. Why not just agree it was a phase so he could go home or at least make up with his parents for now so they would continue to pay for him to go to school for two more years? I didn't really know much about Noel's situation, so I had no place judging, but I wondered what I would do in his shoes. Would I keep the peace, at least until the end of college? Would I defy my parents the way Noel had? I didn't know. But it must have sucked to be on his own like that.

Joe was gone when I got to my room—he'd left me a note on the whiteboard telling me he'd gone to "study" with Vanessa—so I picked up *In the Wind*.

In this section, Jerry wrote about meeting a guy named Paul, whom he described as being tall and thin with longish blond hair—gee, who did I know who looked like that?—and also being so beautiful Jerry couldn't take his eyes off him. This was the first time in the book Jerry actually named one of his affairs, and it became clear soon enough that he fell in love with this Paul fellow. They got an apartment together in Greenwich Village in the early eighties, right when AIDS was tearing apart the community.

What struck me about this part of the book was how brave Jerry acted. He had kind of a fuck-you attitude toward anyone who questioned his choices, including his conservative family back home. When Paul was diagnosed with AIDS, Jerry finally broke down and told his family what was happening to him. He expected condemnation, but his parents, while judgmental about his lifestyle, still said they loved him.

I cried like a baby when Jerry described Paul's death.

Jerry somehow escaped contracting the disease, but many of his friends in New York did not. A few, he wrote, were still alive at the time he was writing the book, but many had succumbed. It was so sad to me, and I went to bed that night with the feeling still lingering. What must Jerry have felt late in the night in the weeks after Paul died, with so many of his friends gone too?

And why was I being such a wuss about just accepting what I felt? Jerry had not only come out to his family in a time when being gay wasn't nearly as accepted as it was now, but he'd stared certain death in the face and survived. What had I done? Made tentative friendship overtures to a guy I liked and lied through my teeth to all my friends.

I lay awake most of that night and remembered glimpses of things I'd suppressed: checking out other boys in the locker room, a late night in my bunk at summer camp when a friend and I had jerked each other off, my complete fascination with the beefy student teacher who'd taken over my eleventh-grade history class for six weeks. But somehow it had never occurred to me I might not be straight. I'd been talking about dating girls with my friends and my family since I hit puberty. Boys dated girls. That was what was supposed to happen.

It wasn't even like I hadn't known gay people growing up. My mom had a cousin in California who had been with his male partner for thirty years. My family fully embraced them. My parents had gay friends they socialized with regularly when I was a kid. And yet it had never occurred to me I would ever be in a relationship with a man.

But how could I not know?

Maybe I was bi. That entered my thought processes too. All those women I'd dated… and then lost interest in. On the other hand, I couldn't guarantee dating someone with a penis was the magical cure for my ambivalence about relationships. Even if I did make a move on Noel, would he sustain my interest for more than a month?

I didn't know the answers to any of these questions, and I felt sick all night contemplating them. When my alarm went off the next morning, I wasn't any closer to answers, but the nausea was so bad I had to run to the bathroom to throw up.

When I emerged from the stall, Fred was standing there. "Party too hard last night?" he said with a significant measure of compassion. As RA, Fred was trying to fulfill some kind of weird hybrid parent/mentor/ best friend role for everyone on the floor.

"No. I didn't drink anything yesterday. Stomach bug, maybe."

"Oh, too bad. You need me to take you to Health Services?"

"No, I'm all right." A trip to Health Services would probably only serve to make me feel worse. That place gave me terrible anxiety. "I think I just need to lie down for a while."

"Okay. Well, let me know if you need anything."

Fred started to walk out of the bathroom, but something else occurred to me. "Hey, Fred?"

His face lit up. He looked so happy to be needed. "What can I do for you?"

"Are there LGBT organizations on campus? I'm asking for a friend. He's… questioning his sexuality."

I was certain Fred could see right through the old "I'm asking for a friend" canard, but he smiled and said, "Yeah, there is one. I think they meet on Thursdays. Want me to find out? For your friend?"

"Yeah, that would be great. Thanks. Uh, no hurry or anything."

"Okay. They probably have a website too." He smiled. "Feel better, Dave. I'll be around all afternoon if you change your mind about Health Services."

"Thanks. I appreciate it."

I retreated back to my room. Class, I decided, was out of the question, so I slid back into bed and pulled the covers over my head, hoping I could work all this out before Joe came back. I figured I just needed a little more time to think and the answer to all my open questions would present itself.

CHAPTER 6

THE FIRST weekend of May was always Spring Fest on the North Quad. It was basically a weekend-long party. On Saturday the quad became kind of a low-rent carnival, with junk food, games, and a bouncy castle. Sunday they brought in live local bands to play hour-long sets from about noon until dusk. Students from all over campus—and some of the other local schools—flooded my little residential area, and most of them spent a good part of the weekend totally wasted.

So Joe and I started early, drinking beer in our room midday Saturday while working up the energy to go eat cotton candy and play around in the bouncy castle. Vanessa showed up too, and drank with us.

"So, Dave," she said, already kind of tipsy, "now that you and Britney have broken up, do you have your eye on anyone in particular?"

"No. And the semester's almost over anyway. What's the point?"

She narrowed her eyes at me. "Dude, I'm not telling you to get married. I was just curious."

I sighed. "Are you trying to say I'd just be a third wheel if I hang out with you guys all weekend, so you want me to find a girl to hook up with?" It came out sounding a little more angry and defensive than I'd intended.

"No," said Vanessa, looking offended. "Of course not. I was just asking."

Joe shot me a "What the hell?" raised-eyebrow look over the top of his red plastic cup.

Once we were rocking the appropriate level of inebriation, we wandered outside to the carnival. Kareem stood by the bouncy castle with a ponderously large puff of pink cotton candy in his hands. When we approached, he offered us some, so I pinched off a bit of it and tried it. Super sugary but not bad. Standard cotton candy, in other words.

"It's not even that warm," Kareem said, "but Kayla Gregory and her friends are in the bouncy castle wearing only bikinis."

This piqued Joe's interest. He started to lean toward the entrance to the bouncy castle, but Vanessa snagged his arm and pulled him back. "Nice try, buddy," she said.

My phone buzzed in my pocket. I pulled it out and saw a text from Noel. *I'm on my way to North Quad. U around?*

Kareem grabbed my phone out of my hand. "Ooh, is some hot new girl texting you?" He read the text. "Who the hell is Noel?"

"He's my friend who came to the last lounge party. I told him to come meet me at Spring Fest so we could hang out."

"Noel." Kareem took a bite of cotton candy straight from the puff and stared contemplatively out into the distance. "Nope, I don't remember a Noel."

"That's because he doesn't have boobs," Vanessa said. "He's the cute gay guy. He was wearing red pants."

Kareem looked at us with a blank expression. "Nope."

"You're really friends with this guy?" Joe said.

"Is that a problem?" I asked, a little snippy.

"No. Whatever," said Joe.

I grabbed my phone back from Kareem and texted Noel that I was near the bouncy castle.

"I heard you and Britney broke up," Kareem said, "mostly because I was trying to mack on Britney's roommate the other day. Pretty sure that girl's a lesbo. She wanted no part of all this." Kareem waved a hand over his body.

"So if a girl doesn't want you, she must be a lesbian," said Vanessa.

"That's what I just said," said Kareem.

Vanessa rolled her eyes.

"Well, this is a charming, homophobic conversation," I said.

Kareem shrugged. "Who's homophobic? No big deal if she's a lesbian."

I sighed, feeling uncomfortable now. Kareem was annoying me, even though I usually found his hijinks entertaining. Joe glared at me like I'd done something wrong. Vanessa smiled, looking happily oblivious. Suddenly I wanted to be on the other side of the quad from these people. I wanted to be spending the day with Noel.

He arrived five minutes later, just as Kareem polished off the last of the cotton candy. Kareem and Joe were having a rather heated conversation about the NBA Playoffs. I had no horse in that race—the Celtics had been eliminated, so I'd checked out of the rest of the basketball season—and I was chatting with Vanessa about how nice the weather was when I saw Noel heading our way.

I could tell when Joe spotted him because he paused his conversation long enough for Kareem to plow over him with some counterargument about how the Spurs were destined for greatness, something I knew Joe would never abide.

But I didn't care.

Noel smiled at me and—okay, this was a cliché, but it was true—everything else around me faded away.

Today he had on salmon-pink high-waters and a gray T-shirt that looked really soft. He wore nice docksiders, and his hair was perfect, falling softly over his forehead. He was so beautiful. I wanted to spend all afternoon looking at him. I wanted to touch him. I wanted to see what he looked like without all those pretty clothes on.

Damn it.

"He's *pretty*," Vanessa said, awe in her voice.

I chose not to comment. That is, I agreed, but I kept it to myself.

"Hey," I said when he got to us. I smiled. I couldn't help it.

He grinned, showing off his perfect teeth. "Hi! This looks fun."

"Have you never been to a Spring Fest?"

"I didn't come last year, no."

"Oh, I'll show you around."

"Dude," said Joe. "It's from here to the other side of the quad. What is there to show?"

I wanted to tell Joe to fuck off. He scowled at me. What the hell had gotten up his butt? I gave him the finger.

"If we're gonna bounce around in the castle, we should get in this line instead of standing here like idiots," said Vanessa.

So Joe, Vanessa, and Kareem got in line, and I said, "I'm gonna go find something to eat." Noel followed me to the other side of the quad.

"Is it not cool with your friends that I'm here? Is this some kind of North Quad solidarity thing?"

I waved my hand. "No. I don't know. Joe's been weird all day. We welcome outsiders, normally. Everyone at WMU knows North Quad Spring Fest is the best party of the year."

"I've heard. Jason has been talking about it for weeks."

"Jason?"

"Guy I've been seeing. He lives in West Quad, but he hangs out up here all the time."

My jealousy was white-hot, so powerful I stumbled. Noel reached over and grabbed my elbow, pulling me back upright before I could trip. The touch was… well, geez, this was also a cliché. But clichés exist for a reason. His hand was warm on my arm and there was electricity and all of it, and I was in very deep trouble.

There were four guys grilling hot dogs and miscellaneous other things on a couple of portable grills in one corner of the quad. We grabbed a few dogs, and then we left the quad and I took Noel over to the grassy area behind one of the dorm buildings where we usually played touch football and ultimate Frisbee. There were a bunch of students just lounging around. We found an empty patch of grass and sat beside each other as we ate.

"So how does this usually go?" he asked. "Spring Fest, I mean."

"The carnival will go on for the rest of the day. Then once it gets dark, there's a DJ in the quad, and everybody dances and gets really drunk, basically."

He laughed. "Sounds fun."

"I'm sorry my friends were so rude. Or just Joe. I'm sorry he was rude."

"It's all right."

"It's really not. I just… I don't want you to feel like you can't come here and hang out."

He smiled. "Thanks."

"So, yeah, anyway. We've got some beer back in my room, but there's usually some kind of mixed drink that shows up at some point in the afternoon too. And Jorge over there probably has a number of illicit substances." I gestured in Jorge's direction. He and a few of his cronies were sitting on a quilt that looked like it had been stolen from someone's granny's house. Jorge wasn't even trying to hide the joint in his hand.

"Not my thing," said Noel.

"Me neither. Just saying."

He finished off the veggie dog he'd taken and then leaned back on his hands with his knees up, the picture of casual and relaxed. I felt a lot more tense, wondering what to say to this guy who, let's face it, I totally lusted after.

"So," I said.

He laughed. "It's a great day."

It was. The sun shone high in the sky, the air was warm, and a gentle breeze brought the scent of grilled meat and newly bloomed flowers our way.

"I'm looking forward to this semester being over," I said, hoping to get some conversation going.

"Lot of hard classes?"

"Don't ever double major. I don't know why I thought it was a good idea. Especially since I have two artsy majors. I don't have exams, but I have to write, like, six papers at the end of every semester."

"That's rough." He looked me over. "I had you pegged as a jock when we first met."

"I *am* a jock. I run fall track."

"Yeah, but you have a lot of other interests too. There's a lot more to you than what's on the surface."

"That's true of most people."

He sat up a little straighter and wrapped his arms around his knees. "Not always true in my experience. Jason? The guy I've been seeing on and off all semester? He lives and breathes comic books. He's a Japanese major because he loves manga and anime. As far as I can tell, that's all there really is to him. I don't really know anything about comic books, but most of our conversations are about superheroes. It's why he hasn't been upgraded from 'guy I see sometimes.'"

"Ah."

"Like, he's a hot nerd. I like that. Not a lot of personality, though."

I didn't know how to feel about the fact we were apparently now close enough for him to talk about his love life, but I did like that apparently this Jason guy didn't exactly hold Noel's heart in his hands.

We spent the next hour or so just chatting. I stopped paying attention to the time. The only reason we eventually moved was because we both suddenly got a flutter of text messages. Joe texted me to ask where I'd gone. I didn't especially want to be found; I was enjoying my time with Noel a great deal. Noel said offhand that a friend of his was somewhere on North Quad looking for him.

Before we left to find our respective friends, Jorge offered us a cup from his huge jug full of some red beverage, so we sampled it. By the time I finally went back to the quad, Noel and I were pretty tipsy.

Noel's friend turned out to be no one I should have been jealous of, a curly-haired girl named Ashley. She introduced herself as Noel's fag hag, which made him wince. He clarified, "This is my good friend Ashley. She's a fellow psych major, and she does backstage tech for the Theater Club shows."

She grinned. "Sorry. Forgot you hated the 'fag hag' term."

"It just seems so demeaning. And you're hardly a hag."

Ashley laughed. "Maybe I'm reclaiming the term." She fluffed her hair with her hands. "Anyway, this is supposed to be the best party of the spring. Where does a girl get a drink around here?"

"Come with me," I said.

I escorted Noel and Ashley back to my room. I couldn't tell if Joe was really over whatever thing he'd been wigging out about or if he was just being polite, but he got drinks for everyone—Kareem and Bev were there too—and we sat around the room while we waited for the DJ to come. Noel sat beside me on my bed, and I liked that.

I was never going to be able to explain this to Joe.

Ashley and Vanessa knew each other and greeted each other with hugs and smiles. "Bio 301," Ashley said before she and Vanessa gave each other a fist bump. "Professor Lawson."

"Worst class *ever*," Vanessa said knowingly.

"Oh, I know. Lawson's accent, yeah?"

Both girls dissolved into peals of laughter.

Joe seemed sullen, but Vanessa, at least, kept conversation going. After she and Ashley relived the glory of one of the worst classes they'd taken at WMU, she turned her curiosity on Noel.

"Why psych?" Vanessa asked.

Noel smiled. "I'm fascinated by it." He glanced at me, perhaps recalling our previous conversation. "I'm interested in how mental disorders are diagnosed, first of all. But also, I have an uncle who is a psychiatrist, and he was always telling us these stories about his patients. Like, he had this one patient with schizophrenia who was convinced these three little green aliens were following him around all the time. I always wanted to know what kind of bad wiring in the human brain could cause him to believe that."

For a moment I reflected on what Noel said. This was somewhat different from what he'd told me but probably also true. It made me wonder about what he was willing to confide in me and to a room full of mostly strangers.

"That's really cool," Vanessa told him. "Are you planning on grad school?"

"I think so, yeah."

Vanessa grinned. "Are you in the LGBT club on campus? What the hell is it called again?"

I wanted to kick Vanessa for being so nosy, but Noel smiled. "It's calling itself the Queer Student Union these days, and yeah. I'm a member, but I haven't been to a meeting in a while. The guy who runs it is too militant for me."

"How so?" I asked.

He glanced at me again. "This guy doesn't even have straight friends." He gestured around the room. "Like, he calls all straight people breeders in a disgusted way. Wants nothing to do with marriage equality and those kinds of laws because he thinks gays getting married dilutes gay culture or something like that, as if gay culture were this monolithic thing."

"Weird," I said, for lack of anything more constructive.

Noel shrugged. "I mean, he's entitled to his opinion. But I kind of want to get married someday."

Something about his hopeful tone made me smile.

Vanessa moved on to quizzing Bev, who had followed Kareem back to my room. Noel turned toward me and smiled before looking back to those assembled and striking up a conversation with Ashley about some of their mutual friends. I couldn't figure out what he was trying to tell me, but I got the sense he approved of Vanessa. Or at least he was willing to tolerate her probing. And Ashley seemed to blend right in with this group. These all seemed like positive signs.

A little while later, the telltale bass thump echoing around the quad outside our window heralded the arrival of the DJ. Joe made another round of drinks, which everyone carried outside; Spring Fest was the one time of year campus security more or less ignored the open container laws of the Commonwealth of Massachusetts.

Joe actively hated dancing, but once we were outside, he made an attempt at an awkward shimmy for Vanessa's sake after the song changed and Vanessa squealed, "This is my jam!" Kareem started grinding on Bev, and Ashley ran into someone else she knew, which left me more or less alone with Noel.

That was when things got weird.

I wanted to dance with him, but I knew if I did, everyone in the whole damn quad would be aware of what I was up to, and I really was not ready for that. I took a fortifying sip of my drink—the ratio of vodka to juice had shifted significantly toward more vodka the later in the evening we got—and started bobbing my head to the music. I looked around to see if any other guys were dancing together, and there were a few clumps of straight dudes shuffling around. Would it be weird to dance with Noel if we didn't touch? Would everyone know by his clothes that he was gay and I probably was too because I was hanging on him so much?

This was too much, suddenly.

"Dave, you okay?" Noel asked.

"Yeah, sorry." I looked down at my cup, which was somehow empty. "I spaced out for a sec. Uh, I'm gonna go see if I can find a refill."

"Okay. Oh, hey, Jason is here. Go get a drink and I'll go say hi."

Well, that was just what I needed. I walked to the edge of the quad, as if I were headed back to my room, but I turned around and saw Noel sidle up to some guy with dark hair—the guy I'd seen him flirting with at the Mac that one time. The guy was skinny and had about a week's worth of beard growth. They greeted each other with smiles and hugs.

It occurred to me: Noel had sex with this guy. In fact he'd had sex with him regularly.

I couldn't really picture it. That was, I could totally picture Noel naked, but with this beardy guy in the Iron Man T-shirt? No.

Then Noel put his arms around Beardy Jason's neck and their hips pressed together, and then nudity was all I could see. The two of them. Naked, grinding against each other just like that, Noel getting off on it. I was hard. I was disgusted.

I pretty much ran back inside. When I got to my room, I poured myself a shot of vodka and downed it immediately. I'd been drinking all afternoon and had a decent buzz going, but I needed more. I needed to obliterate the image of Noel with Jason, of them kissing or… groping… or whatever it was they did behind closed doors. I hadn't the first clue, but I imagined it wasn't so different than what girls and guys did together when they made out, mostly rubbing against each other until it got to the actual penetrative sex parts… and I *knew*, but I didn't really. For a moment all I could see was beautiful Noel, naked, with his head thrown back in ecstasy and then that goddamned comic book nerd with his hands all over Noel, all over *my* Noel….

Christ, I had to get a grip. I did another shot.

Because I wanted to forget I had even a passing interest in Noel or that meeting him had thrown everything I'd ever known into question.

I was being melodramatic. I'd had this inkling about where my interests lay for a long time, probably, I'd just been pushing it back. Noel hadn't really changed anything so much as poked something already there, but now I sat on the floor of my room, a little drunk, pouring my third shot and freaking the fuck out because I wanted Noel fiercely, and there was no fucking way on earth I could ever have him. Lord, he deserved better than a coward like me.

Vanessa walked in then. "Woah," she said when she saw me.

I poured another finger of vodka into my red plastic cup and then picked up a bottle of whatever mixer was closest—some kind of red juice—and made like I wasn't the most pathetic student at Western Massachusetts University.

"Where's Noel?" she asked.

"Dancing with his boyfriend." If I'd been sober, I probably could have kept the edge out of my voice.

Vanessa's eyebrows shot up. She sat next to me on the floor. "Are you okay?"

I shook my head. "No. No, I'm really not."

She put an arm around me. "Oh, Dave. What is it?"

"I don't know. Maybe it's all the vodka, but I feel like I'm losing my mind. I can't really explain it any better than that."

"Is there something going on with you and Noel?"

"No. Nothing. We're friends."

"And he has a boyfriend."

I nodded.

"Do you want there to be something going on with you and Noel?"

I leaned back and looked at Vanessa, wondering if I could trust her.

She sighed. "If you're not ready to tell Joe, I won't say anything to him."

"I don't know," I said. "Maybe. But I'm not gay."

"Nobody said you were."

I leaned back against my bed, resting my head on the mattress. From my vantage point, I could see Joe's bed and the wall of posters, some of which had women in bikinis on them, and I knew I was supposed to find the women exciting, but I didn't. My body didn't want those women— they looked shiny and plastic and fake. I looked at Vanessa. She was pretty, but I didn't want her either. No, what I wanted was down in the quad, probably full-on making out with another dude by now.

"What if I were gay?" I asked Vanessa.

"It wouldn't matter."

I frowned.

"I just mean," Vanessa said, "we'd all still be your friends. Even Joe. If you were gay instead of straight, nothing would change."

I knew she was wrong; everything felt like it was changing.

"I'm sorry you're having a hard time," she said. "Can I do anything?"

"No. I'll be okay."

She got up and made herself a drink. "You ready to go back out there?" she asked.

"I suppose."

I stood up and immediately was dizzy. "Oof," I said.

"If you vomit later, I'm not holding your hair back," said Vanessa.

When we got back outside, Noel stood at the edge of the quad. Beardy Jason gave him a kiss and a wave and then was off again.

"He's not staying?" I asked as I got to Noel.

He started and looked at me. He smiled, at least. "No. There's some kind of *Star Wars* screening at the Mac, and apparently seeing a movie he's already seen eighty times is more important than hanging out with me." Noel shrugged.

"That jerk," I said.

Noel laughed. "Honey, it's fine. I was having a good time hanging out with you. And Jason and I aren't that serious." He held up his cup. "Some girls gave us mudslides. Apparently they stole one of those ten-gallon tubs of ice cream from the dining hall."

"Classy," said Vanessa.

Ashley wandered back over. "Was that Jason?" she asked.

"Yep," said Noel. "He turned down all this fun to hang out with his geek friends at the Mac."

Ashley raised an eyebrow. "Right. And you're still with him because...."

Noel sighed. "I dunno. It's kind of slim pickings for cute gay guys at WMU."

Ashley patted his shoulder. "You don't have to keep dating the so-so guy just because he's there. It's okay to hold out for somebody special."

"That's good advice," said Vanessa.

I stayed silent because I was certain anything I said would give too much away.

The song changed again. Ashley grinned and grabbed Noel's hands. "Dance with me!"

Vanessa and I stood at the edge of the quad and watched them dance. Ashley got a little handsy with Noel, but he played along. He was actually a pretty great dancer with a good sense of rhythm. Although it was hard to be objective when he was moving his hips that way, because they made me think of him thrusting and....

God. I covered my eyes with my free hand.

"You really do have a crush on him, don't you?" Vanessa said.

"I'm not gay."

"Okay. But maybe you're bisexual. Or not. I don't know. What I do know is the world is not always black and white, and sometimes you just feel what you feel."

What I felt as I watched Ashley and Noel dance together was that I wanted his hands on me the way they were on Ashley, and I knew he didn't even like her in that way.

The song ended and Ashley spun around to grope some other guy. Noel and the guy acknowledged each other with a brief clasp of their hands. Ashley and the guy started dancing too hard, though, so Noel drifted back toward us.

"You know that guy?" I asked, taking him in. The guy and Ashley were dancing like crazy people and grinning at each other. I deemed the guy objectively attractive if you liked them dark-haired and scruffy.

Which apparently Noel did. He said, "Dated him for, like, five minutes freshman year. He's hot but has the IQ of a banana."

Vanessa snorted. "Well, I'm gonna go find Joe. I'll see you boys later."

I watched her go, feeling frustrated and sad. I took a sip of my drink.

"You okay?" Noel asked.

"I wish people would stop asking me that. I'm fine."

"And kind of drunk."

"I want to dance." The words just tumbled out of my mouth. Maybe it was the vodka talking, but I was getting pretty tired of standing on the sidelines.

"All right," Noel said. "Let's dance."

I followed him into the crowd of people. The DJ put on a song I knew vaguely, but clearly everyone else in the crowd loved it, because a wave of cheers passed around us. But whatever. I was past caring. I threw my arms in the air and bent my knees and kind of swished my hips around. I didn't really know how to dance, but that was hardly a prerequisite for dancing at a place like this. Most of the kids around me looked like idiots, joyfully and drunkenly swaying to the beat.

Noel nodded and got into it too, but he clearly had a much better sense of rhythm than I did. His moves were all smooth and on beat. He shifted his hips and bowed his shoulders and threw his arms out in a way that made sense.

"I love this song," he said to me.

He danced and I watched him. I made sad, failed attempts at copying his moves. He made faces like he was really into the song or else just trying to make me laugh. I did laugh, because I was drunk and because I really liked him.

Then I reached for him.

He let me. I put my hands on his hips and stepped closer to him, bringing our bodies together. He bit his lip. He didn't touch me. We danced like that for a minute, mirroring each other, my hands on his hips, his arms at his sides. I moved into his personal space, making my meaning clear. I danced *with* Noel. He put his hands on my shoulders. Our hips touched and my body was all electrical pulses and goose bumps. My heart pounded. I got hard. I leaned closer.

The song ended. The bubble burst.

Noel gently pushed me away. "You really sure about this, Dave?"

"I am."

"You're drunk sure."

"Who the hell cares?"

"I do."

So, okay, this was not the way to do… whatever I was doing.

"I think I need some water," I said.

"Then let's find you some."

THE NIGHT went on in that vein for a while. I hung out with Noel, we ran into people we knew, we danced a little, we drank a lot. Eventually we tracked down Ashley, and then we rejoined Joe and his party, which had collected our friend Mike and a couple of our regular touch football buddies. Joe determined our room wasn't a big enough space to hang out in, so we ended up in the lounge on our floor, piled on the couches. Noel and I sat next to each other, leaning on each other's shoulders.

Ashley and Mike lived on the same floor, it turned out, and the two of them flirted like crazy. I wasn't sure anything would come of it—Mike didn't date much despite joking almost constantly about hooking up with girls, and Noel had implied Ashley was kind of seeing a guy who lived in East Quad. While they made eyes at each other, the rest of us excitedly gossiped and talked about people we saw hooking up and sports and classes and whatever the hell. I barely listened. I liked the feeling of Noel pressing against me, of the warmth of his body in proximity to mine, the way his chest gently vibrated as he talked. It was exciting in a way that hooking up with a girl hadn't been in a long time.

I was also wasted; there was no denying it. Sound rushed around me, and I felt like I was underwater. The room spun. It was on the edge of unpleasant, but if I didn't move much, I was all right.

Kareem and Bev took off at one point. Ashley got a text from the guy in East Quad and wandered off. Mike and the other guys made some noise about trying to catch the end of some game. Eventually Joe and Vanessa got up too. Joe gave me strict instructions not to go back to the room for at least half an hour, and Noel assured Joe he'd keep me away.

"Doesn't look like he's going anywhere for a while anyway," Noel said.

When Joe left, Noel and I were alone in the lounge. I laid my head on his shoulder because it was there.

"Noel?" I said.

"Mmm?" He put an arm around me.

I snuggled a little closer. This was nice. I felt anchored against him. "Are you drunk?"

"I think a little, yeah."

"Me too."

"Are you saying that as a disclaimer?"

"Huh?"

He sighed and I felt his chest move against my face. "Tomorrow, are you going to tell me what happened tonight means nothing because you were drunk?"

"No. If anything happens tonight, it's because I want it to happen."

He sighed. "What is it you want to happen tonight?"

I pulled away so I could face him. "Can I tell you a secret nobody knows?"

Even through the alcohol haze, I was aware of how silly I sounded. But he nodded and looked at me solemnly.

"I think I'm…." But I couldn't say it.

That hung in the air for a moment.

"What do you think you are?" he asked eventually.

I still didn't think *gay* quite fit. There were still women in the world I found sexually attractive. I'd been completely head-over-heels for the girl I'd dated freshman year before she dumped me to go out with a townie. But I definitely wasn't straight. I could face that now, in this drunk moment.

"Queer," I said. "I've never told anyone."

He nodded slowly.

"Queer," I repeated. "It makes me sound strange, but I don't think there's anything strange about me."

"There isn't," Noel said. He leaned a little closer to me.

Oh Lord. I wanted to kiss him. He had such nice lips, on the thin side but still just right there and very kissable. I'd never kissed a boy before and I wondered if it would taste different than kissing a girl.

The world tipped and shook around us, but I focused on his mouth and said, "I really like you."

"I really like you too."

"But you have Beardy Jason."

He laughed softly. "Eh. He's nothing special. He's not like you."

We stared at each other for a long moment. I heard what Noel said, but it whizzed by me. I figured I should take this opportunity to ask for what I really wanted, but what was that? If I'd nearly had an aneurism about dancing, walking around campus as a couple would surely kill me. But if he dug me as much as I dug him, maybe he'd let me see what he had to offer.

"I want to see what it's like," I said.

"What what's like?"

"Being with a man."

He stared at me, his expression unreadable. "You've never…."

"Never."

"But you want to…."

I kissed him. I put my hand on the side of his face to keep him there, and I pressed my lips against his, tentative at first, but then I opened up to it. I took his lower lip between both of mine, sucking gently. He responded, moving his lips against mine. I licked into his mouth, wanting to taste him. He tasted of rum and chocolate ice cream and something else I couldn't name. I liked kissing him a lot, and the simple connection between us made me hot everywhere. And, hell, I'd been hard since we'd sat down on that couch together. Making out wasn't helping matters.

He put a hand on my thigh but otherwise didn't move closer. He kissed me back, snaking his tongue into my mouth and moaning softly, but he made no move to take it further. I couldn't tell if this experience was as mind-blowing for him as it was for me. Because the thing was, this moment felt nearly perfect: the way our lips fit together, the taste of him, his warm body near me, his scent. I was turned on, but more than that, I was suddenly free of the anxiety I often felt when I hooked up with someone. This was... well, this was the way things were supposed to be. And maybe Noel was who I was supposed to be with.

He pulled away gently and smiled at me.

"Maybe this happens to you all the time," I said, "but that was a hell of a kiss."

"I agree. And it doesn't happen all the time."

"I want to do that again."

I leaned forward to kiss him again, but he put a finger on my lips. "Listen," he said. "You're drunk, maybe not completely of sound mind. I think we should leave this here for now. But if, when you're sober, you still want to kiss me, I'd be happy to oblige."

"Okay," I said.

"It hasn't been quite half an hour. We should probably wait a little longer before I take you back to your room."

"Okay."

I leaned on the sofa, and then I settled my head back on his shoulder. He put an arm around me and held me there. I closed my eyes and inhaled, loving the way he smelled, sort of minty, like nice cologne and toothpaste, but also like the sweet sourness of alcohol.

I'd had a lot to drink that night, huh? I tried to make a quick mental calculation but lost track, wondering how I was even still coherent and not, like, puking my guts out in one of the shrubs that lined the quad. But no, I was wrapped up in Noel's arms and could not have felt more content.

The room was still spinning, but for a brief moment, I thought Noel could make all the whirring stop. He could ground me, make me whole. But maybe that was all drunk hyperbole.

Or maybe I had just learned something important.

CHAPTER 7

I WOKE up the next morning alone in bed in my room without a clear recollection of how I got there. Joe slept across the room in his bed, also alone, rolled onto his side so that I faced his back.

I must have fallen asleep in the lounge with Noel. That was the last thing I remembered. I'd kissed him and then fallen asleep. I'd kissed him. Had I really done that?

I felt giddy at the memory. It had been new and exciting, and I wanted to do it again.

The clock indicated it was just after 11:00 am. The tinny, off-key buzz of a band doing a sound check out on the quad wafted into the room, alerting me to the fact that the day was about to get started. I wondered if I could talk Noel back to the North Quad to hang out with me and kiss me some more. I didn't care about the consequences right then.

I picked my phone off the plastic bin that operated as my nightstand and sent him a text: *U awake?*

Yup came the almost instantaneous reply. *U feel ok?*

Surprisingly, yes. There was a vague pain in the back of my skull but no a full-on headache. Nothing coffee and a greasy breakfast couldn't fix. *I feel great!* I texted back. *U want to come see some bands?*

Sorry, can't.

Oh.

I mean, what else could I say? I pictured him in bed with Beardy Jason, and suddenly I did feel kind of nauseous.

But then I got: *Just got a call from future landlord. Have 2 go 2 South Hadley 2 sign papers and set up stuff at new apartment.*

I let out a sigh of relief. I texted, *If you're back by dinner, maybe you want to get something to eat?*

His response took a few minutes. I rationalized he probably was just getting ready to leave and not looking at his phone, but what if he hated me and my drunk ass now? What if, by kissing him, I'd fucked everything up? I knew he was with Jason, after all, even if he said it wasn't serious. What if I'd made a huge mistake? What if he wasn't really into me?

Eventually he texted, *How much of last nite do u remember?*

All of it, I said. Well, not the part where he must have taken me back to my room and put me to bed, but the important part I remembered. In a rare moment of bravery, I followed up with, *I'm sober now and I still want 2 kiss u.*

He texted me back eight smiley faces. So that seemed like a good sign.

Out on the quad, someone moved a speaker or microphone, and the feedback squawk was ear-piercing. Joe stirred and grumbled something. I decided to get up and go shower.

When I got back to the room a little while later, Joe was up and sitting at his desk, checking something on his computer. I pulled on clothes and sat on my bed to lace up my sneakers. I picked up my phone and saw a text from Noel begging off dinner because he'd forgotten he had to work that night. I thought about texting Kareem to see if he wanted to get something greasy for breakfast from the dining hall. I could have asked Joe, who sat right there, in the T-shirt he'd been wearing the day before and a pair of plaid boxers, but the vibe coming off him wasn't especially friendly.

Then again, maybe I imagined it.

"You going to breakfast?" I asked.

"Probably."

"Anytime soon or…?"

He turned around and looked at me. "There's something I don't get."

"Okay." I finished tying my shoes and put my feet on the floor.

"Why is it all of a sudden you're best friends with this guy none of us have ever met before, and he's all over you last night even though you're not even gay, and you're just going along with it?"

"He wasn't all over me." As far as I could remember anyway.

"Uh, dude. How drunk were you? He basically carried you back here from the lounge and put you to bed. He fucking tucked you in. What the hell was that about?"

"I don't know." Now that he mentioned it, I had a vague recollection of Noel tugging my covers over me and kissing my forehead. It had been sweet.

"Everything with you is fucking weird right now. I don't know what the hell is going on in your head."

"Nothing. There's nothing going on in my head. Nothing is new or different or weird. I like hanging out with Noel. That's all. Why? Is the fact he's gay a problem for you?" I said all this on one long breath, which was probably the only clue Joe needed that something was off here.

"No," Joe said. "I don't give a shit if he's gay. Unless he's hitting on you."

"Why do you care? If he does something I don't want him to do, that's my problem, isn't it?"

"Do you want him to hit on you?"

I had no idea how to answer that, so I just stared at Joe.

He grunted. "Fuck it. Forget I said anything."

"If you don't care if he's gay, what the fuck is your problem?" I asked.

"Nothing! Nothing is my problem. Just like there's nothing in that pretty little head of yours."

"Fuck you."

He let out a breath. "Look, I'm sorry, but it's weird, okay. He's... he's not like us."

"Maybe that's what I like about him."

"Fine. Like I said, forget I said anything." He stood. "I'll go to breakfast. I need some goddamned coffee. Just give me ten fucking minutes to get dressed."

SO THINGS were kind of back to normal, or I thought they were anyway.

Somehow, in all the weekend activity, I'd completely forgotten the following Tuesday was the day Jerry Grossworth would be the guest speaker in my English class. I'd finished *In the Wind* by then and had gone back and reread the passages that had spoken to me the most, so I was actually really excited to hear him talk.

Jerry was a middle-aged guy, in his late fifties if my math was right, and he had one of those faces I suspected had once been quite handsome but was now lined with age and not so firm. He had a kind smile, though, and I liked the way his eyes crinkled when he looked at us all.

"You are part of an entirely new generation," he informed us as he began his talk.

He spoke off the cuff about his reasons for writing the book, namely that he hoped his story could help others in similar positions, especially those trapped in the less accepting corners of society.

Then he said, "The book is fifteen years old now, and sometimes I think I'd like to write an epilogue. I was in a pretty dark place when I wrote *In the Wind*, although I intended for the message to be inspirational. You have to let go of everything holding you back in order to be happy, so writing was really my way of letting go of some old memories. Shortly after I finished the book, I met Greg. We were married five years ago."

A smattering of applause sounded through the class.

"That's hopeful, right?" Jerry said. "My parents wouldn't talk to me for a while, did not approve of my so-called lifestyle, and the first man I ever loved died of AIDS. My twenties were a rough time. But I've seen and done so many great things since I finished writing that book. I found love again. I've been around the world. I lived to see real acceptance of LGBT people in America at large, definitely not enough yet but more than I thought I'd see in my lifetime. That's what I want you young people to take away from my experiences. There's so much hope in the world."

When he said that, the class burst into a more resounding round of applause.

Professor Strong opened up the floor to questions. I wanted to ask something—I wanted to talk directly to the man who had written the book that had basically changed my life—but my mind went blank. Instead I tried to come up with a question while my classmates hogged Jerry's attention. Most of them asked follow-up questions related to the events of the book or asked him what he'd meant by a particular turn of phrase. I had a question forming, relating to my own drama of course, about deceit and coming clean to your loved ones even if you hadn't lied *per se*.

I hadn't lied until recently, at least not about my sexuality, because I hadn't understood it. But I had been lying to Joe about what I was going through and what Noel really meant to me, and for that, I judged myself harshly. Still, in the classroom, sitting fifteen feet from Jerry Grossworth, I wanted to ask the question "Do you think it's deceptive to stay in the closet, even if you aren't ready to come out yet?" I realized this would probably make my classmates assume I was in the closet. That kept my hands in my lap, although part of me thought asking was more important than keeping quiet.

Professor Strong, more aware of the forward march of time than I was, wound down the discussion before I could ask anything. "Mr. Grossworth is speaking tonight in Auditorium B in Addison Hall at seven," she said, casually putting her arm on Jerry's shoulder as if they were old friends. "I know a few more of you had questions you didn't have time to ask, but if you come to the presentation tonight, Jerry may be able to answer them then."

She dismissed the class then. So instead of asking my question, I left the room and texted Noel.

You doing anything 2nite?

I was most of the way down the hall toward the men's room where we'd first met when he texted me back. *Volunteered to help with a QSU event.*

It took me a moment to work out QSU stood for Queer Student Union, which was silly because Fred had stopped by my room that very morning to give me the info on the group, "in case your friend still wants to attend their meetings." He'd handed me a pamphlet with a website link and their meeting schedule. Thank goodness Joe had been at class; I never would have been able to explain that one.

With Jerry Grossworth? I texted back to Noel.

Yes.

I want to go. Can we sit together?

He texted me back a smiley. Then: *You bet, cutie.*

I imagined I had hearts in my eyes and little birdies swirling around my head. Dear Lord, I was in sad shape.

I so didn't care.

NOEL MET me that night in the back of the auditorium. I hadn't seen him since The Kiss, but we'd kept up a steady stream of text messages and I felt giddy whenever I thought of him, so I reasoned things between us were mostly good. He grinned when he saw me, and that made me feel warm inside. I grinned back. He hugged me in greeting, just a quick little hug, but still, that was new for us, and it felt Significant.

"I saved you a seat," he said. "Members of the QSU got reserved seating up front in exchange for helping out, but we got to bring guests. You're my guest."

"Oh, cool." I looked around for Noel's beardy boyfriend but didn't see him. "What about Jason?"

Noel shrugged. "This isn't really his sort of thing. Come on."

He took my hand—took my hand!—and escorted me down to the second row, which had been roped off with red yarn. Someone had taped a Reserved sign to the yarn. A few people were already seated in the section.

A blond guy with a nose ring walked up to us. "Hey, Noel," he said. Then he lowered his voice. "Who's your cute friend?"

"Paul, this is my friend Dave. Dave, this is Paul. He's one of the QSU officers."

I moved to shake hands with Paul but realized Noel still held my right hand in his. I supposed that meant Paul would pick up on the fact that perhaps Noel and I were more than friends. Butterflies flitted in my stomach at the thought.

If nothing else, though, being at an event honoring a man I so admired for his bravery made me realize how foolish I was being. I didn't know a soul in this auditorium, save for Noel, and this was obviously a queer-friendly space. What reason did I have to hide?

"I just have to check on something," Noel said, guiding me into the seat he'd save for me. "I'll be right back."

I looked around while I waited. The crowd looked mixed. I did recognize a few people from my English class, including a girl I'd dated for a hot minute sophomore year and a few people I knew were friendly with Joe and Kareem. My being here had some plausible deniability—I had just read this guy's book for class, and Noel was my friend, so it made sense for us to sit together—but I couldn't help but feel like a spotlight was shining down on me, with a big red arrow that said "Queer! This kid here is queer! Alert!"

Noel returned a few minutes later and settled into the chair next to me. He smiled and said, "I read *In the Wind* a while ago. It's a little dated, but I liked it."

The words were so tepid considering all this book had done for me. But I didn't want to give too much of myself away. "He gave a talk to my English class this afternoon. I wanted to ask him a question, but we ran out of time."

"What were you going to ask?"

My first instinct was to snap, "None of your business," because the question felt private now, but I swallowed and said, "Maybe not even a question. I just… I've been thinking a lot for the last month about, I don't know. Everything."

"Uh-huh."

"Well, so basically, I'm not ready to talk about this with my friends yet, but I feel like I'm lying if I don't."

Noel frowned, and I was sad for that because I knew I had said something he didn't like. "Are you worried about Joe and them?"

I nodded. "And my family. And the whole, uh, coming out thing." I let out a breath. "This all still feels so new to me. A month ago I was dating a girl and had no idea the reason I felt so weird about that was because of all this." I gestured between us. "I think my family would be okay, probably, and Joe too, but what idiot gets to be twenty years old without knowing he's not really straight?"

A crease formed in Noel's forehead. "I'm the first person you've ever even mentioned your feelings about this to?"

"Yes. You're the only person."

"Dave...."

We were interrupted by some shuffling on stage. A tall, skinny guy with a buzz cut and a lot of tattoos walked out on stage and introduced himself as Chris Hendricks, the president of the QSU. He talked—at length, in a highly repetitive manner—about how thrilled his organization was to welcome Jerry Grossworth to campus. After a good five minutes of this, Jerry himself ambled onto the stage and took the microphone from Chris.

Jerry gave a longer, more detailed version of the talk he'd given to my English class. Enough of it sounded the same that I thought maybe this was a canned speech he gave to college campuses all over the country. He talked about what New York had been like in the eighties, about AIDS, about being out and proud even with a close-minded family. He talked about writing the book and about his husband. Then he talked about his next project, a book of essays, due out in a couple of months. We as an audience sat there, rapt.

This man inspired me. He made me want to be a better person. He made me want to find whatever bravery I had hidden in the depths of my soul so I could just be who I was always meant to be. I thought if I could be brave like that, then maybe Noel would really want me as more than just a make-out partner. He'd want me enough to give up Jason. He'd be proud to have me by his side. Not that he was ashamed now, exactly, but I didn't think I deserved much of his respect, let alone his pride or affection.

But I could get there. Jerry Grossworth made me believe it was possible. And I wanted it, so much.

When Jerry opened up the room for questions, Noel elbowed me, but I couldn't make my hand go up in the air. Instead I listened to other people stand up and tell their stories. A woman said she was a senior and had been inspired after reading *In the Wind* to finally admit to her best friend that she had more than friendly feelings for her. They'd been a couple for three years. A man said he had never known another gay person his entire life, but then he read *In the Wind* in high school and felt hopeful more people like him were out there. There were a dozen stories like this in that auditorium, stories of hope and change and love.

I'm not proud of this, but I cried.

I didn't realize it at first, not until my eyes began to itch. Then a tear slid down my cheek. I lifted my hand to wipe it away and the gesture caught Noel's attention.

"Oh, Dave," he whispered.

"So much hope," I said. "There's so much love in this room."

Noel smiled. "I know." He reached over and wiped away my tears with his thumb. "I know."

There was a reception afterward with just the QSU students and a handful of faculty members. Noel got me in and then insisted he introduce me to Jerry. Noel had already met him earlier in the evening, so I guess they were old friends now. He introduced me as "My friend Dave." I shook Jerry's hand. He told me to call him Jerry.

"I saw you in Elizabeth Strong's class today, yes?" Jerry said.

"Yeah." I was surprised he'd picked me out of the crowd. Maybe I'd looked especially agitated. "I had wanted to ask you something, but we ran out of time." Yikes, I was super nervous suddenly. My stomach flopped as I spoke. This was just what I needed, I thought, to vomit all over poor Jerry Grossworth's shoes.

Jerry smiled. "What did you want to ask me?"

I glanced at Noel. "Well, I...." I took a deep breath. "Look, this is the situation. I've only recently started to come to terms with the fact that I'm... queer."

It was incredibly hard to say. My heart was pounding so hard I could hear it.

Jerry nodded. "I know what that's like."

"I've hardly told anyone. I can't believe I'm telling you."

Jerry gave me his kind smile. There was something very fatherly about him.

I needed some kind of support, so I reached toward Noel. I knew he couldn't tell what I needed, so as he looked at me with a puzzled expression, I hooked my finger into one of his belt loops. I needed his proximity more than anything else. "I just... I'm not quite ready to tell the world yet, but I feel like a big fat liar if I don't."

Jerry nodded. "We all do these things on our own time," he said.

A nonanswer. I sighed. "Or it's dumb. I'm sorry for bothering you."

Jerry shot me the kind smile again. "You're not bothering me. I like speaking at colleges because there are so many young people who are seeing the world the way I once did, only you have a different world before you. I was about your age when I started discovering things about myself I hadn't known were possible, but my world was much darker than this one is." He tilted his head. "People come out for a lot of reasons. Because they're tired of lying, maybe. Or because they fall in love." He glanced at where my hand now rested on Noel's waist.

Noel coughed.

I didn't know anything about love. All I really knew was I wanted Noel in a somewhat intangible way. I wanted him near me. I wanted him to talk to me. I wanted him sexually. That wasn't love. That wasn't anything beyond a vague yearning.

Jerry patted my shoulder. "I think you'll be all right." He winked and then moved on to chat with someone else.

I found that unsatisfying. I turned to Noel. "Do you think I'll be all right?"

"Yes, I do." His tone was so forceful I almost believed him. "I mean, do things as you're ready for them. This is all really new to you. If you want to come out, I'll help, or I'll listen. Okay?"

"Yeah."

I moved. I didn't intend to hug him, but I let go of his belt loop and moved my hand around to his back. He put an arm around my shoulders. And then we were hugging, our bodies pressed together, and it was the most comforting, anchoring thing in the world. And I thought, yeah, maybe I would be okay. If nothing else, I had Noel.

CHAPTER 8

JOE WOULDN'T be caught dead at a musical, but I managed to talk
Vanessa and a down-for-anything Kareem into attending the WMU
Theater Club production of *Guys and Dolls*.

The Theater Club was basically acting for nonmajors. They
tended to put on more mainstream fare—musicals or else the same
kinds of plays your high school drama club did, like *A Streetcar Named
Desire* and *The Odd Couple*—than the theater department did. The
club members put on these shows for the hell of it, so they were more
fun to watch than the theater department's shows, which tended to be
pretentious, avant-garde, and incomprehensible, at least to me. The one
theater department production I had gone to had been a modernization
of an obscure Elizabethan-era play; the play itself read like low-rent
Shakespeare, but the actors danced around in shiny vinyl catsuits with
bright neon belts that were supposed to symbolize... something. That
was never really clear to me. I only went because I'd been dating a girl
in the theater department at the time and she'd insisted. Otherwise I
avoided theater department shows, but the Theater Club productions
were always a good time.

So I settled in to watch *Guys and Dolls*, and not only because
I'd get to see Noel sing to everyone that they should sit down and stop
rocking the boat.

While the house lights were still on, Kareem flipped through the
program and said, "Oh, I think the girl who plays Adelaide lives in Emerson
Hall. Jenny Schuster? She's the short girl with curly brown hair?"

Didn't even ring a bell. "Who?"

Kareem waved his hand and then pointed at the stage. "Jenny. She
goes to our gym, dude."

"So does everyone in North Quad." That, and Kareem, Joe, and I
only actually managed to go to the gym maybe once every other week.

"Is she the one who dates Chip the Pizza Guy?" asked Vanessa. Chip
was a staple in the North Quad dorms. He seemed to be the only guy who
delivered pizza from this one place just off campus, so everyone knew

him. He was also a WMU student and a Theater Club regular—a quick glance at the program indicated he was playing Benny Southstreet.

"I think so," said Kareem. "Yeah, because every time I see them together, I think about how weird it is that he's, like, two feet taller than she is."

Vanessa laughed. "Good for them. Do we know anyone else in this show?"

"Noel," I said. "And Kat." Kat was the RA on the sixth floor of Emerson House.

Vanessa sighed. "It's a shame Joe thinks he's too butch for musicals."

Kareem guffawed. "This one's got gangsters and cabaret singers, right?"

"Yeah," I said.

"Whatever, Joe," said Kareem. "Too butch, my big black ass."

The lights dimmed. The small pit orchestra started playing the first notes. The stage lights illuminated a colorful set I supposed was meant to look like Times Square in the 1920s. And out walked Noel, Chip the Pizza Guy, and some other dude I didn't know. They launched right into "Fugue for Tinhorns."

The show was fantastic. If I hadn't already loved the musical, I would have by the time this production ended. The leads—I recognized Jenny once she came on stage as Adelaide, and she played against a cute guy I'd never seen before as Nathan Detroit—were engaging, the singing was pretty solid, and even though Noel played a secondary character, I liked watching him whenever he was on stage.

He was magnetic, handsome, and charming. He had a gorgeous singing voice, too, something I hadn't anticipated, even though he'd told me he loved to sing. It was a bright tenor, and the beauty of it couldn't be disguised even when he adopted a wise-guy New York accent. Well, the accent wasn't that great—it was hard for a boy from North Carolina who had been living in Massachusetts for two years to wrap his mouth around the distinctive hard consonants and cawfee-tawk vowels of New York, I supposed—but the rest of his performance was fantastic. Maybe I was biased, but I thought the theater community was really losing out on something because Noel didn't want to do this professionally.

At intermission Kareem got up to go to the bathroom and Vanessa and I loitered in the audience. A lot of the audience cleared out, but those behind began to chat loudly with each other.

"For what it's worth," Vanessa said quietly, "I think Noel is really talented. He seems like a good guy."

"He is, yeah."

"And you have a crush on him."

"Van, I…."

"It's okay. You can tell me. I won't judge."

I sighed. "I… yeah."

"Does he know?"

"Noel? Yeah. He knows."

Vanessa grinned. "And…?"

"I don't know. We kissed once, but that's it. I like him, but I'm not sure what I want yet."

Vanessa practically glowed, she was so giddy. She put her hands on my shoulders and shook me gently. "Oh my God, this is so awesome. You kissed him? How was it?"

"It was good." I couldn't keep the smile off my face.

She hugged me. "Oh, Dave, I'm so happy for you."

I gently nudged her away. "Don't be happy for me yet. It's nothing. Nothing has really happened. It's just a thing I'm thinking about. Yeah, I like him, but I'm not…." I almost said I wasn't gay, but that felt like a lie. I peeled her hands from my shoulders. "Anyway, maybe it's just a silly fleeting thing and it'll go away and I'll be my old self again once the semester is over. Spring-induced hallucination. All those trees blooming behind Emerson are making me have some kind of allergic reaction."

I didn't believe that, and Vanessa clearly didn't either. She crossed her arms and frowned at me. "Well, whatever. You want to date him, I'll support you. You don't, I'll support you. You don't have to be afraid."

"I'm not. I'm just… trying to figure this out. It's complicated." I looked toward the stage. The tech crew, clad in black pants and T-shirts, were moving set pieces around. I recognized Noel's friend Ashley—her insane curly hair stood out against all the black clothing—and we gave each other little waves. I turned back to Vanessa. "I don't know how else to explain it. But it's not as easy as you're making it sound, and I honestly am not really sure what I want to happen yet."

"Okay."

"So don't tell Joe. Not until I'm ready to say something. Which I'm not, because this is nothing."

She pressed her lips together in a way that showed she was clearly trying to suppress a smile. "Okay."

"And just… don't be auditioning to be my fag hag, okay? It's not like that. I'm not going to suddenly be interested in shopping and pink cocktails just because I'm… whatever it is I am."

"I would never." Vanessa made a show of looking appalled. "Besides, I prefer the term 'fruit fly.'"

And okay, that made me laugh.

Kareem returned then and asked, "What's funny?"

"Your face." I told him.

He stuck his tongue out and made his eyes bulge, proving my point. The house lights dimmed, so we sat back down.

After the show we lingered in the lobby, chatting with other audience members we knew and waiting for the actors to join us.

Ashley came by and said hi, but then she got pulled away with the other tech people, laughing the whole time. Apparently they felt pretty confident they'd put on a good show. "Noel is on his way out," she told me as she left. She said this while winking. Winking! I prayed Kareem hadn't seen.

Most of the cast filtered out about twenty minutes after the curtain. I watched Noel travel the gauntlet through people he knew, accepting hugs and kisses and even a rose from a girl who I hoped knew better. He kissed her cheek.

I realized quickly enough I was just part of the gauntlet. Quite a few people gathered in the lobby were people Noel knew well, had probably spent a lot of time with him, and everyone seemed to really like him. What wasn't to like? He was cute and friendly, and he greeted everyone warmly. When a beefy guy gave him a hug, he laughed and accepted it, looking thrilled to see whoever this guy was, and my jealousy score went off the meter.

He walked up to me with the same broad smile he'd given to everyone else. "What did you think?" he asked.

"You were great!" I said, probably with too much enthusiasm.

He thanked me. He still had on stage makeup, smudgy eyeliner and rosy cheeks. He winked at me and patted my shoulder, and then he moved on to the next person he had to greet.

What was with all the winking?

To say I was disappointed would be an understatement. Conscious of Vanessa and Kareem looking at me, I tried to stay engaged in conversation with the people around me while watching Noel proceed across the lobby. I fretted that I thought about him a lot more than he thought about me, that our evening with Jerry Grossworth notwithstanding, we'd made no progress, no steps forward. I'd been thinking about Noel pretty much nonstop since that night, and nothing had changed between us. There'd been no second kiss. And Noel, of course, had all these friends to hug him and congratulate him. Gay friends, fashionable friends, friends who were from his home planet and not mine, people he belonged with. I wondered if he'd even spared a thought for me since the last time I'd seen him.

And, of course, there was goddamned Beardy Jason, who gave Noel a smile and a big kiss on the lips in greeting.

Who was I? No one, that's who.

Vanessa, Kareem, and I stopped at the Mac for milk shakes on the way back to the dorms. I was well into my chocolate shake when I got a text from Noel.

So glad you could come tonight! Sorry for not talking longer.

Well, there was that. I glanced at Vanessa, who seemed to be using her straw as a spoon to fish a big blob of ice cream out of her shake. *It's okay*, I texted to Noel. *You were really good. I mean it. Great singing voice. I had no idea.*

I glanced up at the table. Kareem was similarly engrossed in his phone, and Vanessa was now staring at me with her eyebrows raised expectantly. I shook my head.

Noel texted, *I wish we could have talked. Where are you now?*

Wait, did he want to meet up? *The Mac. With friends.*

I regretted adding the last part almost immediately. I wanted to see Noel badly, but I couldn't figure out how to ditch Kareem and Vanessa without having to explain myself. My heart pounded now, and I wasn't quite sure I could face him. Part of me wanted to drop everything and run across campus with "Born Free" playing in the background, so I could launch myself into his arms and kiss him and… all of that, but part of me couldn't move my butt out of the uncomfortable plastic chair in the Mac because all of this scared the shit out of me.

There was a long wait for the next text. Eventually he said, *I told Jason I wanted us to be just friends.*

Wait, what? *Really?* I asked.

Yeah. Not fair to string him along if I want to be with you.

That message was like a punch in the face. He wanted to be with me? My stomach flopped, but I managed to text, *You weren't blowing me off just now?*

No. Jason and I had plans after the show and I didn't want to keep him waiting.

Then a moment later, he said, *I wanted to end it.*

Because of me? I asked, still not believing it.

And some other reasons.

That was enough for me. A happy warmth spread through my chest. I looked up before I responded and realized Kareem and Vanessa were both staring at me.

"Dude," Kareem said. "You just giggled."

"Sorry," I said. I texted Noel, *I gotta stop ignoring my friends, but let's talk later.*

He texted me back a smiley face.

I wanted to talk now. I wanted to call him and tell him I was on my way to his dorm, and then we'd... well, I wasn't sure what we'd do, but it would probably be awesome.

"Have you already moved on from Britney?" Kareem asked, clearly onto me.

"What? No," I said. "And the semester's almost over. What's the point?"

"You and Joe have the slick bachelor pad set up, don't you?" Kareem said.

Vanessa laughed. "Oh, it's slick all right. Based on what Joe has told me, it's all shag carpeting and secondhand furniture."

It was true. I'd learned when we went to sign the lease that the carpet in this place left something to be desired. It was a decent-enough neutral beige color, but my shoes sank into it when I walked across it. Given that the apartment had been home to a long series of WMU students, I could only imagine what now lived in the depths of the carpet. We had a nice TV for the place, sure, but I couldn't imagine anyone being impressed by our tiny living quarters.

I said, "Who is even going to be out here this summer, besides me, Joe, and Vanessa?" And Noel, though I didn't add that. I didn't know if it was public knowledge.

"Bev and I are talking about going to Cape Cod in August," said Kareem, much to my relief. I had never been so glad for his inability to stick to one conversation topic for longer than two minutes.

"That's going well," I said.

"So far."

Kareem launched into a story about taking Bev out on a date to the Pub, our little town's generic American-food restaurant and the most popular first-date location near campus. I always thought the place was overrated—and hamburgers cost half as much at the Mac—but Kareem had bought whatever they were selling about it being romantic. Vanessa cooed as he told his story, telling him he was adorable, which he denied through a smile.

I spent his whole story thinking about Noel.

CHAPTER 9

EVEN THOUGH I wanted to, I didn't see Noel again that week, and then it was finals, so everyone's schedules were wacky. I picked up a few extra shifts at Hale's on top of everything—my parents had offered to pay my apartment rent during the school year as they had for room and board in the dorms, but if I insisted on staying in Western Mass for the summer, I was on my own—so I spent the first week of finals either at work or in my dorm room typing out papers.

Noel and I texted almost constantly. He'd send me photos of secondhand furniture he was thinking about buying for his apartment, or he'd fret about a final, or he'd just text to say he was thinking of me. Texts like the latter always made me happy, like something inside me was melting. I'd text him back with funny customer stories from Hale's or movie quotes, half of which he didn't get, or just to say I was thinking about him too.

I also decided that if I was going to embrace this liking-guys thing, at least internally, I should look my fill and try to work out what I found appealing or what my type was.

I spent a whole afternoon at the library, camped out at one of the big tables on the fifth floor, and this pair of guys, both of them skinny and dark-haired with some scruffy beard growth, sat across from me. I kept sneaking glances at them as I pretended to pore through the film encyclopedia on the table in front of me. I liked the look of both of them. One wore glasses and had a rounder face and was a little heavier than the other, who had a square jaw and the same rough build as Noel, thin but broad shouldered, kind of rectangular. Yeah, I would have made out in the stacks with either guy.

Or I'd sit in the Mac eating burgers with Joe and sneak looks at the guys around me. I seemed to be drawn to certain body types—guys who were thin or fit but had clearly masculine bodies—and I seemed to have a preference for darker hair. Then a beefy blond guy would walk by our table and I'd think, yeah, he could get it. And Kareem had this friend who was black and bald and had the most beautiful skin I'd ever seen and wore these cute dark-framed hipster glasses, and I wanted to make out with that guy whenever I saw him. And, of course, there was Noel and his wispy blond hair, and he was the star of a number of my more illicit fantasies.

Joe, meanwhile, seemed to be quizzing me. One evening at the Mac, as we were studying for the final in the history class we were taking together, Joe kept interrupting to say things like, "Hey, there's that Becky girl from class. She's pretty cute, right?"

"Sure," I'd say.

I tried. Becky, for example, was aesthetically pleasing. She was petite, but her body looked soft and feminine in a way that was appealing, and I did want to touch her skin to see what it felt like, and I liked her honey-colored curly hair that hung past her shoulders. Before Noel and the current crisis, I might have asked her out. So I wasn't totally straight, but I wasn't totally gay, either, was my conclusion.

"Oh, hey, that girl is barely wearing any clothes," said Joe, gesturing toward a willowy girl wearing booty shorts and what seemed to be a plaid bikini top.

"She has nice tits," I said, because she did.

Joe barked out a laugh. "Yeah, she does."

So maybe I was an equal-opportunity perv.

I had no idea. Maybe I was bisexual. Maybe it was a waste of time to put a label on it. All I knew was my way of looking at the world had changed irrevocably that semester.

Joe just grinned and chucked me on the shoulder with his fist, so I guessed I passed his test.

So finals… happened, for better or worse, and then my parents drove out with my dad's van to help me and Joe move into our apartment. We didn't have much stuff between us—the contents of our dorm room fit in my car, although just barely—but my parents did gift me with the double bed from their guest room plus an old dresser and a lamp and various odds and ends they were "donating" to my first apartment, I figured so they could finally replace them.

It was weird and exciting to be moving into an apartment. It was like the dorms in a lot of ways, just with more doors, privacy, and silence. But it felt like such an adult thing to have a space like this to myself, one I was paying rent for—albeit with my parents' help—and that I was responsible for.

As Joe and I carried boxes and suitcases into my bedroom, Mom stood in the middle and directed traffic. It became clear pretty quickly she wanted to decorate my room as if I were as incapable as I'd been as a kid. She told me where to put the furniture, which boxes to unpack first, which posters I should put up. When I rolled my eyes at her, she grabbed the hat off my head and hit my arm lightly with it. Then she peered at the hat.

"This hat is filthy. Don't you ever wash it?"

"It perfectly conforms to my head. Washing it would change the shape."

Dad came in and ruffled my hair. "The delivery truck with Joe's mattress just got here. The delivery guys are on their way up."

"Great!" I said. "Mom can inflict her interior design aspirations on Joe."

She narrowed her eyes at me. I snatched my hat back and pulled it onto my head.

"Really, Dave," she said. "One of these days, you'll meet a girl who will make you wash that hat. Then what will you do?"

I shrugged her off and walked out of the room, though I did spare a thought for Noel, who had made fun of the hat often enough.

Joe, who'd been in hearing range, put a hand on his head to hold on to his own hat when my mother approached him.

Once all of our stuff had been delivered and placed in the apartment to my mother's standards, we stood around admiring our work. It was small but already felt homey.

My mom got a little teary. She wiped at her eyes. "Now, you know, you can come home at any time this summer."

"Mom. I'll be working full-time at the restaurant. I'm taking an extra English class. I'll be busy."

She nodded. "I know. It's just that my baby is all grown-up, but I'm not ready for it. How can you be old enough to have your own apartment?" She hugged me tightly. "I'm so proud of you, sweetie."

"Ah. Thanks, Mom."

I did wonder, a little while later as we ate dinner at the Italian restaurant near the apartment complex, how proud my mother would be if she knew everything that had been going on in my head. I had forged some kind of peace with Joe, who seemed reassured again that I was straight and harmless and the same guy I'd always been, but that was a façade. My mother, I knew, still hoped I'd meet a great girl at WMU and get married after graduation. That was the path she'd taken with my father, despite the fact they'd both been somewhat radical in their college days. Perhaps they'd had that in common. I grew up hearing stories about how they'd protested vague things like corporate greed and foreign policy to the USSR when they were in college. My dad was arrested at a rally against the Reagan administration when he was a junior, and he remained proud of this fact. And my mother once marched with Gloria Steinem. Yet I'd had a perfectly traditional childhood.

Still, my parents had been married for twenty-five years and were nauseatingly good together, so I had been convinced at eighteen that I'd meet the love of my life in college. Maybe I still would. My parents' dormant radicalism at least gave me some hope they might accept a child who was not so traditional.

Explaining everything to them would have to wait, because I didn't want to rock the boat with Joe present, so I ate chicken marsala and chatted amiably with my parents about how the semester had gone.

Just before dessert was served, my phone buzzed. It was a text from Noel. *How did the move go?*

"Ooh," said my mother.

"What?" I asked.

"Is that a girlfriend texting you?"

It took a lot not to roll my eyes at my mother again. "No. A friend."

Joe crossed his arms over his chest. "Noel, right? Noel is texting you?"

"Who is Noel?" asked Mom.

"A friend. And yes, he just texted me. Wanted to know how the move went. That's all."

"I just thought based on your facial expression…," said Mom.

"What was my facial expression?"

"You just looked like you'd gotten a text that made you very happy."

Well, yikes. I put a hand over my face for a moment, as if that could keep me from betraying my emotions. "Oh. No. Nothing like that. I mean, I'm not *un*happy Noel texted me, but it's not, like, a romantic thing."

I hated the dishonesty. The truth, of course, was that hearing from Noel made me extraordinarily happy. I texted him back, *Move was good! At dinner with parents. Call U later?*

Please do! he sent back.

CHAPTER 10

PERHAPS THE main advantage to apartment living was having my own bedroom with a door that closed. Joe kept such unpredictable hours that I was used to having to be prepared for him to walk into our dorm room at any time, so it was an adjustment, getting used to having my own private space.

I did what any red-blooded boy would do under such circumstances: I watched a lot of porn.

Up to this point in my life, I hadn't seen any gay porn and had only the vaguest ideas about what men did with each other when they got together sexually. If I was honest with myself, I'd say I had looked at plenty of men in straight porn in a lustful way. Certainly there had been pictures and movies I'd seen where the woman wasn't doing much for me, so the big muscular guy she was fucking on-screen was more appealing by default. Probably I could have justified my wandering gaze by explaining he represented some kind of fantasy fulfillment on my part, like I'd even know what to do with hulking shoulders and a ten-inch cock. But there had also been male porn stars I enjoyed looking at just because they were hot.

So, to cut to the chase, since I thought about Noel more than any other thing in my life and because I had a door that closed, I watched a lot of gay porn. Partly I was trying to ascertain if these things really did turn me on—and boy howdy, did they!—but partly I was trying to prepare myself, because I wanted to have sex with Noel. I wanted to approach that having some idea of what to expect.

Truthfully this whole enterprise scared the bejesus out of me on just about every level.

But still, while trying to sort out what was real and what was fake in the videos I watched, I did learn a few things. And watching one hot guy give a blow job to another hot guy was not a hardship. Whether any of this knowledge had any practical application to my real life remained to be seen.

A FEW weeks after the semester ended, I got a text message from Noel as I left work at Hale's: *I'm hungry and bored.*

I'm Dave, I texted back.

Ha ha. What are u up 2?

Leaving work in Northampton.

I can be there in 20. Can we get something to eat?

The chef at Hale's had made me a sandwich during my break, but that was three hours before. I hadn't felt hungry, but my stomach growled at the prospect of food. I texted Noel to meet me at a restaurant on Main Street.

We hadn't really seen each other much since the semester ended. We'd had dinner in Amherst one night after we'd both moved into our respective apartments, but other than sharing a meal and good conversation, we hadn't done anything. I'd wanted to, but I'd chickened out. I got the impression Noel was letting me do things at my own pace, so while he'd made it clear he wanted to be with me, he hadn't made a move either. So, tag, I was it. I was the offense. The ball was in my court.

The restaurant I picked was a casual vegetarian place sandwiched between a stationery store and a shop that only sold things made out of hemp. The restaurant was pretty typical of Northampton, a lazy college town that was home to all manner of eclectic shops and restaurants. I loved spending time in this town—Joe and I sometimes came for brunch on the weekends and the local concert venues attracted some great bands—so I was happy to do so with Noel.

He arrived at the restaurant about ten minutes after I did. He sat across from me with a smile. "How was work?" he asked.

"Good. You?"

Noel had gotten a job at a pricey boutique near Amherst College and he had some kind of research-assistant job at WMU; all those work hours were part of the reason why we hadn't seen each other. I still hadn't figured out his schedule, so I didn't know which job he'd gone to that day, but it almost didn't matter.

"Pretty well," he said.

We made small talk while we waited for our food. Given my affinity for the Mac's hamburgers, I obviously was not a vegetarian, and Noel wasn't either, but this place served really delicious food. I'd found it the semester I dated a vegan girl. I think I sufficiently impressed Noel with how classy the place was.

As we ate, I tried to work out how to broach the topic I most wanted to bring up.

I false started a few times. I'd say something like "Hey, what are you doing after this?" and he'd say, "Oh, nothing really, why?" and I'd be all, "Oh, no reason," even though the actual reason was "We should go somewhere we can get naked together." I almost wished I could order booze to put some liquid courage into my system, but my twenty-first birthday wasn't for another few months and everyone in Western Massachusetts was anal about carding because there were so many colleges in the area. So booze was not an option. I forked food into my mouth instead, though at a certain point, I stopped tasting it.

"Is there something in particular you'd like to do after dinner?" Noel asked as we were finishing off our entrées. "I mean, since you keep asking."

"I don't know how to ask this without sounding like a creeper," I said.

He laughed. "Ask me anyway."

I took a deep breath. "So, okay, the thing is, I want to have sex. With you."

He went completely still for a moment. Then he nodded slowly.

The lighting in the restaurant was so bright and cheerful, it felt like the opposite of a place to be having serious and/or sexy conversations. But here we were. I lowered my voice so we wouldn't be overheard. "I get that it's a big leap from 'friends who kissed that one time' to sex, and I understand if you don't want to. I mean, no pressure. But I want—no, I need—to find out what it's like to be with a man. And honestly? I'm really attracted to you. A lot. I mean, I've had a crush on you since we met. That's probably pretty obvious."

He sat there staring at me, which was the most unnerving thing.

"You think we should…," he said but then held up his hands for me to fill in the blank.

"Just throwing that out there."

"Are you angling for an invitation back to my apartment?"

I couldn't tell if he was for or against this plot of mine. "No. I mean, yeah, I guess, because you live closer to here than I do, but, like, we could go to my place too. Joe's at his parents' in Boston until Thursday. So we could go anywhere if you wanted… some privacy. I mean, only if you want to."

He frowned. His hesitation gave me a complex. I bet he'd just taken one look at Beardy Jason and then they'd been doing it on one of those long, skinny dorm beds without a second thought. Maybe I was okay to kiss but not to take home. He didn't really lust after me in *that* way.

"Or forget it," I said on a sigh.

"No. No, that's not…. I'm not going to forget this. You asked me for something, and I need some time to digest your question. Basically what you're saying is you like me and you want to have sex with a man."

"Yes."

"But I'm not…. I mean, it wouldn't matter which man you had sex with, would it?"

Oh. I hadn't thought of it in that way. Perhaps I'd phrased my proposition poorly. "It would matter. A lot. I'm not just gonna pick some rando off the street. Even when I sleep with women, I don't operate that way." I looked at my empty plate. A quick glance at the waitress indicated she was giving us space to have what probably looked like a very serious conversation. "Especially for, you know, the first time. It would have to be with someone I trusted." I paused to look him over. I had no clue what he was thinking, and his face gave nothing away. "I want it to be with you."

He nodded without giving me a real answer. "Did you drive here?"

"Yeah. Did you?"

"No, I don't have a car. I took the bus."

He waved down the waitress. My heart pounded as I pulled my wallet out of my pocket. I had no idea what was going to happen when we walked out of the restaurant. Would he just walk to the bus stop and never talk to me again? Had I taken this too far?

"Where are you parked?" he asked when we walked outside.

"Public lot behind Hale's."

He gestured down Main Street, so I led him to my car. We didn't speak. I was baffled. Did he want to come home with me? Did he just want a ride home? Were we going to have sex after all?

I unlocked my car and he climbed into the passenger seat. When I got in behind the wheel, I asked, "Where to?" and shut the door.

He turned to me. "I didn't want to say this outside."

"Okay."

"And I can't even believe I'm going to say this, because basically, part of me is like, 'hey, a hot guy I really like wants to have sex with me, let's do it,' but part of me is like, 'he just wants to experiment.' I mean, I'm not just here for your whims, Dave. I'm a person with feelings and thoughts of my own."

"I know."

"I do really like you. But like you keep saying, this is all really new for you. I keep going back and forth on whether it's worth it for me to do all this with you if you're just going to...." He bit his lip and shook his head.

I didn't know what he thought I would do. I said, "I've never been in a gay relationship before, but straight ones tend to play out in a certain way. Two people meet, they date for a while to get to know each other and see if they're compatible, they spend time together because they want to, and at some point they have sex. Is that about how gay relationships go?"

He shrugged. "Sure."

"So why can't that be what happens here? We both like each other. I'm not saying we have to have sex tonight. I want to, but I can wait."

"But I thought...."

"Look, you want to know the real honest truth? I've been kind of thinking about boys in sexy ways since I was thirteen, but I was too chicken to admit it to myself, so I've been pushing all those feelings away for a long time. Or I rationalized them. Giving and receiving a hand job from another boy at summer camp? Oh, no big, that's just what boys do."

He smiled faintly and looked out the front windshield. "I don't think that's what *all* boys do."

"That's my point. So this... these feelings, they've been with me all along, but it wasn't until I met you that I started to confront them head-on. As it were."

He turned back. "Why?"

"Why? I don't know why. Because I saw you crying in a bathroom? Because you're so fucking beautiful I just want to spend all day staring at you? Because spending time with you has made me realize I feel things I can't just tamp down and forget about? Because you're The One? I have no idea. Maybe all these things are true. All I know is I was in a lot of denial, but since meeting you, I can't deny how I feel anymore. I don't know if I'm gay or bi or queer or what, but I do know I want you. Can you appreciate how big a deal that is?"

"I can, but...." He shook his head. "Do you want *me* or do you just want to act on these queer feelings you're having?"

"You," I said. To seal the deal, I leaned over and kissed him.

Kissing Noel was as awesome as I remembered. His lips were warm and slick. When I licked into his mouth, I tasted something savory and sweet. He let out a breath that tickled my mouth and then put a hand on my shoulder, perhaps to steady me. I put my hands on his cheeks and held him there and, really, just kissed the hell out of him.

He pulled back gently. "Are you sure?"

"I'm sure."

"Better drive to my place, then, since it's closer and all."

NOEL RENTED out the top floor of a house in South Hadley, not far from Mount Holyoke College. It wasn't a big apartment; it had a medium-sized living room furnished with some beat-up secondhand furniture that might have been in the room since 1986, a tiny kitchen with really ugly linoleum floors, a closet-sized bathroom, and a bedroom really only big enough to fit his bed.

As he gave me the tour, he kept apologizing for how shabby everything was. It didn't bother me at all. My apartment wasn't exactly the Taj Mahal either.

When we were in his bedroom, he sat on the bed with a heavy sigh.

"Are you all right?"

He shrugged. "I keep thinking, I wish this was nicer. I wish I could afford better furniture or an apartment with cleaner floors. I got this place at a bargain, especially since it was already mostly furnished. And it's what I can pay for. I hope to put some money away for next semester, too, because it looks like I might be paying my own way for the rest of college."

My heart sank. I'd forgotten his parents had disowned him. I had known they had cut him off, of course, but I hadn't really felt that fact until seeing his living space. I blurted out, "You can pay for school while working retail?"

"No. But I talked to the bursar's office about reapplying for financial aid. And I have a small trust fund from my grandmother. My parents haven't been able to touch it since I turned eighteen. So I can do it, but I have to be thrifty."

I sat down next to him, feeling a little deflated. "I'm really sorry you're going through all this. And here I am thinking about stupid things that aren't important like vegetarian restaurants and sex, and you're trying to figure out how to finish college."

"Sex is important," he said. "And I'm happy for the distraction. It's nice to be able to think about something other than my parents for a little while every day."

All right. I figured I could run with that. "Have you been thinking about me every day?"

He smiled shyly. "Maybe. A little."

I took his hand and held it between both of mine. I felt like I had to make most of the first moves, to show him I was serious. Now that he smiled more forcefully at me and we were in his bedroom and I had some sense for what was about to happen, I was hard and aroused. My skin tingled everywhere he touched me.

"I'd be happy to distract you," I said.

He reached for me, then put his free hand on my shoulder blade and pulled me forward a little. Then he kissed me. He moaned as he did so, the moan of someone who had been working all day and finally got a chance to relax. He took his other hand from mine and slid his arms around me. I grabbed his waist and felt the tension draining from his body.

I pulled back and said, "This should be as much for you as it is for me. I want to be with you and I want to know what that's like, but only if you're totally with me. If you want me, I'm here for you. Even if you just want to forget your problems for the rest of tonight."

"I want you for more than just that," he said.

I smiled. "You want me, period."

He smiled too. "Yeah. You want me too. Period."

"Yes."

We kissed again. He pulled at me more and lay back on the bed. We were soon lying side by side. I touched him anywhere I could reach. I needed to know what his body felt like. I could see him just fine in the yellow light from the bare-bulb fixture hanging from the ceiling, but I wanted to know what he felt like under my hands, against my skin.

We each toed off our shoes. He had on those salmon-pink highwater pants again and a neatly pressed blue-and-pink plaid shirt. But not for long. I undid the buttons so I could touch more of his skin. He writhed against me.

"We don't——" he said breathlessly as he moved against my hands. "We don't have to go, uh, all the way tonight."

That was both a relief and a disappointment. "Do you not want to?"

"No, I do. I… well. Let's… let's see what happens. I don't want to rush you."

He was holding something back from me. I could sense it. I couldn't begin to guess what, though. I reminded myself that the sum of what I knew of gay sex came from porn, and I knew better than to think anything I'd seen was exactly accurate. The mechanics of one particular sex act were still elusive to me. "I don't think I'm ready for, ah, you know. Anal. Yet," I said.

He smiled and ran a hand through my hair. "Good to know."

"You've done it?"

He nodded. Then he whispered, "I like to bottom."

Holy smokes! It was crazy arousing, picturing him that way. What if he were beneath me or on top of me instead of beside me? What if I were inside him? What if I were driving myself into him over and over again? What if he were moaning in ecstasy, what if his body were squeezing mine, what if….

"That's so hot," I said.

He laughed. "I'm glad you think so. But we can take things slow, all right?"

Somewhere in there my hat got loose—I hadn't even remembered it was still on my head—and Noel tossed it aside.

He kissed me, so I shoved his shirt off his shoulders. He had on a thin undershirt, so I nudged at his arms, and he leaned back and pulled it off.

Everything was new, and yet it wasn't. I'd been in plenty of sexual situations before, just never with a man. Noel lay back on the bed and lifted his arms above his head. I looked him over. He was fit, though his muscles weren't really defined. His chest was all flat planes, and he had those broad shoulders, and his body was so masculine and basically perfect. I ran my hand over his pecs, over his nipples, over the sparse hair there. His skin was surprisingly soft and warm. He arched his back slightly, as if he were pushing against my hand.

I liked what I saw. It was difficult to analyze or quantify. I couldn't seem to stop touching him. I pinched one of his nipples experimentally and it hardened immediately. Watching him sent a shiver down my spine, made me harder than anything.

That confirmed a lot of things for me, as if there was even a question anymore.

I kissed him. He thrust his fingers into my hair and groaned into my mouth. I climbed on top of him, and to see what would happen, I thrust my hips against his. I could feel his hard cock through the layers of clothes between us. That was so exciting, my skin went electric. I shifted so my cock pressed against his, and my brain went blank while sensation overwhelmed me. I stopped analyzing altogether. I just felt.

Noel pulled my undershirt over my head and ran his hands confidently down my chest. He mirrored some of my movements, pinching my nipples and skimming his palms over my skin. I threw my head back, closing my eyes to feel what he did to me.

"So sexy," he said, tugging on a lock of my hair.

I opened my eyes and saw him gazing up at me. He looked awestruck. He looked how I felt gazing back down at him. His white-blond hair was mussed, his cheeks were flushed, and his blue eyes seemed to glow. He was so goddamned beautiful, so fucking hot, and my arousal was becoming urgent, unnerving.

"Take off your pants," he said, reaching between us to tug on my fly.

So I shoved off my waiter pants, a pair of simple black trousers. That left me in just my blue-and-yellow paisley boxers, which read "my mother bought these for me" not "I'm wearing sexy underwear," and that was mildly embarrassing. I hadn't been expecting anyone to see them when I'd gotten dressed that morning. He raised an eyebrow at me, but I straddled him, which seemed to effectively distract him.

He leaned up and kissed me, so I tugged on his shoulders and rolled over so he was on top of me. He was taller and heavier than any girl I'd ever been with, but I liked that about him, liked how hard his body felt, how he was a little hairy, how he tasted different from anyone I'd kissed before. I really liked his weight on top of me, pressed against me.

He wriggled out of his pants, which left him in a pair of blue briefs, and I could see... a lot. His cock was hard and pressing against the material, and it was certainly nothing to be ashamed of, and I wanted to just stare at it for a while. Because it was right there. Because the air around us was beginning to smell of sweat and man. Because he was hot for me and I was hot for him, and the evidence of that was plain.

"I want to see you totally naked," I said.

He smiled. He knelt over me, his knees outside mine, and he hooked his thumbs into the waistband of his briefs. I couldn't look away. My heart pounded in anticipation. I was going to see all of him. He smiled at me wryly, and then, with aching slowness, he started to peel his briefs down. He was revealing his penis as if it were the most precious gift, and I believed it was. God, every part of him was beautiful, and I looked up at his face, down the long column of his neck, his flat pecs, his torso with hair that was blond and soft but got darker below his belly button, and then there was his cock, which he showed me as he pulled off his briefs.

His cock was hard and jutting away from his body. It was long and thick and pink. He might have been slightly bigger than me, but that didn't matter to me just then. He was looking down at my crotch. My hard-on was poking through the hole in my boxers.

"So you're into this, is what you're saying," he said.

"Yeah, I... yeah. Come here."

I pulled him into my arms and we kissed again. I was hyperaware of his naked body pressing against me. He reached between us and slid off my boxers, and then the two of us were naked together. My heart was racing, my blood rushing in my ears. I opened my legs so he could settle between them. He shifted his hips and our cocks pressed together. That was... I'd never felt anything like it. My brain shorted out. It was all just pleasure, electricity pulsing throughout my body, magic. Had I ever been this aroused? This excited? It was all unknown still, what would happen in the next moment. And yet it was like coming home.

We thrust against each other, each looking for friction. He reached between us and wrapped a hand around both of our cocks. "How does that feel?" he asked.

I couldn't really do much more than moan. "Good... that's... oh God."

It was intense, surreal, amazing to be pressed against him this way, but I wanted to experience everything. With one hand, I grabbed his ass, cupping one cheek. His skin was soft and smooth there too, and I liked the shape of his ass against my hand. With my other hand, I reached between us. I swatted his hand out of the way and then wrapped my hand around us. Feeling his cock, hot and hard, pressing against my own, against my hand, that was too much.

"I'm gonna come," I gasped, suddenly on the edge.

"Me too. Come. Come now. Come with me."

He thrust against my palm and the head of his cock ran along the shaft of mine, and that was it. I was overwhelmed, my world went white, and then I was coming against him. I groaned and jerked, and it was cathartic in a way, as if I'd been waiting years for this moment to just let go. Hell, I did let go. I let go of all the old nonsense I'd been hanging on to, I let go of my inhibitions, I let go of everything.

He cried out a moment later and came all over my hand, my stomach. I watched him through the haze of my own dissipating orgasm. So beautiful.

We held each other as we came down together. He kissed my temple. "How... how was that?"

"Intense," I said. "Overwhelming. Amazing."

He barked out a laugh. "Amazing?"

"I'm having a moment. I've never done anything like that before, and you know, my mind is blown. Why? Was it terrible for you? Because I have zero experience with guys, but I could get better."

He smiled and pet my hair. "No, it's not that. I liked how you explored me, actually. It's been, well, a long time since I've felt anything like that. Normally the guys I bring home just cut to the chase. This was more fun."

"Oh. Good."

"Is anyone going to miss you if you spend the night with me?"

My heart fluttered a little. "No. Like I said, Joe's in Boston. No one's home. And even if he were there, it wouldn't matter. He's never asked questions when I don't come home. And I don't have to be at work tomorrow until the dinner shift."

He smiled. His hand running over my head was making my scalp tingle.

"So basically, we should do this again," I said.

"Tonight?"

"Tonight. Tomorrow. Next Tuesday."

He laughed. "Yeah. I agree. I... I'd really like that."

"Good," I said. I hugged him.

We lingered in bed until we got sticky. Then we cleaned up, put on our undies, and went to the kitchen. He poured us both glasses of water. When he handed one to me, I held it up. "We should toast," I said.

"To what?" he asked with a smile.

"To us. To the great summer ahead of us."

"Yes," he said. "To summer. To us."

We clinked glasses.

CHAPTER 11

EVERY TIME I mentioned I had gone out with Noel, Joe scowled at me, so I stopped telling him who I was going out with.

We didn't see much of each other anyway, between work and the class I was taking and the fact he spent the night at Vanessa's more often than not.

Noel and I were in my living room one evening in early July, watching TV, eating fatty snack food, and generally having a good time. He kept making punny comments about the characters in the show we were watching, and I kept laughing even though his jokes were corny as hell.

"This character Ben reminds me of this guy Aaron in the QSU," Noel said, "although Aaron is a lot twinkier."

"Twinkier?"

"You know, like a twink?"

I just stared at him, no inkling about what he was talking about. "Like a Twinkie? The yellow snack cakes that somehow never go stale?"

Noel laughed. "No, like…. Okay, so, gay guys use a lot of slang to describe each other. Like, you know, a bear is a big burly hairy guy?"

"Okay." This was news to me.

"And a twink is a young, pretty, skinny guy."

"Like you?"

"Yeah, I guess so." Noel smiled. "But the stereotype is twinks are shallow party boys."

I leaned close to him. "And that's *not* you?"

He pushed me away, giggling a little. Still, I felt like I had a lot to learn here. There was quite a bit of culture and slang Noel was privy to that I had never heard before. I had no intention of really changing myself—discovering my latent interest in men hadn't changed the way I spoke or inspired me to become more artistic or anything like that, and one would have had to pry the Sox cap from my cold, dead hands—but I felt incomplete and unprepared suddenly. It was as if I had shown up on the first day of the movie shoot without learning my lines, but Noel had been studying the script for months.

Noel watched the screen for a moment, so I did as well. Even the gay character on this TV show—played by an openly straight actor—seemed to know more about being gay than I did.

"I'm such an idiot," I said.

"What makes you say that?" Noel took a handful of popcorn from the bowl sandwiched between us.

"I don't know anything about being gay."

Noel munched on the popcorn for a moment before he said, "Sure you do. You're attracted to men, aren't you?"

"Yes."

Noel turned to face me. "That's pretty much all there is to it." He tilted his head and raised his eyebrow.

"Easy for you to say, seasoned pro."

He lightly punched my shoulder before offering me a cookie from the box on the table. We ate for a moment, watching the show. A laugh line hit just right and we both started giggling, and because I was already kind of fragile, it really cracked me up.

"Why are we laughing so hard?" Noel asked, caught up in the giggle loop as much as I was.

"It's all really funny, isn't it?"

So, of course, right then was when Joe waltzed in, took a look at the two of us laughing, and glowered.

"Did you need something, Joe?" I asked, taking a deep breath to calm down.

He shrugged and sat in the chair near the TV. "What are you watching?"

"New sitcom about three different newlywed couples who live in New York," said Noel. "It's kind of cheesy, but I like it."

Joe narrowed his eyes at the TV. "Oh, I heard about this. One of the couples is gay, right?"

"Yeah." Noel frowned. "This couple is pretty well neutered—like, they don't even touch each other on-screen—but it's kind of nice to see gay people on TV who aren't *total* cardboard stereotypes. They have actual personalities that aren't just 'fussy queen' or 'fashionable sidekick.'" He made finger quotes.

This exchange would have been okay if Joe had been able to keep his face neutral. Instead he looked at the TV and grimaced. He watched a scene, which was, granted, a bit flat and not especially funny. Then he just got up and left the room. He went into his bedroom and closed the door softly.

"Joe is not… he's not the most homo-friendly person I've ever met," Noel whispered.

"No. I know. It's why I haven't said anything to him yet. About… you know. I mean, I'm homeless otherwise, basically. This was the last vacant apartment in my price range in the whole Pioneer Valley."

Noel frowned at me. "You really think he'd kick you out?"

"I honestly don't know." I thought it was possible, though. I could have listed all of the things Joe had said over the years that, in retrospect, seemed homophobic or even possibly hateful. Yet Vanessa insisted he'd be fine with me if I came out. I had no idea what the truth was. He'd been so surly lately I was inclined to follow my first instinct, which was to keep quiet about all of it. "I'm not willing to risk it just yet."

"I guess that's understandable," said Noel.

"I'm sorry." I felt like such an asshole. Here Noel had been living his truth, never denying who he was to anyone, and it had gotten him disowned. He knew more about being homeless than I did; I had loving parents I could go home to, at least for now. But Noel had fought to make his situation workable. His apartment was shabby, but he had a roof over his head.

He shrugged. I could tell he wasn't so pleased with me. We watched TV in silence.

Joe emerged ten minutes later, wearing sweatpants and a bleach-stained WMU T-shirt instead of his jeans-and-T-shirt work uniform. He went into the bathroom. A few minutes later, he paused in the living room to watch a few minutes of the show, laughed at it, said, "Hey, that's pretty funny," and then went back to his room. He left the door open this time.

So then again.

Noel stood up. "I should get going."

I almost protested. I almost told him he didn't have to go. I almost invited him to spend the night with me. I didn't actually do any of these things. Instead I stood as well and said, "Okay."

"I have to work tomorrow, otherwise…."

Otherwise nothing. If Noel didn't have to work, it's not like he'd spend the night. Not with Joe there.

"Oh, did I tell you?" he said. "Ashley's driving here this weekend. Some nonsense about missing Western Mass. I thought if we were going to hang out together, it would be more fun to go to Boston, but she's coming here instead. So I'll probably be mostly hanging out with her. But I'll text you if you want to join us for dinner one night or something."

"I'm working Saturday night. But text me anyway. Maybe I can meet you guys somewhere when I'm not working."

"Okay. And, well, she's staying on my couch, so...."

So no hanky-panky at his place. "I get it."

I escorted him to the door, which was down a short hallway off the living room—not in Joe's eyesight, in other words—and I gave him a quick hug and peck on the lips. He smiled at me sadly. I already knew what he was going to say.

"Look, Dave...," he said.

"No, I know."

"It's not that I want you to be homeless."

"I know. Just... give me some time, okay?" At his frown I added, "You want to get together after work tomorrow? Before Ashley comes in and takes over your life for three days?"

"I work until ten. Thursday?"

"Yeah, Thursday."

He reached over and squeezed my hand. Then he walked out of the apartment.

So I wasn't exactly writing a book on how to conduct a clandestine affair. I supposed I kept inviting Noel over in the hopes we'd get caught, but then, we never did anything when he was over for Joe to catch us doing.

I was struck with a wave of sadness as I thought about it.

Joe was in the living room when I walked back into the apartment. A brief wave of panic went through me as I wondered if he'd seen me kiss Noel. He faced the TV, so I didn't think so.

Still, I braced myself for him to accuse me of something. Instead he said, "You spend more time hanging out with him than you do with me."

His tone was so neutral, I didn't understand how he felt about the situation. "So? You and I are never home at the same time anymore."

Joe shrugged and took a big gulp from the glass of OJ in his hand. I couldn't figure out what he was trying to tell me.

NOEL SPENT the next week either hanging out with Ashley or working—over text, he'd complained about his hours at the same time he expressed his gratitude about being able to make a little extra money—and I didn't have much to do beyond go to work and watch TV. Joe drifted in and out of the apartment. We didn't speak much, mostly just comfortably coexisted, like ships passing.

One of those evenings, I was watching the Sox game and playing some mindless puzzle game on my phone when Joe came home. He grunted at me before heading to his room. I ignored him as he puttered around the apartment. Eventually he sat next to me on the couch.

"How's it going?" he asked.

"Sox are up one in the fourth against Tampa Bay."

"Yeah? I heard Rodriguez is pitching." Rodriguez was a rookie pitcher the Sox had pulled up from their farm system. Joe and I had agreed months ago that he looked promising. Now that conversation felt like it had taken place a lifetime ago.

"He is, yeah," I said. "Looks great. Only gave up one run so far."

"Glad I put him on my fantasy team. It's the only thing keeping me from embarrassing myself. My team is all old fogeys this season. Kareem's cleaning up."

I laughed. A bunch of the guys from our dorm played fantasy baseball in an online league. I had a team too, but I hadn't really been paying attention to it. "Am I in last place?"

"Probably." Joe tapped the app on his phone. "Oh, no. Eighth out of ten. You're beating Mike and Andy."

"Well, that's something."

"I'm in fifth. Which I guess is not terrible. Let me just...." He tapped the screen of his phone a few times.

"What?"

"I put Mauer on the DL. He's been out with a back injury since Tuesday."

I laughed. I found fantasy baseball and the way actual live players intersected with fake teams to be surreal.

On the screen, the Tampa Bay pitcher lobbed a curveball at Ramirez, who got a solid hit. Joe watched and chanted, "Come on, come on," while we waited to see if it would fall into the glove of one of the outfielders. It did, ending the inning. Joe groaned.

At the commercial I asked, "How's Vanessa? I feel like I haven't seen her in weeks."

"You haven't," he said, a little pointed. Then he sighed. "We're all working a lot."

"Yeah," I agreed.

"Anyway, she's good. Her cousin is getting married up in Lenox a couple of weekends from now, so I have to go to that. We're staying with her aunt, who I guess lives near the actual Alice's Restaurant. Like, from the Arlo Guthrie song. Weird, right?"

"Sure." I was only peripherally aware of the song.

"So. How's Noel?"

I didn't like how loaded the question seemed. I was pretty sure Joe was onto us, even though I still hadn't told him I was… whatever I was. And really, besides that one time we'd gotten naked with each other, all we'd really done so far that summer was hang out. Joe's question indicated to me, though, he thought he knew something. "Fine," I said. "Noel's working tonight."

Joe nodded. "You got hot plans this weekend?"

I shrugged. "I took over a shift from that waitress Jen, so I'm working a double on Saturday. That'll suck ass, but it's an orientation weekend at WMU." Joe knew as well as I did orientation weekends meant the parents of incoming freshmen taking them out to nice dinners and getting teary about how fast their babies were growing up. I usually made good tips those weekends.

"Jen? Is she the one with the… hair?" He gestured above his head.

"Yup." Jen had a wild mane of curly black hair. She was a grad student at WMU, in a subject I could never remember. One of the sciences. I knew from past conversations Joe found her attractive, even though he could never remember her name.

The game came back on, and we watched it quietly for a few minutes. Joe got up and grabbed a bag of chips from the kitchen. He sat back down, opened the bag, and offered it to me. It was a comfortable silence—or not silence, since the noise of the game was punctuated by us crunching on chips—but it didn't feel strained or awkward like so many of our encounters had recently.

I chose not to analyze it too closely, though it occurred to me that while watching baseball, we were in familiar territory.

He said, "My sister has decided I should give a reading at her wedding, but she won't tell me what I should read. Says I should pick something that suits them."

"That's weird."

"I think it's a trap."

I laughed. "Well. Any ideas?"

"Nope. You? You're the lit major."

I thought about it for a minute. "You want traditional or outside the box?"

"Eh. Nothing that would inspire my sister to stab me but nothing too obvious either."

"What about a movie speech?"

He immediately launched into the president's speech from *Independence Day*. He had a grin on his face the whole time he spoke.

"Not sure that's the direction you want to go in for a wedding," I said.

He smirked. "All right, Mr. Film Major. What have you got?"

"Let me think about it and get back to you." My mind was already racing, though. I thought about great declaration-of-love scenes, even ones in, let's say, movies that weren't the sorts my film studies professors showed in class. My personal favorite was John Cusack with the boom box in *Say Anything*, but that wasn't a speech.

Joe nodded and opened his mouth like he was about to say something, but then the screen caught his attention. "Oh, holy… woah, did you see that?"

The Sox completed a mighty double play, handily tossing the ball around the infield to tag out the runners at first and second to end the inning. "Nice," I said.

Joe socked me on the arm. It felt like old times.

But then during the next commercial break, he said, "This summer has been so weird, man."

"No joke."

"Just… be careful, okay? Don't… don't work too many hours and get strung out. It's the summer. You should have fun."

"Easy for you to say. I gotta pay for books and shit in the fall."

"Sure, but, you know. Unless you are having fun? With Noel?"

I shrugged because Joe was probing for more information than I wanted to give. "Sure, he's fun to hang out with."

"I just don't get what you have in common with that guy. Does he even like sports?"

"No, but he likes other stuff that I like. We watch movies together." I wanted another example, but my mind went blank. Instead I added, "We never run out of stuff to talk about." Which was true, but I couldn't think of how to explain to Joe how that happened. "Or maybe he's fun to hang out with because we're so different, you know? He's interesting."

Joe sighed. "Yeah. I'll bet he is."

"What the hell is that supposed to mean?"

He held up his hands. "Geez, don't get so defensive. Look, I don't get it, he's not really like us, but whatever. He's your friend. Just don't… don't go all gay on me without saying something."

"What?"

He grunted. "Look, forget it. Just… it's weird, you spending all this time with this gay guy. Like he's your boyfriend."

I turned toward the TV and pretended to watch the game intently, though I stopped seeing what was on-screen. I wanted to ask Joe if Noel being my boyfriend would be an issue, but I couldn't make my mouth form the words.

"Fuck it." Joe stood. "I'm gonna go watch the rest of the game in my room. Night, Dave."

"Good night, Joe."

He walked out of the room.

CHAPTER 12

SO JOE notwithstanding, the summer continued apace.

The unpleasantness between me and Noel—I couldn't figure out how else to describe it, because it wasn't really a fight, but Noel seemed bothered I hadn't told Joe about us yet—dissipated quickly. He invited me out to Sunday brunch with him and Ashley when she was in town again, and we went out to the restaurant at the farm on Route 116 that made fluffy pancakes with apples and maple syrup harvested right there.

Over coffee Ashley explained she was from Brookline and didn't get along very well with her parents, so she had more or less invited herself to crash with Noel whenever she had a weekend off work. When Noel cracked a joke about charging her rent, I didn't think he was completely joking. I knew, because we'd talked about it a little, that he was happy for the company, but on the other hand, we'd had very few opportunities to be alone with each other.

Still, I was happy to spend time with him in any way we could manage it. Also I loved brunch.

"So this guy came into the shop last week," Noel said as our plates were put in front of us. "It's his first anniversary with his girlfriend and he wants to look nice."

Through a mouthful of delicious apple-cinnamon pancakes, I said, "For a date at the Pub, I'm guessing."

"Actually I got you a customer, because I suggested he take her to Hale's." Noel grinned. "Anyway the guy was kind of awkward. Talked a little too loud, wore clothes that didn't quite fit. So I decided this was a project."

"Oh, here we go," said Ashley.

"Hey, I like clothes. I mean, don't you ever walk across campus and want to give half the WMU student body a makeover?"

"No," Ashley and I said in unison.

Noel rolled his eyes. "Well, I wanted to make this guy look good on his date. Apparently his girlfriend is kind of a fashionista, and although she doesn't try to dress him up or anything, he wants to try harder for her. Isn't that cute?"

"That is cute, sweetie," Ashley said. "So what did you pick out for him?"

"Flat-front khakis that are actually the right length for him and a cotton button-down that had sort of a blue swirly pattern on it. He looked hot when I was done with him." He rubbed his palms together. "Mission accomplished."

"Cool," I said. "Joe and I ate at the Pub a few weeks ago, and we saw this couple there dressed to the nines. This area needs nicer restaurants if people are going to go on dates like that."

"There's always Linetti's," said Ashley.

"Not many college kids can afford Linetti's," said Noel. "Anyway, I felt like I had done my good deed for the day. I kind of forgot about him, but he came in yesterday to tell me the date was a big success. His girlfriend was impressed with the clothes."

"Congratulations on getting someone laid," said Ashley. "Now if you could just do the same for yourself."

Noel frowned at that. He glanced at me. He and I had been fooling around a little at his place on nights when we were both free, but it was mostly just making out on his sofa. We were, I supposed, taking things slow, because we were going at my pace. I was stuck somewhere between "I want to try everything" and "all this new stuff is terrifying."

I grinned at Noel sheepishly.

Which was apparently all Ashley needed to put two and two together. "Wait, are you guys…. Dave, I didn't even know you were gay."

"I didn't either," I said.

"So you're not together," she said.

I looked at Noel, who shrugged.

"We are, actually," I said, "but, like, it's early days, you know?" And vague as that was, it felt good to tell *somebody*. It wasn't a big coming out or anything, but now somebody knew my secret.

"Amazing," said Ashley. "That's awesome."

"Calm down, Ash," said Noel. "We're not getting married or anything. Just… dating."

"Still. Jason was a loser, and I'm glad you dumped him. I like Dave. So try not to fuck this up."

Noel laughed. "Hear that, Dave? You've just been endorsed."

"Thanks," I said, not sure what to think of all this.

Ashley turned to me. "No, really. You're way more down-to-earth than the guys Noel usually dates. I like that about you."

It was a nice compliment and all I really could do was blush. Noel reached over and touched my hand briefly, which only made me blush harder.

"Aw," said Ashley. "You two are adorable. I'm surprised I didn't see it sooner."

"You don't think we're mismatched?" I asked before I could think better of it. "I mean, he's all pretty and fashionable, and I'm a dorky jock."

Ashley shook her head. "Honey, you're the fantasy. You're the *jock* who doesn't know how hot he is but who is also totally out of reach."

"No," I said, waving my hand to dismiss the thought.

"She's right," Noel said.

"What? Really?"

Noel smiled at me, but he ducked bashfully. "I mean, I thought you were hot when we met. You've got that sportsy thing going on. And I like your hair even though it's always under a hat." He lifted one shoulder in a sort of half shrug. "I don't know."

Crazy. I invested so little time in my appearance I was pretty genuinely surprised to hear this. I supposed I'd never had too much trouble finding a date. I was all right–looking. But I was pasty and I had stupid hair, and now I was worried Noel thought I was just as clueless about fashion as his wayward customer.

I shook my head. "You guys are nuts. But thank you." I reached over and touched Noel's hand. I left my hand on top of his this time. "I thought you were really striking when we first met. I mean, if that wasn't obvious. I couldn't stop thinking about you." It was a strange thing to admit in front of Ashley, but I wanted him to know I found him hot too.

He smiled.

"Adorable!" Ashley declared.

A FEW nights later, I decided to pick Noel up from his job. I strolled into the store, which was small and expensive and the sort of place that made me feel like I was wearing rags, and spotted him near a rack of brightly colored shirts. I realized with some dismay as I approached that these were men's shirts. Yikes. I really hoped Noel never tried to dress me. Out of respect for the nice clothes, I pulled off my Sox cap and rubbed my head to get my hair to fluff out of the hat shape.

A bright smile lit up his face when he saw me. "Hey, Dave. Fancy meeting you here."

I smiled back. I couldn't help it. "You're closing soon, right?"

He pulled his phone from his pocket to check the time. "Yeah. The store is closing in about five minutes, and then I'm off at nine thirty."

"Excellent."

Noel tilted his head. "Uh, what are you—"

"Would I look totally insane in one of these shirts? I would, right?" I fingered the sleeve on an electric blue button-down.

"You would look different," Noel said.

I was wearing a faded, dark blue T-shirt and khaki shorts, which is pretty much what I wore in the summer whenever I wasn't at work. "I mean, I guess I could stand to spruce up my look."

"Sure. You can dress how you want, though. I mean, someone should light that Sox hat on fire, but you wouldn't be you without it."

"Well, I was just thinking, you know, if I'm going to be seen around town with you, I could put in a little more effort."

He smiled. "You want to be seen around town with me?"

Yes, but maybe not in a boyfriendly way. "Sure," I said.

Someone dimmed the lights in the store. Noel's radiant smile faded. "My boss isn't going to let you hang out in the store while we close. Can I meet you out front in a half hour?"

"Sure. I can find ways to entertain myself for a half hour."

"Maybe less. We were slow today, so it shouldn't take long to clean up and close the store. If you wander off, I'll text you."

That gave me enough time to walk back to my car, which I'd parked somewhat illegally on the edge of the Amherst College campus, and pull it up to a spot that had been recently vacated in front of the store. I hadn't really had a plan, but one formed now, and I knew exactly what I wanted to do with Noel when he got out of work.

It was a hot night, so I turned up the AC. I flipped through radio stations while I waited. The AM sports station I usually listened to wasn't coming in clearly, so I flipped through the music channels. A Kelly Clarkson song I liked came on, so I started singing and banging out the drum beat on my steering wheel. I was belting out the chorus when there was a knock on my window. I started and turned, but it was Noel.

"You're totally tone-deaf," he said as he opened the passenger door.

"We can't all be Sinatra. Get in the car."

He got in and fastened his seat belt. I pulled out and did a U-turn in a nearby driveway, clearly headed in the opposite direction from Noel's apartment.

"Where are we going?" he asked.

"If I tell you, it won't be a surprise."

I drove us toward the WMU campus. Noel must have clued in to where I was headed, because in my peripheral vision I saw him turn and raise his eyebrows at me.

"Have you ever been to the maze?" I asked.

"Maze?"

"The one behind the stadium."

Noel laughed. "When would I have ever gotten anywhere near the stadium?"

"You've never been to a football game? We made the Sugar Bowl last year. I was at the game when we clinched our bowl appearance, and Joe and I rushed the field with everyone else to tear down the goal posts. It was awesome."

"I went to a hockey game once, but only because my roommate freshman year made me. He had a crush on this girl in the pep band."

"Next semester we'll go. Our football team is looking pretty good. There was an article on the ESPN website last week on all the great talent we scouted last season."

Noel shook his head. "Can you see me at a football game?"

"Sure, why not?"

We were quiet for a moment as I pulled into the stadium parking lot. It was completely empty. I chose a spot on the west side of the lot, parked, and got out of the car.

Noel got out and looked up at the stadium. "It never even occurred to me to go to a game. Is the bowl thing important?"

"Yeah. Sort of a mini Super Bowl for college football. Our football team is good. So is basketball. WMU made the Final Four a few years ago. It's fun watching them during March Madness."

"These are English words you're speaking, right?"

I laughed. "Come on. Forget about sports. I've got something else to show you."

"Is it your penis? Because you didn't have to drag me to campus to show me that."

I grabbed his hand. "Come on, funny guy."

The maze was not an especially well-kept secret. I thought it might have been an art project from some alumnus, abandoned for all time. During the regular school year, there were usually about a dozen kids, some of them drunk, who came after dark to navigate the maze. An old girlfriend had shown it to me on a date, and that was probably how word passed around. It wasn't advertised in any of the campus literature, but plenty of people knew where it was.

No one was around now. The maze was located about thirty yards from the stadium, close to the rows of trees that went around the perimeter of campus. It was made up of metal posts and chain-link, and each wall was about ten feet tall. From the outside, especially in the dark, it just looked like a big chain-link block, maybe ten yards wide, but there was an entrance at the front. The only light was the moon and the orange lights in the stadium parking lot.

"What on earth…." There was awe in Noel's voice.

"This is the campus maze. You go in at the front there and then have to figure out how to get to the middle. Then, once you're in the middle, you take a different path out the back. It's not the most difficult maze you've ever been inside, but there are a few dead ends, and it's hard to see in the dark." I grinned.

"I've never been inside any maze."

"Come on, I'll race you to the middle."

Noel laughed and ran alongside me to the entrance. "No fair. You've done this maze before."

"In the dark all things are equal."

To be honest I always got lost in the maze. Something about the darkness and the sameness of each stretch of chain-link made it hard to navigate every time.

Noel and I decided to split up at the entrance. The only sound was the shuffling of feet on the grass. I ran through the maze as best as I could recollect, but I hit a dead end pretty quickly.

After about five minutes of this, Noel called out, "You still here, Dave, or did you leave me to the wolves?"

"Still here." Although where "here" was located in the maze, I had no idea. "Beat you to the middle."

"Not if I get there first."

I made a couple of turns I thought were familiar, but then hit another dead end. "Marco!" I called out.

His laughter rang out into the night. "Polo. Where the hell is the middle of this maze?"

I found the middle not long after that, and as I did my victory end-zone dance, Noel ran up behind me and tackle hugged me. We laughed together, and then suddenly we were kissing. And kissing. And *kissing*. But just as I was about to throw myself on the grass and tell him to take me right there, he pulled away and said, "Beat you back outside!"

I ran after him and caught up easily—he was fast and had long legs, but I did fall track—and then we held hands and worked on getting out of the maze together.

Once we cleared the chain-link, Noel used his free hand to smooth his hair off his face and looked up at the moon. "Full moon tonight."

"Yeah."

He looked at me and smiled. "Thanks, this was fun. And kind of romantic. Us alone in the dark, with only the moon to light our way."

I leaned over and kissed his cheek. "Did you have dinner? I think the pizza place on Route 9 is still open."

"I did eat, but I wouldn't say no to a slice of pizza with you."

I smiled and squeezed his hand and led him back to my car.

A FEW days later, I made a decision.

I'd felt restless all day. I made it through my shift at Hale's on autopilot, but I still noticed the gay couple who came in for dinner and were all smoochy at their table. It annoyed me at first, but I realized soon enough it wasn't that I was grossed out or anything, it was more that I wanted what they had, to be with my man in the way these guys were together. It left me feeling frustrated and horny.

As I ate a plate of chicken and rice during my break, it occurred to me what I really wanted. And since I couldn't do it in person—both because I was at work and because this was something I'd been thinking about for days but couldn't figure out how to say to Noel's face—I texted the object of my affection.

I'm ready.

He was probably at work, so I wasn't expecting an immediate response, and yet within a minute, I got, *For what?*

You. All the way.

It was so hard to just type the damn words, and my hands shook as I did it, but it was still vague and stupid and I realized as soon as I typed it how ridiculous it was. I felt sixteen again.

But he texted back, *Tonight?*

We didn't have a prayer. I couldn't see how this would ever work out in the long term. Most days I wasn't really cool with admitting to myself I might be gay. He deserved a much better man than me. I was a coward.

But I was a coward who knew what I wanted.

I drove to Noel's place after my shift. He grinned at me when he opened the door.

Maybe it was just a summer fling. Maybe whatever was happening between us was doomed to failure. But when it was just me and Noel standing in his doorway, I did not care. I had this night and I planned to make the most of it. I was going to experience whatever I could, spend as much time with Noel as possible, before it all blew up in my face. But I pushed all that aside when I stepped over the threshold. Tonight was just for Noel and me.

It took a moment for me to realize his hair was damp and he wore only a threadbare terrycloth robe.

"I see you dressed up for me," I said.

"I figured I'd pick an outfit for the occasion."

So he clearly hadn't misunderstood my intentions. I smiled at him.

He took my hand and led me through the apartment, toward his bedroom. He paused outside the door. "Did you want a drink or a snack or…."

A drop of water escaped his scalp, traveling slowly down the side of his face, down his neck, then over his collarbone, until it disappeared under his robe. I was utterly mesmerized by that drop, jealous of it because it slid so easily over Noel's skin. I reached over and traced its path with my finger until I got to the edge of the robe. I slid my hand under the robe, touching his skin, reveling in how soft it was. I inhaled deeply, taking in the scent of soap and Noel. Simply being near Noel made my heart race and my skin tingle. Hell, being near Noel made my cock hard. "Let's go straight to bed," I said.

He grinned.

He undressed me quickly, tossing each piece of clothing aside as he removed it. I pushed the robe off his shoulders and was happy to see he was completely naked underneath it. His cock was hard and pointing toward my belly button as we stood facing each other.

I wasn't sure what to do. I'd never been the most assertive guy in bed, and I supposed many years of sleeping with women I wasn't always that into had put me in the habit of letting my partners take the lead. Here, I was even more out of my depth than usual. Despite the fact I wanted Noel more than I'd wanted anyone I'd ever been with—because I was really gay or because he was The One, I didn't know—taking the lead felt unnatural, and besides, I didn't know how to be with a man. Oh, I'd figured out plenty in the weeks we'd been making out, and this was hardly the first time we'd seen each other naked, obviously, but the actual mechanics of the act we were about to commit…. I'd seen porn, but those guys came prelubed, and I knew better than to think I could just shove it in.

Noel led me to the bed. He lay down on it and spread his legs wide. He was beautiful and enticing. My arousal was a tangible thing, pulsing through my body and floating around us. His arousal drew me to the bed like a magnet. I crawled over Noel and kissed him hard, settling into the space between his legs and thrusting my hips so our cocks rubbed together. This I knew how to do.

"What should I—"

He put a finger to my lips. "I'll show you."

He leaned up and kissed me. I sank into that kiss, pressing my lips against his, licking into his mouth. He tasted like heaven. I forgot about everything except for Noel and how our bodies fit together, how we slid against each other.

But then he pushed at my shoulders, and before I knew what was happening, he had rolled us over and pinned me to the mattress. He looked down at me and smiled. Then he kissed me again, writhed above me, shoved his fingers into my hair. He moved his mouth, hot and wet against my skin, over my face. He bit my earlobe hard enough to make me cry out. I put my arms around him and arched my back to press more of my skin against him. God, I loved holding him. I loved how he felt in my arms. I loved how my skin came alive under his touch. He moaned as our cocks brushed against each other. Then he kissed my lips again before he sat up.

He reached for his dresser, which barely fit in the room, and grabbed the big bottle of lube that was sitting there. Next to the bottle were a handful of condoms. I wondered fleetingly how much time he'd spent preparing for this.

He turned to me and hesitated. He brandished the bottle. "Are you really ready for this?"

"Yes!" I said. Lord, was I. Watching him move around the room, watching his chest heave, his skin flush with arousal, made my own body react. I was hot everywhere, I was hard, my own skin was pink. "Yes, I'm ready. I mean, if you are too."

He nodded. "I, uh, took the liberty of, uh, getting prepared before you got here."

I had a sudden mental image of him in the shower, scrubbing his skin clean, plunging his fingers into his ass, getting off on the feeling. It was overwhelming, though not quite as overwhelming as him kneeling over me, so fucking sexy, and looking at me expectantly.

I nodded at him. I couldn't speak.

He grabbed a condom from the dresser and tore the wrapper off. He rolled it onto me. His hands were warm; I had to think unsexy thoughts to keep from coming. He didn't help matters by pouring lube onto my cock and running his warm hands over it again. I muttered something unintelligible. He poured lube over his fingers and quickly put his hands behind him. He reached toward his ass. I watched in awe as fantasy became reality and he ran lube over the entrance to his body. Then he straddled my hips. He raised his eyebrows.

"Yes," I moaned, lifting my hips closer to him. I was drawn to him so strongly it felt like there were strings pulling us together. I held my breath in anticipation.

Deftly he took my cock in his hand and then lowered himself onto it until he was fully seated. I sank in slowly. His body was hot and squeezed me tightly. It was like nothing I'd ever felt before. It wasn't like being with a girl. It was tighter. It was hotter. It was awesome.

He sat for a moment before he started to move. His erection flagged, so I reached for it, taking him in my hand and stroking him the way I'd learned he liked. He preferred a lighter touch than I used on myself. I stroked him to the rhythm he set while rising up and sinking back down over my cock. I watched myself disappear into his body as I stroked him.

I reached with my other hand and gently squeezed his balls. He moaned and leaned back, propping himself on his hands.

I closed my eyes for a moment to appreciate it. The sensation was intense, his body squeezing and sliding against my cock. I moaned, savoring it. I opened my eyes again. His face was twisted up with pleasure. He bit his lip, perhaps to keep in a moan. He was fully hard again, fucking my hand as he fucked himself on my cock. It was the most perfect thing I'd ever seen, so goddamn gorgeous, and I loved every moment of it.

My heart fluttered, my skin felt like it was on fire, and his body squeezed me. Then he moaned and whispered, "Yeah, like that. God, I'm close. Keep touching me like that."

I could only do as I was told.

His face went ecstatic and he groaned loudly, crying out as, suddenly, his body clamped down on me. Jesus, that sent sparks through my system. He came, bucking his hips as he rode me, spurting out ribbons across my chest.

It was the hottest thing I'd ever seen.

I was right behind him, everything overwhelming me until I saw stars. I thrust up into him one last time and came hard, pumping into the condom as I clutched at his hips to hold him there.

After, he cleaned me up and then settled back into bed with me. He curled up against me and draped an arm over my chest. "Was that... was that okay?"

"Okay? God, that was the greatest thing that ever happened to me and I can't wait to do it again!"

He laughed and snuggled closer to me. "Oh good. It was... it was awesome for me too. You're... you're a good partner." He buried his face against my chest for a moment and then lifted his head again. "That sounded cheesy even in my head. I just meant it doesn't always go so smoothly. It was so great, Dave. You're great."

"I think you're great too."

He smiled and settled back against me. "Thank you for making what should have been a terrible summer much better."

"I'm happy to do it."

I put my arms around him and held him close. He said, "I'd offer you a snack, honey, but I don't want to get up just yet."

"It's fine." I felt the pull of sleep myself. "We can eat later. This is, like, the third time you've totally blown my mind with all the sexy stuff. I need some time to wrap my head around what just happened." I closed my eyes and settled into the pillow.

"Mmm," he said.

We slowly drifted off together.

CHAPTER 13

DESPITE BEING hot, the summer between semesters had a strange snow-globe quality to it, where everything was perfect and beautiful; stress and worry went on vacation. My lit class was pretty easy, and I could do my job in my sleep. So I breezed through most days, especially if I was with Noel, and I pushed all my other concerns aside. I wanted that feeling to go on forever.

Noel's twentieth birthday fell at the end of July. I wanted to do something special for him to show how much he was coming to mean to me, but I was stumped.

Vanessa helped me arrive at the perfect gift.

I was at home one morning, pouring myself a bowl of cereal, when she came out of Joe's room and walked into the kitchen.

"Hello," I said. "Fancy meeting you here."

"Hey, stranger. You've made yourself scarce this summer."

I shrugged. I'd actually been home quite a bit, but I didn't feel like arguing.

She puttered around, opening cabinets and the refrigerator and then the cabinets again until she seemed to decide on something. She pulled out a frying pan and a carton of eggs. "You want an omelet?"

"Sure. You making one for Joe?"

"Yeah, but he's still dead to the world." She started cracking eggs into a bowl. "You got anything to put in the omelets?"

"Cheddar cheese. Green peppers in the bottom drawer, I think. Maybe some spinach."

Vanessa raised her eyebrows at me, looking impressed. "You boys eat spinach?"

I patted my stomach. "I gotta start eating better and training for fall track. I can't really cook or do much more with it other than put it in salad, but it's good for me, right?"

"Sure. Next thing, you'll be buying kale."

As Vanessa started to cook, I munched on cereal. The eggs sizzling smelled so good I was hungry all over again. She sprinkled cheese over the skillet and said, "Since you like musicals, did you hear about the Student Activity Committee trip?"

"What? No."

"There are flyers up all over campus. There are, like, eight plastered to the front door of Dickenson. Isn't your class there?"

I put my now-empty bowl in the sink. "I don't generally read flyers. They're the paper equivalent of white noise."

She rolled her eyes and used the spatula to fold the omelet in half. "Well, the SAC is organizing some kind of bus trip to New York City for those of us stuck here this summer. It's next Saturday. The trip includes a ticket to the matinee of *Wicked*. Only twenty bucks per person."

"Wow, really?"

"Yeah, I guess the SAC had some money left over from the last academic year that they have to use or lose by the start of the fall semester for mysterious budgetary reasons I don't understand. So they organized this trip and are paying most of the expenses. I want to drag Joe, but he won't have any part of the musical. I argued we could just use the tickets to spend the day in New York, but he thought that was a waste."

I watched her cook while I turned this information over in my head. I could afford two tickets for this trip. "I bet Noel would like that."

She turned and shot me a little half smile. "Yeah. I bet he would. How are things going there?"

I glanced toward Joe's door, which was still closed. If he really was still asleep, I felt okay to talk. "Things are good, I think. His birthday is next week, so this might be a really nice present."

"So are you guys, like, a thing?"

I shrugged. I mean, we *were* dating in the sense that we'd been regularly eating meals and spending time together as one does on dates, not to mention we'd been sleeping together fairly regularly too. I was trying to be covert, only spending the night at Noel's when I knew Joe would be out all night, too, or sometimes sneaking back into the apartment in the wee hours of the morning. I was still being cagey about where I was going when Joe asked me what I was up to. In my defense, though, Joe was still weird whenever I slipped and mentioned Noel.

"We're something," I said. "I don't really know what yet. We've been hanging out a lot."

She nodded. "Yeah, Joe mentioned that." The way she looked away indicated Joe had told her a lot more, but she wouldn't relate that back to me. Instead she said, "Okay. But you want to gift him with the magic of Broadway."

"Yeah."

I did. When we hung out, he almost always deferred to what I wanted to do. It meant I was exposing him to a lot of my interests—my favorite movies and restaurants chief among them—but we didn't spend a lot of time on his interests. But he liked musicals, I knew that much, so I thought this might be just the thing.

"Sounds like you're more than just 'something,'" Vanessa said.

Joe stumbled out of his room a moment later. I motioned to Vanessa that she was not to share any of what we'd just discussed, but as we sat down to eat, she blurted, "Dave wants to take Noel on that New York bus trip."

"I mean, just 'cause he likes musicals," I said. "It's not, like, a date, or whatever you're thinking."

Joe and Vanessa both scowled at me, though I figured for different reasons.

"I'm definitely not going, then," said Joe.

I was content to let it drop. Part of me wanted to argue in Noel's defense or ask Joe what his problem with Noel was, but I was so tired of having this dumb Noel-related cold war that I concentrated on eating my omelet.

But Vanessa asked Joe, "Do you not like Noel?"

Joe grunted. "I don't really know him. I'm sure he's fine. Dave sure likes him." There was an edge to his voice.

I glanced at Vanessa, trying to mentally convey that this was not something I wanted to poke at.

She must have understood my telepathic thoughts, because she changed the subject.

I WENT to class Tuesday and actually paused to look at the flyers decorating the main entrance of Dickenson. I used my thumbnail to peel the masking tape off one of them so I could take it, because there were five others taped to the door.

The trip they were organizing was on a bus that would leave from the big driveway in front of the Mac first thing on Saturday morning. We'd get to the city in time to have lunch on our own, meet back at the theater for the show, and then have a few hours in the city before everyone had to get on the bus back to WMU. I thought it might have been nice to spend the night with Noel in a hotel in the city and make more time for tourism—and sex—but that was beyond my current budget. The twenty dollars the SAC was asking for I could do, though.

On my way to class, I pulled out my phone and called the number on the flyer and managed to buy what turned out to be the last two available tickets. I spent most of my class trying to decide whether to give Noel the tickets in advance or spring them on him Saturday morning. Then I realized he might have to work Saturday and all this planning would be for naught.

I texted him after class and arranged to meet for dinner. Then I picked up the tickets from the Student Activity Office in the Mac, dropped by a stationery store to find a fancy envelope to put them in, and drove to a restaurant in South Hadley near Noel's apartment.

I whipped out the envelope as we were finishing our entrées. I'd scrawled *Happy Birthday!* with about seven hundred exclamation points on the front of the envelope.

"My birthday's not until Thursday," he said, though he looked touched and held the envelope as if it were made of delicate glass and wonder.

"I know, but if you're working Saturday, I need you to get out of it, and I thought you might need a couple of days to find someone to cover your shift at the store. I wanted you to see the reason you have to take off."

"Okay." He raised an eyebrow but then slid his thumb along the envelope's seal.

I'd put both *Wicked* tickets and the paper slips that would get us on the bus in the envelope. He slid them out and stared at them for a moment. "What is… wait. Oh my God. Tickets to *Wicked*. On *Broadway*."

"We have to take the bus down with whichever other randos bought tickets from the SAC, but yeah. Eight hours in New York City, with tickets to *Wicked*. Meals are on me. What do you say?"

He clutched the tickets to his chest. "I *was* scheduled to work Saturday, but I'm already mentally rearranging my schedule next week to work extra shifts so I can trade with someone."

"Happy birthday," I said softly.

"Thank you so, so much. This is such an awesome gift." He hopped in his chair. "This is going to be *amazing*." He looked at the envelope again and fanned out the tickets and bus slips. "There are two here. Who should I bring?"

"Um, I think the person who gave you the tickets who also likes musicals is the logical guest."

He grinned. "I'm kidding. Of course you're coming." He put the tickets on the table and ran his hands over them reverentially. "Thank you, Dave. You didn't have to get me a birthday gift."

"I wanted to."

"Yeah."

We spent the next five minutes smiling goofily at each other.

WE BOARDED the bus promptly at 8:00 a.m. Saturday morning. I didn't know any of the other kids on the trip, which I figured was just as well; I felt like I had the freedom to be a little bit couple-y with Noel. I'd even dressed up for the occasion; it was hot, but I wore khakis and one of my shirts with buttons, a dark gray short-sleeved number. Maybe not exciting or particularly fashionable, but dressy for me.

Noel had been giddy since the moment I'd picked him up at his apartment that morning. He was dressed to the nines too: crisp white shirt, plaid pants, and even a cute blue bow tie. He was still all smiles as he settled into the seat next to me. "I've never been to New York before," he said.

"I've been a few times, but with my parents. So this will be different, I think. And I expect the GPS on my phone will get a good workout. I always get turned around in big cities. I mean, I get lost in Boston every time I go, even though I've been there a hundred times."

"Not a city boy, eh?"

"I don't dislike cities. I'll probably live in one after I graduate because that's where most of the media jobs are. But I'd be happy on, like, a farm or something. Or at least some place with a lot of woods for me to hike around in."

"Yeah. That sounds like something you'd like. But I'll take the city any day."

"Yeah?"

"Yeah. Fashion, excitement, *theater*. I've only been to Boston a couple of times, but I really like it."

I could easily picture Noel in a big city with other fashionable people. I imagined in a few years he'd have this life where he met people for drinks at classy bars where they talked about art and literature and theater, or he'd go to brunch with his boyfriend, or he'd be successful enough to buy trendy clothes. I didn't see a lot of room for myself in that kind of life, but who knew?

After the woman who ran the SAC did a quick head count, the bus pulled away from the drive.

We spent the next three hours chatting about whatever, mostly movies and theater. I had seen a few musicals live, but most of the classics he really liked I knew only from their movies. He'd been hoarding original cast recordings since he'd been old enough to save allowance money, and he read Broadway-related websites all the time, something I hadn't even known when I bought the tickets. I'd actually worried *Wicked* was too obvious a choice, since it was such a long-running show, but Noel was over the moon about seeing anything on Broadway.

Our excitement mounted as we arrived in New York. Noel, who had the window seat, practically pressed his nose to the glass to watch all the buildings go by.

The bus dropped us off near Port Authority about two hours before the show. Everyone got off and promptly dispersed. Noel and I decided to walk. He pulled a piece of paper from his pocket.

"This guy, John from the Theater Club, is from Manhattan. I asked him for some suggestions for places to eat that aren't too expensive or too touristy. He suggested we go to Ninth Avenue."

I got out my phone and opened the map app. "That way, I think."

So we walked. Noel's level of giddiness was even greater now that we were actually in the city. He practically buzzed with it and grinned ear to ear. I laughed with him and couldn't keep the smile off my face either. I wanted to get caught up in that enthusiasm, to be a part of it. I was thrilled he was so happy.

Somewhere between Eighth and Ninth Avenue, we walked by an apartment building where a couple was making out on the stoop, and it wasn't until we were almost past them that I realized they were both guys. That startled me at first, but then I took a deep breath and decided those guys made me feel safe enough to take Noel's hand. He smiled at me when I did.

We walked up Ninth until we got to a burger joint with a little rainbow flag hanging from the awning.

"So, okay. I thought about going to this place John recommended because all the waiters there are super-hot gay guys, apparently," Noel said, "but I looked at the menu and it's kind of pricey. And I know you'd be happy with something simple. So what do you think?"

I could always eat a hamburger. "This looks fine."

As we walked in, Noel bit his lip but then said, "There's a place I do want to go for dinner. It's um… it's a gay bar. Is that okay?"

I found the prospect kind of exciting, actually. We weren't home. No one knew us here. I could just… be myself. "Noel, it's fine. I'd love to go to a gay bar with you."

He smiled, looking relieved. "Oh good. I've never actually been to one before." He lowered his voice. "John says this place won't card us."

"Good to know."

Usually I reserved all physical affection toward Noel for when we were behind closed doors, but the anonymity this city afforded us made me feel brave. So as we ate, I flirted outrageously with him, which seemed to delight him, and I touched him, held his hand, played footsie. He giggled through a lot of our meal.

"God, this is fun," he said as we finished eating. "It's so nice to be with you this way."

"This is kind of a gay neighborhood, right? It feels safe here."

"Yeah." He leaned back and looked off into the distance.

I could almost read his mind. I imagined he wanted us to act like this in public all the time. I was getting there, warming up to more PDA with Noel, but when we were out around campus, I kept worrying we'd run into someone I knew. Here in New York City, I knew no one. But I understood what he must have been thinking, and I didn't want to wreck what had thus far been a really great day.

"I'll get there," I said softly.

He smiled faintly and nodded.

We got to the theater about a half hour before the show was supposed to start. A couple of the other kids from the bus were already milling about outside. A pair of girls recognized us and said hello.

"WMU, right?" asked one of them, a short girl with brown curly hair.

"Yeah," said Noel. "I'm Noel and this is Dave."

The girl smiled. "Amelia. This is my friend Jill. We're both going to be juniors."

"Me too," said Noel. "Psych major."

"Oh, psych is my major too!" said Jill. "I thought you looked familiar. We must have had a class or two together."

A shiver went up my spine; that anonymous feeling I'd been riding on all day was gone. My instinct to step away and absolve all knowledge wrestled against my fear of disappointing Noel on what was supposed to be a day specially for him. So I stood there, motionless for a moment.

Then Amelia said, "You guys are, like, a couple, right?"

Noel glanced at me. I took a deep breath and said, "Yes."

Noel smiled.

"You guys are really cute together," said Amelia.

"Thanks," said Noel, throwing an arm around me. "I think so too."

We chatted with them for a few more minutes. Jill was taking a couple of summer classes, and Amelia had a job at a big box store on Route 9 where everyone shopped, and they shared a room in South Quad, the only dorms open during the summer. I liked them fine, though they both seemed more interested in Noel. Who could blame them, really? He was gorgeous, and he looked particularly dapper today with his bow tie.

The show was amazing. We had mezzanine seats, but we could still see everything well. Noel sat forward in his chair, his attention riveted to the stage the whole time. I caught him mouthing along to the lyrics a few times too. At intermission I stood to stretch and soon found myself pulled into a tight hug.

"Thank you so much, Dave. This is so amazing."

I hugged him back. "Of course. Happy birthday."

Noel pulled away gently. "I still can't get over that you did this for me."

"I wanted to do something that would make you happy."

"Watching a DVD of this musical with you on my couch would make me happy."

"Yeah, but you deserve so much more than that."

Jill and Amelia interrupted us, wanting to know what we thought of the show so far. I held back a little while Noel chatted with them. I mentally turned over what I had wanted to say, which was that Noel was so special and he so humbled me, and he'd been through so much and come out of it strong and beautiful. He deserved all the greatest things in life. He deserved to experience Broadway. He deserved to find a great love.

I didn't feel worthy of him.

But I could try. I could be there for him today, for his birthday. I could be the boyfriend he should have, at least for one day.

I reached for his hand. He kept on talking to the girls, but he squeezed my hand back.

We watched the second act with hands intertwined, and again, Noel was rapt, leaning forward. His delight made me happy, proud that I had given him something he enjoyed so much.

Amelia and Jill had dinner reservations, which was kind of a relief, because I worried they'd want to tag along with us to our next destination. I wanted to see what this place Noel had picked out was like, but not with spectators. So we promised to see them back at the bus, and then we walked west to the address Noel had written down.

The interior of the restaurant was sleek and modern, white tables and colorful walls, lots of pink and purple accents. We snagged a corner booth near the bar. There was a couple at the next table blatantly… canoodling. Not making out, really, just being cute together. This was so far outside of the box I lived in, so far outside of my comfort zone, but it was liberating in a way too.

I sat next to Noel in the corner of the booth. Our shoulders touched. He kept giving me little looks, winks or small smiles, so I leaned on him. Our waiter was a muscle-bound guy in a tight, purple T-shirt, and I assumed he was gay and I felt some wonder at that. What would it be like to be that guy, to be comfortable in my skin the way he seemed to be, to be out in a gay bar closer to home?

We ordered dinner and sodas, not wanting to tempt fate, and then mostly people watched. There were so many different types of men—and women—in the bar that it made me think about all the ways people could express themselves and their sexuality. I remember that Noel had told me the only requirement for being gay was finding other men attractive, and here was evidence of that: fashionable guys, ones who looked fey and feminine, ones who looked muscular and super masculine, ones who just looked like regular guys. I saw a guy in a baseball cap, even, and missed my own, which I'd left at home figuring I should look nice for the theater. I thought back to Jerry Grossworth's book, particularly the chapter about his first time in a gay club, and I felt like I was having a similar epiphany. Anyone could be gay. I could be gay. I wasn't sure that these were my people as such, that I had anything more in common with any of the men in this bar than I did with Joe and Kareem, but I thought this could be my world. Someday, maybe. If I stayed with Noel.

"This is cool," Noel said at one point. "Weird but cool."

I agreed. Although some of the people in the bar were groups of guys—or guys and girls—who were clearly just hanging out and having a good time, there were a fair number of couples. I'd seen the occasional gay couple holding hands around campus, though it was rare—or I just didn't notice, what with my gotta-get-to-class blinders—so seeing these pairs of men being so openly affectionate with each other was strange for me at first. But it gave me a giddy thrill too. While we waited for our food, I put my arm around Noel, and he leaned into me.

We spent most of dinner chatting about the show and what we liked about it. Noel would hop in his seat when recounting his favorite bits; he was especially thrilled by the performance of "Defying Gravity." I had to smile, loving how joyful his expression was.

We had to return to the bus by eight, but the midsummer sun hadn't set by the time we started back toward Port Authority. It made it harder to see the city lights, though Noel was no less captivated by them. I just wanted to watch his face as he took it all in. I didn't even really want to go home, because then all this would end.

When we did board the bus, Jill and Amelia sat across from us. They recounted how amazing their dinner had been. Noel sheepishly confided that we'd gone to a gay bar and the food had been okay but the scenery had been amazing. I nodded in agreement.

Jill and Amelia got lost in their own conversation just after promising to exchange phone numbers so we could all hang out after we got back to WMU. Noel settled against my side and thanked me again. "This has been the most amazing day I've had in a long time."

A happy warmth spread across my chest. "You're welcome. It *was* great. I had fun too."

"Seriously, Dave, I can't—"

"It's okay. You don't have to say anything. Happy birthday."

Once the bus got moving, Noel curled up and fell asleep, his long body scrunched into the chair, his head on my shoulder. I held him and watched the world go by outside the bus windows. I felt happy I'd been able to do this for him, and it had been an amazing experience for me as well, but it seemed fleeting. We'd had a perfect day in our snow globe, but I couldn't help but see the cracks in the glass.

CHAPTER 14

I SHOULD have spent more time that summer training for fall track than I had. I could feel laziness in my bones and muscles, the stiffness that crept in after a long period without much exercise. So I decided one sunny Saturday morning I wanted to do some hiking to get my body moving again.

Joe, who would normally be game for such things, was off at Vanessa's cousin's wedding, so I called Noel. "I'm picking you up in a half hour. Wear comfortable shoes."

"Oh-kay," he said. "What are we doing?"

"You ever been to Mount Sugarloaf?"

"Is that a theme park?"

"No, it's a mountain. It's got a really nice hiking trail to the top."

"We're going to hike a mountain?" His voice rose an octave; he sounded terrified.

"It's a small mountain. I'll pick up food on my way to get you. Sandwiches and stuff. We can hike up about halfway, stop for lunch, and then hike the rest. There's a little observation tower at the top. It's old and rickety but somehow still upright, and the view is spectacular."

He sighed. "I forgot you were so sportsy."

I laughed. "Come on, it'll be fun. It's an easy hike." I almost added I also thought it would be romantic, but that seemed to be pushing it. Besides, Noel was not my boyfriend. The word sent herds of butterflies through me, but I was in no position to have a boyfriend. Noel was just... a friend... who I apparently fucked sometimes.

"Okay, fine," he said.

I did indeed pick him up a half hour later. He was waiting in front of his building as I pulled up. I grabbed the plastic bag with sandwiches and chips and sodas I'd left on the front seat and held it as he got into my car.

"You look nice," I said, because he did. Not hiking appropriate, exactly; he had on a bright white short-sleeved button-front shirt and those damn high-water pants he seemed to like, khaki this time. He wore a pair of crisp white sneakers that looked more fashionable than practical.

"You good to walk in those?" I asked. "The hike is about a mile uphill."

"These are my most comfortable shoes."

I hadn't exactly gone hard-core, either, just wearing my regular old beat-up sneakers—not the good ones I used for track and cross-country, just my everyday shoes—and I'd put on a T-shirt and baggy khaki shorts because it was summer and it was pretty hot. I wondered again if I should put more effort into my appearance now I'd wandered over to the gay side; was that expected? The gay guys of my acquaintance all dressed better than I did. On the other hand, I knew zip-a-dee-doo-dah about fashion.

I handed him the bag of food. "Make yourself useful and hold this." Then I started the car.

We chatted about nonsense on the drive over. He expressed apprehension about climbing a mountain, and I assured him this hike had a low difficulty rating. The paths were all well-trodden and there were plenty of places to stop and rest. When we got there, I parked at the foot of Mount Sugarloaf. Noel eyed me skeptically as we got out of the car, but he insisted on carrying the food up the hill. I grabbed the tote bag I'd put in my trunk, which held a blanket, some paper plates, and a big bottle of water.

"I take it you don't do much hiking," I said as we began the trail up the hill.

"Not really, no."

"This'll be easy. It's walking, just uphill. We can go slow if you need to. I figured we could stop for lunch about halfway up."

He nodded. "This is the sort of thing you do for fun, huh, Sportsy?"

"Sure, sometimes. I jog the trails around here during track season, too, for extra practice."

"I wasn't exactly picked last in gym class, but that's about my general level of athleticism."

I scoffed. "Dude. I've seen you naked. No way you have a body like that just from sitting around your apartment."

He shot me a sly half smile. "Well. I lift weights at the South Quad fitness center a couple of times a week. Sometimes I run on the treadmill." He laughed softly. "Dude." He reached over and flicked the lid of my Sox cap.

I adjusted my hat. "Hey. The hat has practical purpose. It's keeping the sun off my face. Speaking of which, there's also sunscreen in the bag." He was so fair, he probably needed it. I lifted the tote bag to show him.

"I put some on before I left my apartment."

It was a gorgeous day. Sunlight streamed through the trees, making bright patterns on the dusty trail. We were shaded by a canopy of bright green leaves and long, spindly branches. There were some other people around but not many, and once a family on a hike with their dog got far enough ahead of us, I felt like we were alone together.

"The rumor," Noel said conversationally, "is the Theater Club wants to do *Hair* in the fall, but they're worried about tangling with the administration due to the nudity at the end of the first act."

My body's reaction to that was insane enough to be fit for scientific study. Noel naked on a stage? Sure, but only if I could shield the eyes of everyone else in the audience. I was excited and jealous and protective all at the same time. "You would get naked onstage?" I asked.

He shrugged. "If it's part of the show. Julie, she's the president of the Theater Club, she thinks I should audition for Claude. Do you know the show?"

"I've seen the movie. My mom has a weird crush on Treat Williams."

Noel laughed. "I haven't seen the movie, but I've heard it has more plot than the show."

"Wow, really? Because the movie plot doesn't make a lot of sense."

"I saw a community theater production back home, but they changed some of the words and cut the nude scene." He shook his head. "North Carolina, what can you do?"

I didn't know what he meant by that. "I thought North Carolina wasn't as conservative as the rest of the South?"

Noel kicked a rock. "That makes everything worse. There are just as many bigots and assholes in North Carolina as there are in the rest of the South, but acting badly is frowned upon, so they're quieter about it. It's not socially acceptable to openly display your prejudice, I guess. So they won't call you a fag to your face, but they will tell everyone in your town so you can't get a job."

"Did that happen?"

He shrugged again. "I wasn't out in high school. I worked at this little clothing store in town, and, I don't know. You've met me. I'm not exactly a paragon of manly heterosexuality. Some customer complained about the 'little girly boy' working at the store and I lost my job, just like that." He snapped his fingers.

"That sucks."

He looked so sad for a moment, I wanted to hug him.

"It's… North Carolina. It's why I wanted to go to college in New England. I wanted to get the hell away from all that. I thought, hey, Massachusetts was the first state to legalize gay marriage, so let me go there."

He was so astonishing, so smart and brave, and he'd been through so much. It reminded me again how cowardly I was being. On the one hand, Noel's experiences were proof there were real consequences for being gay. On the other hand, this was Massachusetts, not North Carolina, and the laws were different, the attitudes of the general population were different. Hell, the attitudes of my own family were different.

I reached over and took his hand. He looked startled for a moment, but then he laced his fingers with mine. We walked like that for a few moments.

"Anyway, *Hair*," he said, still holding my hand. "The show is kind of subversive. It's dated in a hippie-dippie way, but I don't know. I listened to the soundtrack when Julie told me we might do it. It's got a lot of, uh, naughty words in it. There's a song called 'Sodomy.'"

I laughed in surprise. I hadn't remembered that from the one time I'd seen the movie. Trying to lighten the mood, I nudged his shoulder with mine. "Don't tell me you have a problem with sodomy."

He smiled. "Obviously not." He squeezed my hand. "I mean, probably we'll end up doing *Sweet Charity* or *The Music Man* or something inane like that, but I liked the idea of doing something challenging."

"Those are good shows too." I recited the first few lines of "Ya Got Trouble."

Noel laughed. "Why are you not in the Theater Club?"

"I'm a much better audience member than an actor. I have zero desire to be onstage. And you've heard me sing."

"Fair enough."

By this time, I guessed we were still shy of the halfway point up the hill. It really wasn't too strenuous a hike. The path meandered and had a gentle slope. I was content holding hands with Noel as we strolled under the canopy of trees.

He squeezed my hand and said, "I suppose this hiking thing is not terrible."

"That's the spirit."

We walked a little farther, until I judged we'd passed the halfway point. There was a little grassy area off to the side of the path that looked ideal for a picnic.

"We should stop here and eat the sandwiches," I said.

He helped me spread out the blanket, and then we sat side by side. A nice breeze blew around us, bringing with it the scent of the trees and flowers blooming along the hiking trail. Noel sighed contentedly as he settled on the blanket and took a bite of his sandwich.

"Where'd you get the sandwiches?" he asked. "This is really good."

"There's a little deli in Amherst Center, kind of near the Green. Hole-in-the-wall between the burrito place and the comic book shop. Best sandwiches ever, right? I found it one time when I went into town to get a burrito but the line went all the way to Pleasant Street. I was hungry, so I just found the next closest place that served food. I lucked out."

"I don't eat out very often. I barely know the off-campus restaurants. I mean, I've had those burritos because obviously."

I readily agreed. There was a reason there was always a line there.

"What else is over there? Is that Chinese place any good?"

"It's fine. I dated a Chinese girl sophomore year who said it's not authentic, but she always ate enough crab rangoon to feed eight people when we went, so whatever."

Noel tilted his head. "I keep forgetting you dated women. A lot of them, by the sounds of it."

I had, I supposed. "None of those relationships really lasted. I was... I don't know. Looking for something and not finding it. I liked those girls, but none of them really made me happy."

"So you identify as queer now. That's what you keep saying. Not gay or bi."

"I don't know what I am, if I'm honest. I can't be totally gay, because I did like a lot of those girls I dated. I was crazy about a girl freshman year. But I'm obviously not straight, because I'm really into you. And we have sailed right past the point in the relationship I usually get bored, and yet you still fascinate me. I don't know why that is, but I like it. So I guess you could call me bisexual, but I think 'queer' is a good all-encompassing label. 'Queer' seems to fit as well as anything else."

He grinned. "I fascinate you?"

"Sure. I mean, we don't have that much in common, and yet I love spending time with you. So, I don't know what it means, but I want it to keep going."

"Yeah? Me too."

I reached over and squeezed his hand. "Good."

A number of people ambled past us as we ate. Another couple, a guy and a girl, set up a picnic just on the other side of the trail, but we couldn't really hear them through the thick air, and they seemed to be in their own little bubble anyway.

I had never had that. I'd never had that ease in a relationship, in which I could just be myself with someone and let the world pass us by like it didn't matter. I'd never been with anyone I was so into physically, emotionally, and intellectually that the rest of the world faded away, like it seemed to for the couple across the path.

I'd never experienced that until meeting Noel.

That gave me pause, but then I figured if being with Noel made me happy, then I should continue to be with him.

Which meant I'd have to make some changes. I'd have to come out. There was no way a guy like Noel could stay with a closeted guy, not for the long term.

I looked over at him. He was eating and looking up at the trees. A flock of some kind of small bird—sparrows, maybe—was kind of hopping around on the branches above us.

I wasn't ready. I wanted more time with Noel to myself before I had to share him and share what was between us with the rest of the world.

But good Lord, I wanted him. He looked so perfect. He polished off his sandwich and then leaned back on his hands. He closed his eyes and tilted his face up to the sky. He really was the best-looking guy I had ever laid eyes on, and he was mine, at least for now.

"Hey, Noel?"

He lowered his head and looked over at me.

So I kissed him. Right there on the hiking trail, in public, with other hikers about, I kissed him. It wasn't the sexiest kiss ever, but it was warm and affectionate. He put a hand on my shoulder and rubbed his fingers gently against the back of my T-shirt.

He was smiling wide when we parted.

I finished eating and then we cleaned up, shoving the trash back into my bag. I pulled it over my shoulder and we continued our ascent up the mountain. I asked him about his psych classes and his future plans, though he hadn't settled on anything specific beyond applying to grad school when the time came. He pointed out bugs and other small creatures we came across. A scurrying chipmunk intersected our path, which made him laugh.

A rickety old observation tower stood at the top of the mountain. I'd always wondered if the structure was sound—probably not—but it had remained standing the whole time I'd been hiking up this hill. There were maybe a dozen people around now, but I led Noel over to the staircase.

"It's going to feel like the whole thing is about to collapse, but it will stand. It's worth the climb. The view from the top is spectacular," I said.

"Er, okay."

We climbed the stairs together carefully, and the whole tower shook with the weight of the people going up and down. I was not altogether convinced we weren't about to plunge to our deaths, but this thing had held up for decades, so I figured we'd be fine. When we got to the top, I grabbed Noel's shoulders and moved him over so he was facing the valley. "What do you think?" I asked him.

The whole Pioneer Valley was laid out before us. It was beautiful and quaint in a New England way, with the tops of trees rolling below us like painted cotton balls and white clapboard and redbrick buildings planted sporadically over the landscape. If you squinted, you could sort of see the WMU campus in the distance, its dorm towers and the tall white steeple of the chapel.

"Oh, honey, it's gorgeous," Noel said with a gasp. "I had no idea."

I put my arm around his shoulders because I felt like it was appropriate. Probably the people around us wondered what the jock guy in the baggy shorts and the old grody Sox cap was doing with pretty, fashionable Noel, but somehow, up on top of the world, I did not care at all.

His body was warm, pressed against mine. I liked how close we were, how good he smelled, how soft his hair was. I liked having him near me, talking to him, looking out on the valley below us and marveling in the beauty of it with him. Up here, we were like birds soaring above the trees, and nothing could touch us. Here we were together, and it was us above everything.

Here I fell in love with him.

He put an arm around my waist and laid his head on my shoulder for a moment. "It's charming," he said, pulling away from me slightly. "Thank you for showing me this."

"You're welcome." I was suddenly overwhelmed, warmth rising through my body, crowding my chest, making it hard to breathe. I loved Noel. *Loved* him. I'd never felt anything like it before, and it was scary but it also felt good. He was with me and he made me happy, and up here with just the wind and the trees and a few other hikers, he was all I needed. "You can see why I like this hike."

"Yeah." He sighed softly and gazed out at the landscape before us. He put a hand on the railing and leaned forward a little, closing his eyes against the breeze. Then he opened his eyes and looked at me with a smile.

"Beautiful," I said.

"It is," he agreed, though he must have meant the landscape. I had meant him. "Although now we have to go back down."

I waved my hand. "Eh, down is easy."

I could only hope he felt the same way. I wanted to be able to give him everything he gave me, the hope, the companionship, the sense of rightness that came with our being together. I had no idea what I could offer him, but whatever he wanted, I wanted him to have it. In the way he smiled at me now, I thought I caught a glimmer of something in his eyes that said maybe he might bear some of the same affection for me as

I bore for him. Even a fraction would have been so much. I wanted him to feel what I was feeling.

Maybe he did. He laughed and took my hand. We went down the mountain together.

CHAPTER 15

IN THE midst of a late-July heat wave, Noel and I had a rare day in which neither of us had to report to work at all. Noel wanted to find some cheap ways to spruce up his sad little apartment, so I suggested a sojourn into Northampton. There were a bunch of little shops that sold kitschy home décor at reasonable prices; there was one right on Main Street that Joe and I had wandered into a number of times, mostly to point at things while we said, "That's awesome, but where would I put it?"

So I took Noel to that store because he seemed like the sort of guy who would want some kitsch in his life. I could tell immediately I'd guessed right; he lit up like a kid in a candy store. Or like an artsy guy with an apartment to decorate.

"The first floor is mostly gift stuff. Toys and games and knickknacks. The furniture and stuff is downstairs."

"Let's look around up here first," Noel said, beelining toward a display of action figures. "Oh my God, this is precious." He picked up a Jane Austen action figure. "It comes with a little quill pen!"

"You don't really think 'action' when you think of Jane Austen."

"Says you. Have you read *Pride and Prejudice*?"

"No."

He stared at me for a moment, looking appalled. "Some English major you are. It's my favorite book. I'm lending you my copy when we get back to my place later."

I laughed. "Okay."

Somewhat inadvertently we next stumbled into a corner of the store with racier items. Most of it was hokey and plastic and not really sexy, but I felt mortified just the same. The room was being lit by a lamp in the corner, the base of which was a statue of a naked lady with nipples made of little LED lights.

Noel giggled. "How delightfully tacky."

"Really? You don't think this stuff is kind of gross?"

He shrugged. "Some of it, sure, but most of it is campy and fun." He gestured toward some hula girl bobbleheads, which were next to a box of pasta shaped like boobs.

"I guess," I said.

He continued to browse, occasionally picking something up and smiling. "Oh, you're the movie guy. Did you ever see *Flawless*?"

I racked my brain. It didn't ring a bell. "I don't think so."

"Robert DeNiro plays, well, the sort of character Robert DeNiro plays, only in this case, he's super close-minded. But then he has a stroke, and part of his rehab is to take singing lessons from his neighbor, who just happens to be a drag queen played by Philip Seymour Hoffman. It's pretty amazing."

It did sound amazing. I'd never heard of this movie. "I'll have to check it out."

"You should. In the movie, Hoffman has all these fabulous but kind of tacky drag queen friends. I think something about this store reminded me of that."

We went down to the furniture section a little while later. While Noel contemplated a lamp, I thought about his weird fascination with the campy naked ladies upstairs. Just out of curiosity, I asked, "So have you ever been with a girl?"

He laughed and shook his head. "I'm a gold-star gay."

"Gold star? They give you a gold star if you *don't* sleep with a woman?"

"Yup. They put it right on the corner of your gay card."

"I guess I don't get a gold star."

He took a photo of the lamp with his phone. "I guess if you're bi and you've had sex with both a man and a woman, you get some kind of star."

"Bully for me."

He glanced at me, his expression a little wary, before he moved on to looking at a display of rugs. I followed him.

"Sorry," I said. "Sorry, that sounded bitchy. But, so, last night, I was just googling shit and I was thinking about, you know, whatever it is I am, and I had kind of decided bisexual fits pretty well, and I think I may be more into guys than girls, but I still like girls. So I was, I don't know, looking for more information?"

Noel turned toward me a little. "Sounds like you've got it figured out. What information did you need?" His tone wasn't accusatory, more curious.

"I don't know. Support? I've never met anyone who is bisexual before. Because you're not into women at all, right?"

He examined the pattern on a rug hanging on the wall, tracing a gold swirl with his finger. "I like women fine, but I don't want to sleep with one."

"Right. Part of me still does. I mean, not right now. Just, like, in theory." I swallowed and watched him for a moment, but his profile betrayed nothing. I said, "So, anyway, I was googling, and a lot of what I found was… not encouraging."

He turned toward me. "How so?"

"It runs the gamut from 'bisexuality doesn't exist' to 'just pick one' to some less savory things." I was having mild PTSD flashbacks just thinking about it. More than half of the articles I found were opinion pieces calling bisexuals frauds. On the one hand, I knew what I felt, but on the other, I couldn't help but wonder if I really was a fraud. I'd come away feeling seriously discouraged.

"That sucks," said Noel.

"You believe me, right? That I might be… bi. I guess."

He turned to face me full-on and said, "Yeah. I don't think the label really matters much. You are whatever you feel you are. As long as you're true to yourself and try to be a good person, the label doesn't matter."

His words touched me. "Yes. I don't know why I'm obsessing so much. Thank you."

"Sure. Are you… are you okay?"

"Yeah. Just, you know. It's a lot to think about. I feel like my whole life got turned upside down this summer."

"But it's good, right?" He looked uncertain.

"Yeah, I think so. I mean, probably I should just own my feelings and not rely on the Internet to define me." I laughed at myself. "Man, I sound like a dork. That's someone's philosophy dissertation right there."

"You don't sound like a dork. I get it."

I looked at one of the rugs and concentrated on the weird symmetric pattern for a moment. Then I turned back to Noel. I decided to up the dork factor and did my best Popeye. "I yam what I yam," I said.

He put his arms behind his back and swayed back and forth a little. He bit his lip. He looked damned adorable, and I wanted to hug him and kiss the unsure look off his face, but we were hardly alone in the store. He leaned forward and said softly, "What you are is my boyfriend, right?"

"Yeah," I said. And because he seemed basically perfect to me right then, I added, "Man, you're awesome. I like you so much."

"I like you too, which is why I'm letting you help me pick out which of these rugs I should put in the living room. I like the one with the blue triangles, but is it too much?"

It would have been a lot for me, but it had kind of a retro fifties vibe and it was totally Noel. "Not too much. It's perfect."

BACK AT Noel's place later, after we'd had a vegetarian dinner he'd cooked for me, we were making out on his couch when an odd thought occurred to me. I must have jerked or something, because Noel said, "What?"

"Have you ever topped?" I asked before I could think better of it.

He smoothed a sweaty fringe of hair off my forehead. "I have, yeah. Why do you ask? Do you want me to top you?"

"Maybe?" Although, honestly, I meant yes. I wanted to know what it felt like. But it had taken all of my courage reserves just to ask the question, and I couldn't assert myself now. "Did you like it? I know you like to bottom, but did you like topping too?"

"I… yeah. I mean, it's not my favorite, but with you… with you, I think it would be good."

"Yeah?"

"Yeah. You want to try it, don't you?"

I took a deep breath and tried to keep my voice steady. I whispered, "You are so sexy when you come when I'm inside you. It's amazing. I want to know what that feels like from the other side."

He kissed me and then said, "Look at you, talking dirty."

"Can you show me what it's like?"

He smiled. "Yeah. But let's go to the bedroom."

The bedroom was only maybe ten feet from the sofa—Noel's apartment was the tiniest—but it felt like a long, momentous journey. Once we walked into his room, he ordered me to strip and lay on the bed. I complied eagerly. I was already hard, so my body was clearly on board.

As I settled on the bed, he went to his dresser and grabbed condoms and lube. He put them on the mattress near my head. Then he whipped his T-shirt off over his head. I called out and wooed as if I were at a strip show, which made him laugh.

"You want a show?" he asked.

"Yeah. I love your body." I moved my hand to my cock and gave it a soft stroke.

He grinned. He swayed his hips as he undid the fly of his khakis and slid them slowly down his hips. There was already a bit of a tent in his red briefs. He danced for me while wearing only his underwear, closing his eyes and throwing his arms over his head, moving his torso and hips to some unheard beat. God, he was beautiful. There should have been whole museums dedicated to art of this man.

"You're so gorgeous," I whispered.

He smiled. "You're no slouch," he said. "Yeah, stroke your cock for me. Just like that. So hot."

He made a big show of slowly peeling off his briefs. He tossed them aside and cupped his cock in his hand, which seemed out of character for him, but I loved it. I could tell by the way his skin flushed we were both getting each other riled up, and it was fun and arousing. Just being with Noel alone in his room like this brought me so much joy.

He crawled onto the bed, crawled over me. He kissed and licked me, starting at my belly button and gradually moving up over my sternum to my collarbone, to my neck, to my ear.

I thought of what we must look like, thought of every silhouetted couple in a movie, bright lights behind them as their shadows made love. But that was all artifice; this was real.

He whispered, "Your first time doing this will probably hurt, but it gets better, I swear."

"I read that it's easier to take from behind your first time."

He tilted his head. "You did research?"

"I'm the sort of nerd who has two majors. Of course I did research."

He laughed. He kissed me soundly, and then he backed off and said, "Spread your legs."

I did as he asked. He poured a lot of lube on his fingers and then slid his hand over my cock. He squeezed my balls. Then he started exploring farther back with his fingers. It felt… weird. Not bad, but strange, out of context. The sensation was a little like running into someone in a place you didn't usually see them, like spotting one of the Hale's servers on campus. It wasn't wrong exactly, but his fingers didn't feel like they should be where they were. No one had ever touched me back there, besides myself.

But Noel moved his fingers confidently, with authority. He knew what he was doing. At first it was just light brushes over my hole, his fingers whispering over surprisingly sensitive skin, but gradually he started pressing more firmly. I wanted something to hold on to, so I snaked my fingers into his hair and grabbed some of the strands. He groaned and looked up at me, so I kissed him. I reveled in the familiar feeling of his lips against mine, the gentle pressure, as he continued to explore my body.

"Roll over," he said against my lips.

I did as he said. He backed away a little, though he never stopped touching me. He slid one of his hands along my hip, over my butt, and he massaged my skin as I settled onto my stomach. Then he hovered over me again. He bent his head and trailed soft kisses from the top of my spine to the base of it. That tickled a little, but I liked it. I felt revered, appreciated, maybe even loved as he lavished all this attention on me.

Then he grabbed a pillow. He pushed at my butt, manipulating me onto my hands and knees, and he slid the pillow under my hips. He whispered commands to me—"Lean up, move forward, spread your legs"—and then he kissed me at the base of my spine again. His hands were everywhere, caressing my skin, and he trailed his tongue against my ass crack, and then—

"Woah," I said as he licked my hole.

The sensation was… weird, again. Not bad. Wet. He pressed his tongue against my skin, and that was… good. The texture was strange, but then, oh God.

"Christ," I muttered. Because suddenly, him licking me felt *awesome*.

He grabbed my ass as he licked me, pressing his tongue against my hole, working it inside. I shut my eyes and grabbed on to the sheets for dear life, as if I'd fly apart from the pleasure of it. I pressed back against him, wanting more. More pressure, more pleasure, more of everything.

He leaned away and pressed a kiss to the base of my spine. Then he pressed a finger inside me.

"How does that feel?"

"Good," I moaned, because it was. So good. "More."

He laughed softly, his breath featherlight on my ass. Suddenly the pressure increased and I felt a sharp pain.

"Shh, breathe," he said, moving around to my side and rubbing my back as he stroked the inside of my body. "Relax. If you tense up, it will hurt more. Trust I won't do anything to hurt you, okay? But if it becomes too much, tell me to stop."

"Yes," I whispered. "Keep doing that."

"Yes."

And so it went as he used his fingers to stretch me. By the time he deemed me ready, I was a whimpering mess of longing, hugging one of his pillows and pressing wantonly against his hand.

In my peripheral vision, I saw him grab one of the condoms near my head, and my heart rate kicked up a notch in anticipation. This was really going to happen. He was going to fuck me. And I wanted it to happen. I wanted it desperately.

"You're beautiful," he told me. "Like this, the way you want me, it's… it's beautiful."

I whispered his name.

"Yes, sweetie, I'm right here." He moved around me and settled between my parted knees. He ran a hand up my back. "I'm about to be inside you. Are you ready for me?"

"Yes," I groaned. I was coming apart. I was sweaty and tingly, my body all nerve endings and desire, and there was nothing I wanted or needed more than his cock inside my body.

The blunt head of his cock pressed against me, and I realized it was a lot larger than a finger. I pulled in a breath, bracing myself for what I anticipated would be quite a bit of pain.

But then he rubbed my back, his palm pressing into my skin in gentle circles. "Relax," he said.

So I took a deep breath and exhaled.

He pressed forward.

It hurt. It was a surprise. But as he gradually pressed forward, it felt increasingly good. It was still… weird. But it felt important. Was he this undone every time I fucked him? Because me being inside him felt like a revelation every time, and I loved the way his body felt as he squeezed

me. I especially loved fucking him face-to-face and kissing him as our
pleasure grew.

This was something else entirely.

He slowly built up to a rhythm. There was still a bit of searing pain,
a sense something was happening here that was not what nature intended,
but the more he pressed against me, the better it felt. He was *inside* me.
That was *incredible*. And soon I was pressing back, half fucking the
pillow under my hips, and begging Noel for more.

Breathlessly he said, "Roll onto your back."

"What? But I—"

He pulled out. "I want us to be facing each other when we come."

And that would be perfect. I rolled onto my back, propping my butt
on the pillow. He hooked his elbows under my knees and pressed up. Then
he was sliding inside me again. He moaned; then he kissed me.

It was perfect. We were perfect.

I loved him so goddamn much.

I said nothing. I couldn't have if I wanted to. I wrapped my arms
around his shoulders and held him close as we fucked, as we *made love*,
as we kissed and rutted and did everything. Then the tingles all over my
body became something more, and the orgasm started somewhere at the
base of my spine and spread until I was crying out and coming against
his belly.

Noel moaned my name and pumped his hips a few more times
before he suddenly went very still, holding his breath. He let that breath
out on a great moan, and he kissed me as he came. I could feel his hips
buck and vibrate against me.

We both dripped with sweat as we came back down. He pulled out
slowly and took care of the condom, and then he curled up against me
and pulled me into his arms.

"How was that?" he asked.

"Consider my mind blown. Again." I put my arms around him.

"That's good, right?"

"It's great!" I hugged him. "I've never had sex like this. So good
every time."

He smiled. "I'm glad." He smoothed my hair off my forehead.

"How was it for you?"

"Good. Intense."

"Yeah. Not sure I could do that every time. But I get why you love it."

"So we'll switch things up sometimes." He kissed me.

"Yes. I want to do everything with you, Noel."

He smiled. "Yeah. Me too. I guess I'm pretty glad you stumbled in on me in the Dickenson men's room."

"Me too." I paused to wipe the sweat off his face, to rub his shoulder. "You've changed my life, Noel. For the better."

"I didn't intend that."

"I know, but… whatever happens to us, I'll always be grateful for this time we're spending together. Okay? That sounds super cheesy, but it's true."

"It's nice."

"Good."

We snuggled together and sank into the mattress, not really speaking anymore, just holding each other. I had no idea what would happen to us, but I cared about him a great deal. Whether I could be the man he deserved remained to be seen.

CHAPTER 16

A FEW mornings later, I woke up in Noel's bed. The clock said it was just after eight. I was surprised to be awake so early considering we'd been up most of the night working out new and exciting ways to have sex—I'd given my first blow job the night before, and mostly it involved doing unto Noel as I would have done unto me, and there had been physical evidence he'd enjoyed it. I learned a little while after that Noel gave life-affirming blow jobs, and I looked forward to experiencing one again.

Either way, I woke up in his bed, and he was still dead to the world. I tried going back to sleep but discovered quickly enough this was a futile exercise, so I got up and started getting dressed.

He stirred and blinked at me a few times. "Are you leaving?" he asked sleepily.

"I have class in a few hours. All my books are at home. I should probably go soon."

"Or," he said, "you could get back into bed and let me teach you something new."

And when he put it like that....

I crawled back onto the bed and kissed him. He laughed softly against my mouth and tangled his fingers in my hair.

"Maybe I could suck you off again," I said. "Show me what you like, okay? I want it to feel good for you."

He grinned and then leaned close to nibble on my earlobe. He pulled away from me and tossed the sheet on the floor. He was totally naked and his cock was hard. He was so fucking sexy, I couldn't keep my hands off him.

"Lots of tongue," he said. "Not too hard. And..." He took my hand and put it at the base of his cock. "Touch me wherever you want to. Anywhere. Everywhere."

"Yeah?" I said, moving my hand to cup his balls.

He gasped and arched his back. "Yeah. And maybe you could...."
He shifted his hips, rocking them up so my hand moved a little farther

south. I guessed what he wanted and touched his hole, really just grazed it with the tip of my finger. He hissed. So, yeah, that was what he wanted. I grabbed the lube from his side table and applied a generous amount. Then I gently pressed my finger inside him, and he arched off the bed. As he moaned, I dove, taking his cock into my mouth. I did as he asked, running my tongue up and down his shaft, not taking things too fast or too hard. I sucked on him gently as I thrust my finger in and out of his body. He grabbed my hair and tugged on it. Then he pushed me onto his cock. He pulled and pushed a few times to show me the pace he wanted.

"Curl your finger," he said.

"What?"

"Toward my... like you're telling me to come hither."

It took me a second to understand he wanted me to touch his prostate, but I tried it, and he groaned. "Oh God. Yeah. Like that."

I tried that a few more times as I sucked on his cock. I used my other hand to stroke the base of his shaft. His groans got louder, until he nearly shouted, "I'm coming!" He came in my mouth, his semen a little bitter but not really bad tasting, and it excited me that I'd made him come, that I'd done something that made his body react so strongly.

I swallowed. He panted as he came down from his orgasm. Then he reached over, hooked a hand around my head, and pulled me close. He kissed me hard, with lots of tongue, and he must have tasted himself, but that excited me too, and I was hard and throbbing. I wanted him badly, wanted to press inside him, but I knew better now; he couldn't accommodate me so soon after his orgasm. I was learning. But he grabbed me, flipped me onto my back, and put his mouth on my cock, sucking hard and stroking me fast, just as I liked it—he was learning too. I went off like a rocket within minutes.

I reluctantly went home an hour later. When I got there, Joe was up and eating cereal in front of the TV.

"So you are sleeping with someone," he said.

The walk of shame was irrefutable evidence—I was wearing my work uniform, even, so it's not like I could argue I'd gone out for a run or to buy milk before he got up—and still I said, "What makes you say that?"

"Don't be an idiot, Dave."

He looked angry. His eyebrows came to a point above his nose, and he shoveled cereal into his mouth with surprising aggression. I decided this was not the time to confide in my best friend that I'd been sleeping with a dude. So I deflected. "Why are you so angry?"

"You've never been the type to just hop in bed with a girl, so who is it? No one I can think of. No girls we know are up here except for Vanessa, who is obviously not who you're sleeping with. So. Someone from the restaurant?"

"No. And it's none of your business."

His eyebrows shot up. "Oh, that's mature."

"Dude, stop shouting at me."

"Or it's Noel. Are you fucking Noel?"

"I can't talk to you when you're this pissy," I said, offended by his tone.

"Oh, well, whatever. That's fine. You just spend all night out without so much as a text, so what am I supposed to conclude? Either you're fucking someone or you were kidnapped or were dead in a ditch somewhere."

"You never said anything when I stayed out all night before. I don't get why this is different."

"I knew who you were fucking before. Now you're keeping it a secret? It's me, Dave. We're friends. We talk about shit." He put his spoon down somewhat forcefully. "I mean, what am I supposed to conclude? That this Noel guy has come into your life and turned you into a fag? Because that's kind of what it looks like. You spend more time with him than you have with some of your past girlfriends. I don't know who the hell else you've spent any time with this summer."

"That's not how that works, you know. One man cannot turn another gay."

"So you've been a goddamned fag this whole time?"

I headed for my bedroom. "Fuck you, Joe." I slammed the door.

I was out of sorts for the rest of the day. One could have argued that if Joe didn't like gay guys, he had no business being my friend, but aside from the typical straight-dude thing of saying dumb shit as a result of being mildly paranoid some gay guy would hit on him— and I had pointed out to Joe more than once that if this was the worst thing that ever happened to him, his life was just fine—he'd never expressed homophobia quite this explicitly. I'd never heard him call anyone a fag before. More to the point, Joe was my best friend and had been through most of college. I'd always thought we saw the world in the same way, were cut from the same cloth. His anger mystified me. Unless he really was that homophobic and had just been masking it. Or I hadn't noticed it because I wasn't looking for it before. Or maybe it was fine for other people to be gay, but not for someone who was as close to Joe as I was.

It hurt. Joe's rejection was like a physical pain. His words hung over me like a thundercloud all day, and my chest hurt and my stomach churned whenever I thought about it, which was often. I couldn't pay attention in class because my thoughts kept drifting back to what Joe had said.

Yeah, I'd been a goddamned fag the whole time, I thought. All the years he'd known me, I was queer. And yeah, I was fucking Noel, but I was falling in love with him too, and that scared the shit out of me. It would've been nice to be able to talk about that with my best friend, to hash things out the way we had in the past when I'd had girl problems.

But no. Joe made it clear he wanted no part of that.

I didn't feel like I could go home that night. I got out of class and sat in the Mac for an hour, nursing a milk shake and watching the thin crowds of summer students ebb and flow through the restaurant. Then I called Noel, actually called him instead of texting him, because I needed to hear his voice.

"Joe and I fought. He called me a fag."

"Oh, sweetie. Come over to my place tonight."

So that's what I did.

I KNEW there was a bigger fight to be had between me and Joe, but I avoided it and him for the rest of the week. I knew his schedule well enough, knew which shifts he typically worked and which nights Vanessa was free to have him over, so I only went home to shower and change when I calculated he wouldn't be there. Otherwise I slept at Noel's.

The hours Noel and I spent together were idyllic at times. Some nights it felt like just me and Noel against the world. We'd have increasingly creative sex until the wee hours of the morning, and then we'd stay in bed together until our work or class schedules forced us to leave. He was so sweet and caring, making sure I ate regularly, talking to me about music or movies late at night when I had trouble sleeping, and then running his hands through my hair as I drifted off. I'd hold him as we fell asleep together and think things might be all right.

But they weren't. I might have just lost my best friend.

I finally made a mistake on a Saturday afternoon. I had gone home to do laundry and was in the middle of folding it in the living room when Joe came home with Vanessa in tow.

"Howdy, stranger," Joe said.

"Fine. You got me. Want to call me a fag again?"

Both he and Vanessa winced. "No," said Joe.

I kind of expected him to apologize there, and part of me wished he would just say "I'm sorry" and make a comment on the previous night's Red Sox/Yankees game. I'd seen it; Noel didn't have cable, so we'd gone to the Pub and watched it on the TV over the bar, and he'd spent most of the game quizzing me on the finer points of the sport.

But Joe remained mute for a few long minutes.

He dropped his bag near the door and walked over to me. Vanessa trailed behind him, shooting looks between the two of us. I wanted to think she was on my side, but she stayed quiet too.

"Haven't seen you all week," Joe said.

"Yeah, well."

"You didn't answer my texts."

"Nope."

"Oh, what? So now you're pissed at me?"

"Joe." I sighed. I didn't want to get mad. It ran through my head that he should have known how I'd react to what he'd said. I didn't think we could bounce back from this one; I felt too angry, too betrayed. I said, "How was I supposed to react? You yelled at me and called me a fag."

Joe spared a glance for Vanessa, who took a step back toward his bedroom. "I know," Joe said. "That was… uncalled for. I'm sorry, okay?"

"Joe…," Vanessa said slowly, probably as aware of Joe's temper and his not-exactly-apologetic tone as I was.

Joe looked at her and grunted. I imagined they'd talked about what had happened, and she'd probably counseled him in the way she thought best. I would have put money on her having told him he was wrong for calling me a fag. I could imagine her telling him to make up with me or to not be so adversarial, because she just wanted everyone to be friends and to be happy. I appreciated that about her, but something about her having spoken to Joe about me really bothered me. I liked Vanessa, I knew she meant well, but this was between me and Joe.

"Uh," I said to Vanessa. "Could you leave us alone for a few?"

She looked back and forth between us, "Joe, what do you—"

"I got this, Van," he said.

She frowned but nodded and walked into Joe's room. She left the door open and was probably eavesdropping, but at least it was just me and Joe in the living room.

I looked at Joe, anger roaring through my bloodstream. I was still so upset I couldn't speak.

"I'm sorry," he said. "I shouldn't have said what I did. But I was worried when you didn't come home. Maybe it's none of my business who you're sleeping with, but you could've at least sent me a text telling me you were gonna be out all night. Besides, usually you tell me who you're spending time with. From what I've seen, the only person you've been spending time with this summer is Noel. What was I supposed to think?"

He was right, but I'd had a few days to let my anger and hurt marinate. "You could've asked me instead of assuming. You could've been less of an asshole about it."

"Are you sleeping with Noel?"

I wondered if Vanessa had told him. Of course, she didn't know anything had progressed past the 'dating' phase. I hadn't told her I'd slept with Noel. I looked toward Joe's room, but even if she'd been in sight, she wouldn't have told me if she'd said anything to him.

"I don't want to talk about Noel," I said. "I don't want to talk about anything with you right now. You've been such a jackass all summer, since before the semester ended even, and I don't know what got up your butt, but—"

"*I've* been a jackass? You won't even talk to me anymore!"

"Why should I when you've been acting this way?"

"Boys!" shouted Vanessa from the bedroom. "This is not getting better with you two shouting at each other."

"Stay out of it, Vanessa!" I shouted back.

Joe glowered at me from across the room. He crossed his arms at his chest. When he spoke, his voice was less shouty and more even keel. "I know you've been home when I'm not here because your stuff keeps moving around. Figures you finally learn my schedule because you don't want to see me anymore."

"Can you blame me after what you said?"

"What did I say? I just want to know the truth."

Probably I should have just said, "Yeah, I'm sleeping with Noel, and fuck you if you think there's something wrong with that," but I couldn't bring myself to do it. I probably should have said, "I'm really falling for this guy," but I couldn't say that either. Instead I just stood there, staring at Joe, stewing in my hurt, anger, and confusion. Unable to speak, I went back to folding my clothes.

"Fine, asshole," he said. Then he stormed into his room and slammed the door.

I overheard Vanessa tell Joe, "Both of you need to get the hell over yourselves."

"You said——" Joe started.

"I know what I said. But you could try being honest with him instead of angry." Then they started talking lower and I couldn't make out what they were saying anymore.

That left me alone with my laundry for the time being.

AN HOUR later, as I was tossing an overnight bag into my car down in the apartment complex parking lot, Vanessa ran outside.

I didn't especially want to talk to her, but I didn't say anything.

"Look," she said, "I get that you're both mad at each other."

"What gave us away?"

She grunted. "All right, first of all, be honest with me. You're with Noel, right? You're headed to his place right now, aren't you?"

"Yeah," I said. I felt resigned.

She sighed. "You could tell Joe the truth."

"Are you fucking serious?" I looked up toward my apartment. It was on the other side of the building, the windows facing the lawn out back and not the parking lot, but part of me wondered if Joe was in hearing range anyway. I gestured toward our floor. "He threw a bunch of homophobic nonsense at me, but I'm supposed to interpret that as him giving me a safe space to tell him the truth or whatever other nonsense you're about to tell me? No, Van. I think you're wrong about this one."

She sighed. "I don't think it's you being gay that bothers him."

"No? What part of him calling me a fag sounds like he's cool with me being queer?"

"If you guys could just, for one minute, talk like rational humans instead of shouting...."

I wanted to shout, "He started it!" but instead stood there with my arms crossed over my chest.

"I'm sorry," she said. "I really didn't expect this. I didn't think he'd react this way."

I let out a breath and dropped my arms. "I know, but just...."

Joe's car was parked next to mine. We didn't have reserved spaces or anything, but we always parked in about the same spot, and here was my old silver POS next to his shiny black Camry, same as it had been in student parking on campus. The backseat of his car was littered with his usual ephemera—spare clothes, an ice scraper, a baseball bat, miscellaneous papers—and there was something achingly familiar about it. I'd spent a lot of time in that car riding around Western Mass with Joe, shouting out the lyrics to the rock songs we both liked best, getting lost in the farmland a few miles from campus. Just then I had a vivid memory of us flying over a hill on this one road that went by the bison farm off Route 9—that was something Joe especially got a kick out of, since he'd grown up in South Boston about as far from farmland as anything—and Joe took the hill too fast and wound up bottoming out the car on a bump. We'd laughed at the time, though he'd wound up having to get some repairs done.

But we used to do shit like that all the time. We went to games together, we snuck into bars together, we drove around the back roads of Amherst and Hadley together. We ate brunch, we talked sports, we laughed at the same kinds of jokes.

I missed him then. I missed my best friend. I missed our easy camaraderie. I wanted it back. But most of all, I wanted someone who I could talk to about all the crazy stuff I'd been going through, because Joe used to listen to me talk about anything, but this felt like the last thing I could tell him.

"I want to tell him," I said quietly. "But I just can't. Not when he's acting this way."

She nodded slowly. "He's hurt and angry, too, you know."

I shrugged. What the hell did he have to be angry about except that his best friend had gone gay?

"I gotta go," I said. "I told Noel I'd meet him for dinner by his apartment. I'm supposed to be there in ten minutes, but it's a twenty-minute drive, so…."

"You really like this guy," she said.

"I love him."

And there it was. I hadn't even said those words to Noel, but here I was confessing it to Vanessa. I hadn't meant to, but the words had just tumbled out of my mouth.

Her eyes went wide with surprise.

"Don't tell Joe," I said, opening my car door. "It should be me who tells him, but we both need to cool off before I can."

"Yeah," she said. "I want to help you. Help both of you."

I knew she wanted to be there for me, and I probably should have taken her up on it because I could have used a friend just then, but she was more Joe's friend than mine and I felt a little resentful.

"I know you want to help and I really appreciate it, but… let it be for now, okay?"

She smiled sadly. "Okay. Just… if you need anything…."

"Yeah. Thanks, Van."

I got in my car and drove to Noel.

CHAPTER 17

MY MOM called when I was at Noel's a few nights later.

His place really was a shithole. He had put some effort into sprucing it up with new lampshades and curtains, and of course the rug we'd picked out, but he didn't have the resources to do more than put lipstick on that pigsty—he pointed out paying tuition next semester was more important than interior decorating—so it mostly remained a shithole. I was starting to hate how colorless and busted up the place was, both because I disliked the space and because I wanted better for Noel. I wanted my own apartment back. I wanted to be able to hang out there and watch baseball games on Joe's big TV and sleep in my own bed and be near my own stuff, but it was hard to do those things and avoid Joe at the same time. I didn't dare bring Noel home with me, and I wanted to spend time with him, too, so I sucked it up.

We were eating pizza and watching a movie on Noel's laptop when my mom called. She wanted to come visit sometime in August. Allegedly she and Dad had finally gotten around to cleaning out the basement—one of those projects they said they'd do every year but didn't—so she had some more secondhand things she could bring to my apartment. I told her that was fine, acknowledging to myself I'd have to make peace with Joe because this current mode of operating was not sustainable, but I said to come out during a weekend Joe would be at his sister's wedding.

"I called your landline first," Mom said. "Joe said you haven't been home much. Is everything all right?"

"Yeah. Just working a lot."

"Okay. You'd tell me if something was wrong."

"Sure," I said, feeling annoyed. I had always been up-front with my mom in the past—we'd been close and I felt comfortable talking to her about most of my personal nonsense—but I didn't feel ready to talk about all this just yet.

"Because you can tell me, you know. Whatever it is."

"Everything's fine, Mom." But I said it with enough anger and defensiveness Noel shot me an alarmed look and my mother gasped.

"David! Don't you take that tone with me. It was just a question. I'm your mother and I worry."

"I'm sorry."

"That's better. All right, then. I'll see you in a few weeks."

Once I finally got her off the phone—Mom preferred the "Wait, one more thing!" method of saying good-bye and it always took forever—I turned to Noel. He stared back at me.

"So are you just not telling anyone what's going on in your life?" he asked.

I shrugged.

"How much longer do you think you can get away with that?"

"I don't know," I said. It sucked, if I was honest with myself. I felt completely terrible about the situation, and my inability to do anything about it sat like a bad meal in the pit of my stomach. I wanted to tell people about Noel, but I didn't feel like I could. "I'm not ready to have that conversation with my parents," I said.

"When do you think you will be?" He crossed his arms and leaned away from me.

"I don't know."

That answer was clearly not what he wanted to hear. He got up from the sofa and walked into his kitchen. I heard the water run and the burner on the stove click on, which I took to mean he was making tea. Hot tea in hot weather was one of Noel's particular eccentricities, something I'd learned in all the days I'd stayed at his apartment. He drank tea because it comforted him.

He emerged a minute later, but instead of resuming his spot on the sofa, he stood near the doorway to the kitchen.

He said, "I don't... I'm not a phase you're going through."

"I never said you were."

"You won't tell anyone about me."

"It's not like you're a secret. You were at my place all the time before Joe and I started fighting. You and I go out in public."

He pursed his lips as he looked at me. Then he said, "There's a clear end date on whatever is going on between us, though, isn't there?"

There probably was. I opened my mouth to protest, but any reassurance I was formulating in my mind felt like a lie.

He rubbed his forehead. "Here's the situation as I see it. You met a gay guy and read a book and wanted to see what cock was like, so you and I fooled around. That's about the sum of things, right?"

I hated hearing it boiled down so much. "That's not all it is. I mean, yeah, that's kinda true, but—"

"I'm not just a phase." He glared at me and balled his hand into a fist. "I'm a man, a person with feelings, and I don't exist to be one of your experiments. I've got too much going on in my life, too much at stake, to let you take advantage of me that way."

"I'm not. I care about you. You are absolutely not a phase. I want to be with you, Noel, not with just any guy. Maybe it started as curiosity, but it's become a lot more than that."

He bit his lip. "I know, but… it doesn't feel that way sometimes."

I was floored. I had no idea how to react to that or what to say to make him see that I did care about him. I loved him. I was here with him now because I wanted to be with Noel, not because I was interested in dudes generally. We'd spent so much time together, gotten to know each other so well. I'd taken him to New York, to my favorite hiking spots, to the maze. I'd done those things because he meant the world to me. He had to know that. Surely he knew as well what I was giving up, what I was sacrificing, what I felt just to be here. I risked my whole life as I knew it to be with him.

"You're not a phase," I repeated. "You're the real thing. You're what I want."

The kettle whistled. He grunted and went back into the kitchen. He walked out a moment later with a cup of tea and sat back next to me on the couch, blowing over the cup as he sat. He was clearly upset and I wanted to change that, but I had no idea what to say or do.

Quietly I said, "It's you, Noel. I love spending time with you. You're beautiful and smart and interesting. I wanted to be your friend before anything else because you're so special. I like being with you. No other guy has ever made me feel this way."

He sipped his tea and stared at his laptop.

"I know you don't want to date a closeted guy," I said, "and you shouldn't. You deserve to be with someone who can be with you out in the open. I want that someone to be me, but it's hard. My best friend won't talk to me now and will probably kick me out if I can't figure out how to reconcile with him. My friends are all jock types, and I don't know what they will say to me if I come out. And my parents...."

He nodded slowly. "I know. Believe me. I get it."

"I know you do. I'm sorry. I just need a little more time to sort all this out."

"Okay," he said softly. Then he asked if I wanted to watch a new movie. I thought the conversation was over.

IT WASN'T. Oh, it seemed like things were resolved, but when we went to bed that night, I felt the strain between us. After he switched off the light, I pulled him against me and whispered into his hair, "I care about you so much." I couldn't say *love* yet, especially not when I didn't know if he returned my feelings. Part of me was terrified he'd hear me say it and laugh in my face, which I knew was irrational, but I just had to sit on the feeling a while longer to be sure it was real. Instead of telling him what was in my heart, I stroked his arms, his chest, kissed the back of his neck. "You were never just a phase for me. This is important, what we have."

He sighed and put his hand on my arm. "Yeah. I just wish... I wish things were different. I know this is all new for you and I don't want to pressure you or rush you, but there's a limit on how long I can go on keeping this a secret."

"I know. I just need more time. I want to tell people. It's not like I *enjoy* keeping this secret."

"Okay," he whispered. He pressed back against me. "I care about you too."

I rubbed my face in his hair, held him close, and loved him with all my heart.

CHAPTER 18

DURING THE second week of August, Noel and I had plans for what I thought would be a romantic dinner at Linetti's, a fancy Italian place in Northampton owned by the same people who owned Hale's. As an employee, I got a discount there, but it wasn't the same as eating in my own restaurant, which I hated doing. I had spent enough time there that summer as it was. But I liked Linetti's well enough. Unfortunately I'd timed our date poorly, and we got there just as the dinner rush was starting. One of the area schools—Smith College, by the looks of the mostly female crowd—must have had orientation or something that week, and there was a wait for tables, which hadn't been the case all summer. I was determined to stick to my plan, but the hostess told me it would be fifteen minutes at least, so we lingered in the vestibule in the front of the restaurant.

I'd been trying to prolong the amount of time I spent at home, sleeping there when I sensed Noel needed space and trying to be in the same space as Joe, even though we were both still angry at each other. We were begrudgingly getting along again, though. I worried there might be irreparable damage to our friendship, since Joe made no secret of the fact he did not approve of whatever it was he thought I was doing, but at least we could still talk about the Sox and the pending football season, so it wasn't completely bad at home. Thus I hadn't seen Noel in a few days and was looking forward to spending the night together.

He looked handsome. He'd put on a gray shirt and a pair of tan-and-black plaid pants. I had on my other shirt with buttons—this one was black—and a pair of gray trousers I thought looked okay. I had dressed thinking my limited wardrobe of nice clothes made choosing an outfit easy. On my way out the door, Joe had asked if I had a hot date. I told him I did and not to wait up, but provided no details.

And now, here we were, two nicely dressed men in the vestibule of a high-end restaurant. So who should walk in but Britney and some dude.

"Woah, hey!" she said when she saw me. "What are you doing here?"

"Dinner," I said.

She giggled. "No, dummy, what are you doing in Northampton? Aren't you from Framingham?"

"Yeah. I've been out here all summer. Got a place in North Amherst, and I've been waiting tables across the street." I glanced at my dinner companion. "You remember my friend Noel?"

"Of course!" she said.

I saw the grimace flash across Noel's face when I said *friend*, but it was gone quickly. He smiled at her.

"I moved back up here early," she said. "I'm going to be an RA this year, did I tell you?"

"No. That's great," I said. "I mean, responsibilities and stuff, but you get your own room and you move in early and get all set up. Right?"

"Yeah. So I'll be in Thoreau House in East Quad. Not the most glamorous residential area, but they have the vegetarian dining hall, so that won't be bad." I didn't think Britney was a vegetarian—I wasn't sure, though, so I really had been the worst boyfriend ever—but it was well-known that the vegetarian dining hall had some of the best food on campus. It was better than the Grade F mystery meat they served elsewhere. The chef who worked at the veggie dining hall made a lot of Middle Eastern and Greek food, at any rate, so you could get hummus and falafel anytime, which I appreciated.

"Cool," I said. "I'm living with Joe off campus. Which I guess I just told you. North Amherst. The apartment complex near the high school."

"Yeah, now I remember. I ran into Joe at the end of last semester and he told me. Sounds like a good setup. You'll have to have some parties after the semester starts."

"Sure. I'll let you know."

The dude with Britney cleared his throat.

"Oh, sorry," she said. "Ricky, this is Dave. Dave and I used to go out, but that was a million years ago and he dumped me, so you have nothing to fear from him." She grinned. I wasn't convinced Ricky understood her tone, since he glowered at me. "Dave, this is Ricky. He's an RA in Webster House." Webster was one of the other dorms in North Quad. "He's my lovely date for the evening." She smiled and swayed back and forth a little, as if she could not have been more pleased. He was an okay-looking guy, a bit on the beefier side of the spectrum.

"Nice to meet you," I said. We shook hands.

Noel put his hand on my shoulder. I went stiff almost immediately and panic lanced through me. I wasn't ready to come out to Britney. I barely knew her. Sure, we'd slept together a couple of times, but... and sure, I'd broken up with her so I could be with Noel, kind of....

Full-on panic hit then.

Noel withdrew his hand. "Sorry. Our table's ready."

"Oh, maybe we can get a table for four and all sit together!" said Britney.

I could not think of anything worse. I just wanted Noel to myself and for Britney to go away. Her being there was going to inhibit me and would likely ruin our date. I didn't think I could sustain the façade Noel and I were just friends throughout an entire dinner, for one thing, but also, she was kind of annoying me now. "I don't want to interrupt your date," I said.

"We can double-date. It's fine."

"Oh, we're not—" I started to say, which earned me a scowl from Noel.

And now everybody hated me.

The hostess saved me by pointing out the table she had free for me and Noel only had room for two and was tucked into a corner, wedged between another full table and the wall. "You'll have to wait another twenty if you want a table for four," she said.

"I don't want to wait," Noel said.

"Guess we better get this table, then," I said to Britney. "Bummer. I'll see you later, okay?"

She smiled. "Text me after the semester starts and we'll get milk shakes at the Mac. It looks like we have a lot to catch up on."

I nodded and followed Noel to the corner table. After we were seated and the hostess left us with menus, Noel said, "So we're not on a date. Just so I'm clear."

I let out a breath. "No, we are. I... I'm sorry. I panicked."

"What's the big deal? She assumed we were together and didn't seem to have a problem with it."

"I'm not even out to my friends or family. Am I supposed to come out to my ex-girlfriend or whatever first? And, like, how would that make her feel?" I stopped myself from voicing a bunch of clichés about Britney thinking she'd turned me gay or that sex with her was so bad I turned to dudes next; even as jokes, they struck me as horrible things to say. And likely not true; maybe she'd be relieved that she hadn't done anything wrong because I was really into guys.

Noel frowned and opened his menu.

Apparently the answer to the question about whether I should have come out to Britney was yes, because we spent the next ten minutes speaking mostly in monosyllables. "Water?" "Yes." "Bread?" "Okay." "Appetizer?" "Nah."

By the time we ordered food, I wanted to scream.

"Why can't we just carry on as we have been?" I asked, frustrated now, wanting things between us to be easy, as they had been all summer. I wanted things to stop feeling like they were spiraling out of control. Across the restaurant, Britney and Ricky were seated, and she waved at me.

"Really?" he said quietly. "Really? You'd ask me that question? You'd ask if we can just keep going the same way? Surely you already know the answer."

"At least for the summer," I whispered.

He shook his head. "You say it's not a phase, that there isn't an end date, but you just put one on this relationship."

"Noel, I—"

He leaned forward and whisper-shouted at me. "Did you see what just happened? Out there with Britney? You just denied being in a relationship with me. I'm the dirty secret you've got stuffed in the back of your closet. I risked my whole life—my whole fucking life!—to come out and live how I wanted. I sacrificed everything, and I did it damn the consequences. My family won't talk to me, I have to figure out how to pay tuition for the rest of college, but I'll figure it out, and I'm doing it because being honest about who I am is essential to my continued survival. Do you get that?" He leaned back and let out a disgusted huff. "Of course you don't, because you want to shove me back into the closet. You want to deny there's anything going on between us entirely, and by doing so, you force me into a lie. Can you see why that might be a problem for me?"

He was absolutely right. I knew it. His words shamed me because they were true, and I sank into my chair a little. I was a coward. I was completely unworthy of him. I felt worse than roadkill along Route 9. "I'm sorry."

He leaned forward and pressed a hand to his chest. "I know you're not ready to tell your parents and I know you and Joe are on the outs and I know you're afraid, but you have to know I can't just be your secret forever. I really like you, Dave, and I've had a lot of fun with you this summer, but I can't continue to be with you if you're going to stay in the closet indefinitely."

It was a knife to the chest, but I deserved it. I looked up at him. His blue eyes gazed back at me with intensity, and his face was flushed. He was upset, as he had every right to be. I knew he was right, and I was an asshole.

It was like I'd pushed him back into that bathroom stall where we'd first met. I knew I was hurting him the longer I drew this out.

And still I said, "So, what, you need me to have a plan?"

"Well… yeah. It would be nice if you had 'coming out' somewhere on your agenda for the fall semester. Look, I don't care if your ex-whatever doesn't know who you're sleeping with now. It's none of her business. But you haven't even tried to tell your friends. And that was fine for a while, but the longer we're together, the worse that feels. If this relationship is going to work, it can't stay a secret. You know that. It's not fair to either of us."

"I know."

He nodded and took a sip of his water. "So?"

"So… I don't know."

He bit his lip and looked away from me.

A waiter brought out our food, but it tasted like sawdust. Noel ate but didn't talk to me, avoiding my gaze for the most part and focusing on his meal.

Noel, who I knew with certainty as my heart was breaking, was the love of my life, was mad at me, and I'd made him mad, and I'd hurt him, and I hated myself for it. But what was I supposed to do? Call my parents right then and tell them I was dating a guy? Tell Joe? Tell Kareem and Mike and all those guys? Have a goddamned coming out party?

No. I couldn't do any of those things.

Instead I sat there, paralyzed by the fear of every possibility before me, because none of my options were good. Noel had basically given me an ultimatum: come out or break up. I dreaded both.

I got the check as soon as it became clear this dinner was a disaster and paid it because I figured it was the least I could do. We left the restaurant together. Britney waved at me like a maniac from her table. I waved back, but then Noel tugged me outside.

"I'm sorry," I said again.

"I get it," he said.

We stood on Main Street; the neon lights of the Linetti's sign lit up his face, made him look purplish. I imagined that purple hue was a bruise, one I'd given him, and I wanted to crawl into a corner and die.

He grunted and watched a car speed by, but then he turned back to me. "I know how hard this is for you. I've been there, remember? But you have to understand where I'm coming from. I can't go back into the closet, not after everything that's happened to me. I won't do it."

"No. I know. You shouldn't."

"I'll get the bus home." He turned to walk toward the bus stop.

I couldn't just let him go. "No. Let me give you a ride home." I gestured toward the parking lot.

He bit his lip again and looked between me and the bus stop. He finally let out a breath and his shoulders slumped. "All right. Ride home. But that's it. You're not coming home with me tonight."

Once we were in my car, I said, "I know you're mad at me."

He sighed. "It's not that I'm mad at you exactly. I'm mad at the situation. I want to be with you. I do, but not if it means more nights like this. This is so hard."

I started up the car. "I'm sorry." I didn't think I'd ever be able to apologize enough.

"I know, but…." But he didn't finish the thought.

As I pulled onto Route 9, he said, "It sucks because I like you so much, but tonight made me realize I really can't be your secret. I believe you when you say this is not just a phase, that you like me enough to get invested in a relationship, but I can't just keep going as we have been. Something has to change if we're ever going to move forward. If you could tell me you had plans to come out to your friends, at least, that would be all right. We wouldn't have to sneak around anymore, for one thing. But if you plan to keep me quiet forever, I can't do it. I can't. It hurts too much."

It was hard to have this conversation and drive because my vision kept going blurry. But I focused on the road and said, "But Joe—"

"Yeah, I know. What about your other friends, though? Or your parents? Or anybody."

"I don't know."

He let out a breath. "I really do care about you, but maybe it's better to cut our losses now. Get out before we're both in too deep."

"No." This was the worst because I knew he was right, but I didn't want to let him go. I imagined telling Joe I was with Noel, though, and I could basically see his fist aimed at my face. I imagined telling my parents and having them throw me out the way Noel's had him. I couldn't do it. But I said, "No, I don't want to break up."

He sighed. "It's easy to get caught up in how good things feel in the moment, but sooner or later, if we just kept going the way we were, it would have gone sour. I don't want that for us. But I can't think of any way it'll ever get better if you don't put yourself out there and try. I just can't do things your way anymore, Dave. I care about you, but I can't."

When we got to Amherst, I turned onto 116 and headed south toward South Hadley. I concentrated on the roads and how to get where I was going, distracting myself from what Noel had said, although the truth was plain.

"You're breaking up with me," I said as we passed Amherst College.

"I don't want to, but I don't see any way to go forward without us both getting our hearts broken down the line. Not if you insist on keeping everything the way it has been."

He was giving me an out, an opportunity to tell him I would come out and introduce him to all my friends, but for whatever reason, I couldn't say that. I didn't want to lie. I had no strategy moving forward. I loved Noel, I didn't want to break up, but I didn't want to tell anyone about him either. Joe would kick me out, my parents would have to confront the reality of their queer son, my jock friends would stop talking to me… it was like I could see my whole terrible future playing out before me.

"I can't," I whispered. And I also couldn't help but think he deserved so much better than me.

"Then I guess that's it for us," he said.

Shit. Shit, shit, *shit*. "That's not what I want."

"I know, but do you understand what I'm saying?"

"I do. I just need more time. Can't we stay together for the rest of the summer at least? Make the most of the time we have until the rest of the students come back?"

"What's the point? It will just hurt more the longer we spend time together."

He was right and I knew it. I sped the rest of the way down 116, letting the car do eighty down the mostly deserted road, eager now to get him out of the car so I could totally lose my shit in peace. We rode in silence until I pulled up to his building.

"I hate that it's ending this way," he said. "But you have to know—"

"I do. I'm sorry too. So sorry. Bye, Noel."

"Bye."

He got out of the car. I waited at the curb until he was inside before I pulled away. I was about halfway back to my apartment in North Amherst when I stopped being able to see the road clearly. I pulled over and burst into tears.

Everything in that moment felt bleak. I had nothing and nobody; it was just me with my newly discovered queerness but no Noel and no friends I could talk to about it. So I wept for a good long while, until it felt like I had no more tears, and I thought, this was why Noel was crying in the bathroom that day. This feeling of having nothing must have been what it was like to lose his family.

Except not, because Noel was brave, and I was a fucking wussy-ass coward.

I got it together enough to get home, but I knew I must have looked like a wreck, so when I got to my apartment and unlocked the door, I beelined for my room. Joe called out, "Date must not have gone that well if you're home already!" from the living room, but I ignored him, went into my bedroom, and slammed the door.

CHAPTER 19

I WASN'T feeling much better the next morning. Joe was already up when I got out of bed. I found him fiddling with the coffeemaker in the kitchen.

"You want to talk about it?" he asked.

"No."

"Fine. Just figured I'd offer."

His tone seemed… normal. Supportive. Not angry or resentful. But I didn't want to talk about this with Joe. Instead I said, "Did you make enough coffee for both of us?"

"Yeah. That nasty vanilla creamer stuff you like is in the fridge too. It was on sale, so I bought some."

I recognized that as an olive branch. "Thanks," I said. "My head is pounding."

"I promised Vanessa I'd drive her to the mall today, but I think the Sox are playing tonight."

"I'll be here," I said.

"Maybe I'll pick up a six-pack on the way home."

After that I wallowed for a few days. Part of me kept thinking the easiest thing to do would be to just come out to everyone, prove myself to Noel, and win him back. Part of me thought he'd given me an easy out and now I could go back to my life of dating girls and being totally straight. I knew that last bit wasn't possible or true, but in my darkest moments, I thought it could be, or at least wished it could. My life would have been so much easier if I could forget about Noel and be straight.

I wanted to write a letter to every bigot who had ever argued being gay was a choice, that the "homosexual lifestyle" was something one could take on or give up like vegetarianism or knitting. If it were that easy, I wouldn't have been hurting so much. Because I hurt. I ached. I made a mistake—being with Noel in the first place or letting him go, it wasn't clear to me, but probably both—and I'd acted like a weak coward, and there was not a soul I could talk to about it. All I could really do was sit in my room and play mopey music really loudly and think about how my heart was crushed.

I missed Noel with a fierceness, and in my less lucid moments, I saw or heard something I thought he'd appreciate and got out my phone to text him and usually remembered just before I hit Send that he had dumped me and we couldn't talk anymore. I did text *I miss u* late one night when I was a little drunk on the cheap beer I'd imbibed with Joe while we watched the Sox play the Yankees, but I never got a response, so I assumed we were well and truly over.

Joe, at least, was less hostile. We mostly cohabited and talked about sports, which had been the framework of our relationship for three years, but there was no depth anymore. I kept my distance, unwilling to talk about anything personal, and Joe didn't push but kept shooting me these looks like he wasn't quite sure what to do with me.

But he finally had it with me as he packed for his sister's wedding toward the end of August. Our relationship was strained, obviously, but we'd been civil to each other for the past week or so. He gave me space and didn't say anything angry or negative. I mostly kept to my room and didn't say anything at all. Even when I watched TV in the living room, he let me be.

I was on the couch, eating a box of cookies to ease my pain, as he carried all the crap he needed to the door. There was a huge suitcase, a cardboard box full of who knew what, and a garment bag already stacked by the door, and then he went to his room and emerged with a duffel bag. He paused in the living room and said, "Picked the speech." Then he dumped the duffel next to the door.

"Oh? Which option did you settle on?" I'd picked five movie speeches for Joe to recite at the wedding and gave them to him weeks before. That had been before we stopped talking, before the big fight. It felt like it had been years ago. I'd chosen five because I couldn't narrow it down. They varied from the obvious (*Jerry Maguire*) to the less traditional (*When Harry Met Sally*) to the British (*Love Actually*). I'd also thrown into the mix Mr. Darcy's speech to Elizabeth in *Pride and Prejudice*: "You must allow me to tell you how ardently I admire and love you." That one I included for Noel. I'd rented the miniseries adaptation with Colin Firth the day after Noel had told me it was his favorite book.

"I went with Preston's speech from *Can't Hardly Wait*."

"That's a good one." I could recite that scene from memory. Preston, the sweet protagonist of the movie, is practicing what he'll say to his longtime crush, Amanda, when he finally gets to talk to her, and he says, "Maybe we can find out if there's a reason for all of this… maybe we can find out what that reason is… I think I'm ready to do this. Finally."

God, what was the reason?

It's a nice moment in the context of the movie, although because it's also a teen comedy from the late '90s, it turns out Preston is giving this speech to a couple of stoners who aren't even really paying attention. When Preston does actually talk to Amanda later in the movie, he fucks it up.

That felt about right.

Still, I'd always liked the moment: the hopeful expression on Preston's face, the idealism of the speech, the open question of what Fate intended by throwing people together, and the urgency of this being his last chance to make it right because he can't sit around waiting for something to happen anymore.

Joe dropped his arms and sighed somewhat dramatically. He plopped down next to me on the couch. "I know you don't want to talk about it, but I give up. You've been sad for over a week without any explanation, and I can't take it anymore. I wanted to give you space, but I have to know. We used to talk to each other. What the hell is going on with you?"

"Joe, I—"

"Or don't tell me, just like you haven't told me anything all fucking summer, but just… talk to me, Dave. Just tell me about whatever it is that's happening with you. Or tell me something."

"I… can't."

"But why? Did someone die? Did your dad say something stupid? Did you fail your summer class? Did you get fired? What is it?"

"If I tell you, you'll hate me."

I thought maybe he got it then. He leaned back and opened his mouth, but then he closed it again abruptly. I thought maybe he intended to protest, but instead he shook his head and said, "I won't. I promise. Whatever it is, Dave, and I mean that. Just tell me. I won't hate you. God, you're my best friend. How could I hate you?"

I lost it. I lost my last grip on all the shit I'd been trying to hold inside. I missed Noel, I hated myself for lying and being so goddamned weak and cowardly, and I was terrified my big secret would destroy everything I'd known to that point. I began to cry, which shouldn't have been possible given how much crying I'd done behind closed doors since Noel had broken up with me, but apparently there were still tears left, because I hunched over and bawled. Being ashamed for crying in front of Joe just made me cry harder.

Joe reached over and patted my back. "Come on, buddy. You can tell me."

"If not me, then you'll hate Noel," I said, my voice watery. "I know you kind of already do."

"I don't. Unless he hurt you, in which case—"

"I deserved it."

He balked. "What makes you say that?"

And because he was about to go away for two weeks, which would give me enough time to find another apartment or dorm room or something while he was gone, just in case he ended our friendship, I told the truth. "He dumped me. We've been dating since June, okay, and yeah, I fucked him, just like you said, but I wouldn't come out of the closet, so he dumped me, okay? I'm a fag, Joe, a big flaming fag, and my boyfriend, whom I had fallen in love with, dumped my ass for good reasons, and I haven't been able to tell anyone, and it's the worst." The words all whooshed out of me in one breath before I hiccoughed hard and went back to crying. I was mortified to be losing my shit this way, but I couldn't keep it together anymore.

I braced myself for him to either hit me or storm out. Not that he'd ever hit me before, but somehow I imagined him doing it. Maybe I'd seen some latent aggression in Joe when he'd cheered for his sports teams, or maybe I just assumed anyone who found out I was queer would want to hit me, but for weeks I'd been imagining Joe finding out and putting his fist through my face.

But he didn't. He just sat there with his hands in his lap and nodded. "So let's back up for a minute. You and Noel. Only since June?"

"I kissed him during Spring Fest. We didn't really start dating until a few weeks after that, though."

Joe nodded again. His face was completely neutral. It was unnerving. My heart thudded like it might beat out of my chest, I'd broken out in a cold sweat everywhere, and Joe just sat there placidly. "And you've been dating all summer. So all those nights you stayed out, you were with him."

"Yeah."

"So... you're gay."

"I don't know. Maybe. Or bi. Or queer. Or something. All I know is I'm not straight and I fell in love with a guy."

"How long have you known? About the, ah, not being straight thing?"

"My whole life, probably," I said on a resigned sigh. "But actually, really? Pretty much only since I met Noel. Like, I knew, but I didn't *know*. I didn't understand until I met him. That sounds so stupid, but I guess I'd been trying to shove it down for a long time. But Noel didn't, like, turn me gay. I didn't realize it until recently, but I've felt this way my whole life. I just pushed it away."

Joe's face still betrayed nothing. "So Noel just... brought it out in you."

"Yeah. I guess. And this book I read made me realize... but that's not really important." I wiped my eyes. Whatever catharsis I might have been hoping for turned acidic. I didn't feel any better for having told Joe finally, and he just sat there impassively, not doing anything, which left me to wonder what would happen next. I hated the mystery. My mind kept imagining the worst-case scenario. Losing Noel was one thing. Losing Joe, getting kicked out of my apartment? I didn't think I could face that. "He dumped me because I wouldn't come out of the closet. Well, and some other things, but that was the main thing. He said being with me pulled him back into a place he didn't want to go. Which is fair, because he's been through so much and he's so brave and he deserves so much better than what I offered him. So. That's what happened."

He nodded. He tilted his head a few times as if he were thinking something over. "I kinda knew already. About the gay thing, I mean, not about Noel dumping you, but I will go kick his ass if you want me to."

I laughed softly, and it was snotty and wet through all my crying. "I don't, but thank you."

Finally he turned to me and raised his eyebrows. Whether his expression was judgmental or compassionate, I couldn't have said. "Why didn't you tell me?" he said.

I balked. "Are you fucking kidding me? You've been such an asshole about Noel from the beginning. I'm still not convinced you're not about to throw me out of this apartment. You called me a fag. How the fuck could I tell you?"

He looked surprised. "What?"

"Oh, please. You've been a dick to me since Noel showed up in my life. Don't play ignorant. I know you were mad. You've been saying all this homophobic shit about me turning into a fag and you've been weird around Noel all summer."

An epiphanic expression passed over his face. It was like a lightbulb had just flashed on. "Wait, you think I was mad because you're gay? Or whatever?"

"Aren't you?"

"No. I don't give a shit if you're gay or bi or into elephants. Whatever floats your boat, man."

"But—"

"I mean, it's weird. Don't get me wrong, it's weird. When I first guessed something was going on with you and Noel, it kind of freaked me out."

"Oh."

"But mostly because this thing I thought I knew about you wasn't what I thought. You know what I mean? I mean, we talked about girls all the time, but now suddenly you're not into girls anymore? And you're spending all your time with this guy who is so totally different from everyone we know? I had no idea what was going on."

"That's not... I mean, yeah, but.... It's not that I'm not into girls anymore—"

"I mean, no offense, but it is wicked strange to think about you with Noel. Just really fucking weird." His Southie accent seemed particularly pronounced. *Really fuckin' wee-ahd.*

"I—"

He held up his hand. "But really I was mad because you weren't talking to me. I could tell something was going on in your life, but you never said anything to me about it. And you were spending all this time with Noel, and I thought... I mean, it's fucking stupid, I see that, but I thought he was taking you away from me."

"What?" That didn't make any sense.

"You and me have been best friends for almost the entire time we've been in college. And then suddenly we weren't anymore. You were spending all this time around this other guy, and I kind of knew that something was going on between you because you have the worst poker face, dude. But every time I asked, you said it was nothing, and I thought you stopped trusting me or stopped thinking of me as a friend or whatever the fuck. You were lying to me and I knew it, but I couldn't get you to say anything. And then you were spending all this time with him and not with me, and it felt like I was losing you as a friend."

"Wait, you were mad because I didn't tell you about Noel?"

"Yeah. He was important to you, obviously, or you wouldn't be losing your shit this hard now he's dumped you. But you didn't breathe a word about it to me. You lied to me. Repeatedly. What was I supposed to think?"

It was strange to hear my own thoughts echoed back at me. "He wasn't taking me away. I was still your friend, but you... you were so...." It was taking me a long time to wrap my head around what he was saying. "You were so angry. And you called me a fag! What was I supposed to think?"

"I'm sorry for that. I was mad. I shouldn't have said it."

"You're not mad I'm... queer?"

"No. Not really. Like I said, it's weird, but I'll adjust. I was mad because you wouldn't talk to me."

"So you won't kick me out of the apartment?"

"What? No. No, of course not. But Christ, Dave, don't keep things like that a goddamned secret. I said some boneheaded things, I'm sure, but I didn't really mean them. You want to fuck all the dudes at WMU, be my guest. You want to be with Noel, go for it. But tell me when you do things like that. How can we be friends if you won't talk to me?"

And there went the waterworks again. I couldn't hold it back. A weight had been lifted. "I'm sorry. But you said all these things... and I thought that...."

He shrugged. "You're my friend. That doesn't change if you're... queer. I'm sorry for whatever I said that offended you. Okay? And I'm still your friend."

The conflict felt so stupid now that it was all out in the open. I was relieved, though, and happy to have my best friend back. "I'm sorry for lying. And for not talking to you. I should have... I should have known better. I'm so sorry, Joe."

"Apology accepted. Should we, uh, hug it out?"

I stood up. I wiped my eyes, still embarrassed I'd cried in front of Joe. But it was all out there now. "I won't lie like that again." Because I could see now my lies had caused all of this.

"I understand why you didn't tell me, and I'm ashamed of myself if I made you think you couldn't. But you also know me better than that. I would never—"

"No. I know."

He stood. "I'll be more careful about what I say in the future, okay?"

He reached for me, so I let him fold me into a big bear hug. He patted me on the back a few times. It was weird but not unpleasant.

"All right, then. I gotta go. Vanessa's waiting for me in the parking lot. But just… call me if you need to while I'm gone. Or text. Anytime. Okay?"

"Yeah. I will. Thanks, Joe."

He walked over to his luggage and started to pick it up. "Uh. Is it gonna piss you off if I tell Vanessa?"

"She kind of already knows. Not about the breakup but about the queer thing."

"You told her?"

"She guessed."

Joe smiled faintly. "Worst poker face ever, dude."

CHAPTER 20

I'D ALWAYS really liked teen movies. I couldn't have said why. I had no real desire to relive high school, which for me had been a pressure cooker of hormones and feeling inferior. Perhaps there was something appealing to me about those idealized narratives where everything worked out in the end, even for the outcast kids. Maybe it was the idea that when you were seventeen, you still had your whole life ahead of you and you didn't have adult responsibilities to deal with.

I watched a lot of them while Joe was out of town and I was pretty much alone. I went to work, and then I'd come home and marathon John Hughes's whole catalog. *Pretty in Pink* was my personal favorite, or I'd watch the classics from the late '90s—*Clueless, 10 Things I Hate About You, Can't Hardly Wait, Bring It On*—or some of the more recent ones. I mainlined movie musicals next, and sang along badly to *My Fair Lady* or *Les Mis* or *Cabaret*. I wondered if the queer part of me was the part who had always loved musicals or if that was stereotypical. Hell, I loved movies, period; that was why I'd become a film studies major. Of course, the ones I really loved were too frothy and pedestrian for most of my professors, who made us watch Fellini films with subtitles or drowsy independent dramas or sometimes Scorsese or Coppola if we got lucky. I couldn't imagine any of my professors showing *Sixteen Candles* or *Chicago*.

I had a substantial collection of movies in a number of different formats, and I watched all of my favorites during the first week alone. They comforted me, in a way; they were familiar, for one thing, but also expressed the hope that love would win the day.

My mom came for her visit the weekend after Joe left. She brought with her a handful of additional movies I'd left behind—"We never watch them and I thought you might want them," she said, and she wasn't wrong—and also a lamp the dim living room clearly needed, some extra bedsheets, and a box full of kitchen gadgets and other miscellany she thought I could use, as if I didn't mostly live off leftovers from the restaurant. Then, at her insistence, we ate an early dinner at

Hale's, where she got a little judgy about how the restaurant was run—she'd been working in the restaurant industry for thirty years and had Opinions—before she drove me to the grocery store and helped me stock up on food that wasn't junk. She helped me carry everything back to my apartment, and as we were putting the last of my groceries away, she said, "Is everything okay, Dave?"

I had been waiting for her to ask all day. I'd tried to put on a happy face, though I was still missing Noel and just feeling down generally. But if my poker face was as bad as Joe said, my mother had seen right through all of it.

I shrugged.

"You've seemed kind of sad all day," Mom said. She reached over and adjusted the collar on my polo shirt. "I just want to be sure everything's okay."

Her face was so open. She wanted me to talk with her honestly. I thought of hundreds of nights when I'd been a little boy and she'd opened her arms and let me curl up next to her on the sofa. I'd lean against her soft body and fall asleep. I remembered her patching up my scraped knees and helping me get splinters out of my fingers. I could see her in the stands at my track meets or hugging me after a good report card. I felt safe with her and loved. I didn't want to jeopardize that.

On the other hand, if I had any hope of ever being with Noel again, I had to be honest with my mother.

"No, everything's not all right," I said.

"Oh, sweetheart. Come on. Tell me."

She led me over to the couch, and we sat down next to each other.

"I broke up with someone," I said when she put her hand on my knee. "About two weeks ago."

"Oh, baby. I'm so sorry. I didn't even know you were dating anyone."

"I know. I didn't want to tell you. But I'm still really upset about it, so I guess I'm telling you now."

She frowned and rubbed my knee. "Why didn't you want to tell me?"

I took a deep breath. Here went nothing. "Remember when you helped me and Joe move into this place? And we went out to dinner and I got a text from my friend Noel and you thought I'd gotten a text from a girl?"

"Yes," she said. "Your face lit up so much, I was surprised it was just a friend. Unless you lied and it was a girl."

I closed my eyes. I couldn't face her, suddenly. "No, it was Noel. He wasn't just a friend, though. Mom, Noel was my boyfriend."

She sucked in a breath quickly and took her hand away. "Dave. What are you telling me?"

I opened my eyes but focused on the blank TV instead of looking at her. "I'm not straight. I'm bi, I think. I don't really know yet, but I'm not… not heterosexual. I met a guy named Noel and we started dating at the end of last semester, and we've been spending time together all summer. I fell in love with him, or I think I have, or else this wouldn't hurt so much, right? Because he broke up with me almost two weeks ago, and it feels like the worst thing that's ever happened." I took a deep breath. "Unless you and Dad are going to disown me. Then that would be the worst."

"Oh, sweetie. Oh, Dave, no. We would never—no." She reached for me then and put her arms around me and hugged me tightly. "I still love you, no matter what. Okay? I love you. You're my baby boy, David, and I will love you with my whole heart for all of my life. You understand that? It doesn't matter who you love. Okay?"

"Okay," I said, tears stinging my eyes. "Noel's family disowned him. They found out he's gay and told him not to come home and cut him off financially. His family wants nothing to do with him and he's alone now. I guess I worried…."

My mother stroked my hair. "How terrible for him! But, no. You know we have no problem with gay people. Stephen and Tom were around all the time when you were a kid, remember? We had dinner with Lisa and Susan once a month."

"I know. I guess I just worried… I don't know. It's different when it's your kid, isn't it? I was so afraid. Of what people would think, of what I was feeling. And so confused about… everything. It was like everything was upside-down."

"I don't want you to be afraid of us. We're your parents and we love you."

"Thank you."

She grabbed a stray napkin off the coffee table and used it to wipe the tears off my face. "Now. This breakup. What happened, exactly? Talk to me, Dave."

I took a deep breath. I hadn't realized how much I needed this, needed Mom, until this moment. She loved me no matter what. I loved her too, and I'd missed her when I kept quiet about Noel. In that moment, I realized by keeping my secret, I was hurting myself and the people around me more, that I was putting all this distance between us. My actions hurt not just Noel but me and everyone in my life, and I'd been isolating myself to keep my own secrets. It was counterintuitive in a way—I'd convinced myself keeping this secret was the only way to keep my life together, but the opposite proved true.

So I talked to my mother. "He was upset because I wouldn't tell anyone about us. And he was right, I was a total chicken about it. Joe said all these things I interpreted the wrong way, or, I don't know. I thought he would hate me. I thought everyone would hate me. I didn't feel ready to come out, or whatever. So I lied and kept it a secret, and I hurt Noel in the process. So he broke up with me."

She reached for me and pulled me into her arms again. She hadn't held me this way in a long time. It reminded me of being a little boy, but I didn't mind it. She said, "If you weren't ready, he should have given you time."

"Yeah, but he... he's been through so much. And he's so honest with everyone. I should've been honest for him, but instead I lied to everyone."

"Oh, sweetheart. You're telling the truth now, though. That's important."

"I know, but... I just miss him so much."

She held me a few moments longer and then sat up and smoothed down my hair again. "I know you miss him. It will get better with time. Maybe he wasn't the right guy for you."

"Or maybe he was and I blew it. He's so great, Mom. I wish you could meet him."

"Maybe I will someday. You're telling the truth now, right? Keep telling the truth and see where it gets you. Maybe it'll get you back together with Noel, or maybe it will get you to the person you're supposed to be with, whoever he or she is. Okay?"

"Yeah. Okay. Thanks, Mom."

"Certainly." She leaned down and picked my Sox hat up from where it had fallen onto the floor. She put it back on my head. "You really dated a guy all summer, and he never once made you wash this cap?"

"I think he kind of likes the cap."

She shook her head. "Boys."

CHAPTER 21

JOE CAME back a few days before the new semester started. I'd watched my fill of sappy movies by then and felt a little better about everything. On their arrival back in Western Mass, Joe and Vanessa took me out to dinner to regale me with tales of Joe's sister's wedding and to tell me about eight hundred times how okay they were with my new status as a queer man.

"I told you so," Vanessa said as we walked back to Joe's car after dinner. "Feels good to come out, doesn't it?"

"You don't have to rub it in," I said. "But thanks for, I don't know. Cheering from the sidelines. Being a little pushy even when I told you not to be."

"Anytime. I'm your friend, too, you know. Even if that lunkhead and I ever break up, I'm here for you, okay?"

"Yeah. You're the best, Van."

"I am, aren't I?" She grinned and gave me a soft punch to the arm.

A few nights before classes started, Joe and I went to the Terminal, a bar just off campus that served the most amazing hot wings I'd ever eaten. The crowd was thin since the majority of students hadn't moved back yet and there wasn't any particular sporting event on. The TVs all showed *SportsCenter*.

Joe and I seemed to be repairing our friendship, which I felt good about. I really had missed him a great deal, especially when we'd been living in the same apartment but not speaking to each other. It felt now like we weren't so much just putting up with each other as we were actually building something between us again.

"WMU football picked up this amazing running back this season, I heard," Joe said, munching on a celery stick. "Some kid out of Texas who has reflexes like a cat."

"We'll have to go to football games next semester," I said. "And not just because Vanessa's in the marching band."

Joe smiled. We were generally optimistic, but most of the WMU star players had graduated the previous semester. The athletic department had made noise about changing up the coaching staff, or so Mike told me. He worked as an office assistant in the athletic department, which, from what I could tell, mostly involved sitting at a desk and talking to people who came in and out of the office. He was therefore a great source of WMU athletics gossip.

Still, it surprised me we'd managed to snare a player who'd already gotten so much press attention. One of our recent alumni was on the Giants (boo, hiss!) and another was currently warming the bench for the Patriots, so I knew some of our players went on to the pros. Most just parlayed their athletic scholarship into a degree, from what I could tell.

But more to the point, WMU boasted one of the best marching bands in the northeast, so the games sold out regularly because even when the football team wasn't doing well, everyone wanted to see the band. "Everyone" had included me and Joe the previous year because Vanessa played the trumpet. You couldn't really see her in the formations on the field, but Joe kept saying things like, "She's the third one from the right," as if either of us could tell any of the musicians apart in their boxy uniforms.

At the Terminal, I spent a moment trying to choose between the honey barbecue and the hot wings before me—we'd ordered the latter "wicked hot," as the spiciness gradations went on the menu—and Joe mostly looked at the TV, where the reporters were making predictions about a few different NCAA sports.

Then Joe said, "I guess you want to go to football games for different reasons now, huh?"

I didn't like where this was going. "What reasons would those be, Joe?" I settled on a wicked hot wing. As I bit into it, spice exploded in my mouth. They were buffalo style with an extra cayenne pepper kick, if my guess was right. Super tasty, but it helped to have a cold beer close by. Handily, the bartender on duty that night knew me from track and didn't card me.

"Well, I mean," Joe said, "now that you're gay, you probably want to, like, check out football players, right?"

Oh boy. "First of all, nothing changed when I came out of the closet to you. I'm still Dave. I like football because I like the game. Hot players are a perk, I guess, but that's not why I'd go to a game with you. And I'm not gay *now*, I told you."

"Right, right. Bi or queer or whatever."

I sighed.

"So all those times we watched sports on TV," Joe said, "you've been checking out the guys playing? This whole time?"

"No. Well, maybe a little. I don't know. I'm usually thinking about the game and how the team will win or how badly we're losing or how great that play was. I don't think much about how hot the players are."

"Do you think about me?"

I pursed my lips, not wanting to answer that, not out of embarrassment but because Joe was pissing me off. I knew he was trying to understand, but he seriously could not have gone about it in a worse way.

"No, Joe. Not that way. We're like brothers, right?" I took another bite of my chicken wing. "Besides, you're not my type."

He balked. "Not your type? You think I'm not hot?"

I shrugged. "I think you're my friend, Joe."

He frowned. "Well, Vanessa thinks I'm hot."

"And that's what matters." I selected another wing, a honey barbecue one this time. "Seriously, Joe, nothing has changed, not really. I'm the same person I've been the whole time you've known me. You just have a new piece of information about me now." I didn't feel as light as I thought my voice sounded. Inside I was still a mess. Joe didn't quite understand or accept what had happened. I still missed Noel to the depths of my soul. I dreaded the new semester and whatever nonsense it would bring my way, both academic and otherwise.

"So what is your type?" Joe asked. "Like, just out of curiosity."

"Noel," I said without thinking.

"Really? But he's so...."

"Don't even say it. He's great. Do you honestly want to know what I think?" I tossed the wing remnants in the bowl on the table reserved for bones and wiped my hands on a napkin. "He's hot, okay? Gorgeous, sexy, amazing. He's been through so much, but he's still strong and confident. Proud. He has a sense of humor, but he knows when to be serious. He's so great, Joe, so great, and I miss him a lot, okay? That's what I think. And I want you to stop, I don't know, trying to figure out what I see in him, because it doesn't matter. It just matters that I see it. Okay?"

He held his hands up. "Geez, yeah. I'm sorry."

Someone at the next table shot me a weird look. I hadn't intended to get that personal, especially not in public, but I felt strung out and frustrated.

"I didn't mean to get shouty," I said. "These have not been the best three weeks of my life."

He nodded. "It sucks, dude. I mean, that Noel broke up with you."

I laughed despite myself. I appreciated that Joe could distill it all into a few words. "It does suck."

"I think you need more wings. You want to try the maple ones?"

WE INVITED Kareem over to watch the Sox game the night after classes started. I had hoped this would bring some semblance of normalcy back into our lives rather than Joe tiptoeing around me. Since Joe had come back from his sister's wedding, he and I hung out more than we had all summer, and our relationship was mostly good, but things were still a little strange. He was never careless with nudity the way he had been when we'd lived in the same room, careful to wear pajamas or his robe instead of just his underwear around the place. He was always asking me if I was okay. He swore he was fine anytime I pointed out he was being weird. I thought Kareem, who always had a way of leveling with people and cutting through the bullshit, would at least make my life feel like it had before this crazy summer. Not that I wished to undo anything that had happened, exactly, just that a part of me yearned for how casual and easy everything had been before I'd met Noel.

Of course, I'd probably have to come out to Kareem, which I dreaded doing. He was an easygoing guy, but he came from a super religious family; his mother was a devout Muslim. I had no idea how he felt about gay people.

But he came over and we caught up on what he'd done in his time away from Western Massachusetts. Mostly he'd worked at the mechanic's shop his brother owned in Fall River. His vacation to Cape Cod with Bev had apparently been a disaster, and he didn't think they'd be together much longer, though they hadn't officially broken up yet.

Around the seventh inning, Kareem said, "So what did you guys do all summer? Besides sit on this couch watching baseball."

"We did do a lot of that," Joe said. "And Van and I went to a bunch of weddings. Dave had an interesting summer, though."

"Really? You hook up with a hot townie?"

"Not quite," I said, half wanting to kill Joe, half wanting to hug him for giving me this nudge. "Kareem, there's probably something you should know."

Kareem looked me over. "Okay."

This would never get easier, would it? "I, uh, I did date someone. A guy."

"Really?" said Kareem, drawing the word out slowly, as if he were intrigued.

"Uh, surprise," I said.

"That Noel guy, right?" said Kareem.

I had to laugh. "Did someone just write 'This guy is queer' on my forehead? How did you know?"

"Just a guess," said Kareem with a shrug. "So you and Noel, huh? That's... interesting."

"Not anymore. He dumped me three weeks ago."

"Lame." Kareem shifted on the sofa so he could look at me more directly. "So now that you've had your gay experience, are you going back to women or what?"

"Gay experience?"

"I don't know. Women do it, right? Like, that's what college is for. Experimentation with lesbianism, right? Dudes could be the same. I don't want to fuck a dude, but hey, whatever rocks your cock. You definitely want to get that out of your system now and not when you're forty, because yeesh." Kareem grimaced dramatically.

"No, I'm not... it's not a phase or an experiment or whatever, Kareem. I'm queer. I'm... this is my coming out moment."

Kareem laughed. "No, stop it. Really? I just thought you met a gay guy and wanted to see what it was like. You're not... I mean, you still like women, right?"

"Yeah. I like guys too. That's what I'm trying to tell you. It's not just Noel and this summer, it's my whole life going forward. Not a phase, Kareem. Just me being honest finally."

He stared at me for a long time without saying anything. The longer he went without speaking, the more I worried about what his reaction would be. My stomach churned. All this stress was going to give me an ulcer.

Eventually he shrugged and said, "A'ight."

When he didn't say anything more and then commented on the game, I got frustrated. "Wait, 'a'ight'? That's all you have to say?"

"It sounds stupid when *you* say it, but yeah. Like I said, whatever rocks your cock. You want to fuck dudes, I don't have a problem with it."

"Oh."

Not all of my coming out moments went so smoothly. Mike treated me like I was a leper for a few weeks. Andy started avoiding me. I still had wiggy moments on campus when I assumed everyone was staring at me. But in the end, everyone whose opinion I really cared about was supportive, and that was what mattered.

I didn't exactly announce it to everyone, just people I thought needed to know, but I vowed I'd be honest about my sexuality from then on. No more lying. I promised myself that if someone asked, I'd tell them the truth.

Otherwise, my senior year of college began about as I expected it to. Joe took me out for my first legal drink on my twenty-first birthday in mid-September; it was a little anticlimactic. I freaked out about how much harder my classes were than I'd been expecting. Joe and I watched a lot of baseball while studying together.

Through all of it, I missed Noel. At night, when I was in bed alone, missing him was a palpable ache. I wanted to be able to reach for him, to touch him, to hug him, even to just see him. I'd gotten so used to seeing him regularly that not being able to was like missing a part of my body. Our paths apparently were not destined to cross this semester, because I never ran into him on campus.

Until, that was, one night when I was studying in the Mac. I saw movement out of the corner of my eye and looked up in time to see Noel walk in, dressed like the sexiest farmer I'd ever seen, in a red-and-blue plaid shirt and a surprisingly well-tailored pair of overalls. I knew from flyers I'd seen around campus that the Theater Club was doing *Oklahoma!* that semester and not *Hair*, so I supposed he was dressed in character.

I couldn't *not* stare at him. He was still so beautiful and I still wanted him. I wanted to tell him I'd come out, that I'd learned so much since he'd broken up with me, and I'd hoped it would be enough for him to consider taking me back, but I didn't know how he'd react. Maybe I'd caused too much damage.

I tried to flag him down. He made eye contact with me and I raised my hand. But a brief, pained look flashed across his face, and then he turned away and walked to the counter.

I left everything at the table—my books, my cell phone, some loose change, everything. I crossed the room to the counter and walked right up to him.

"Hi," I said.

I needed him to know all the work I'd done, the promises I'd made. I needed him to know about Joe and my mom and how I was going to be okay, with or without him. I needed him to know if he didn't take me back, there were other men out there that could capture my attention, but he was still the one I really wanted. I wanted him to know I could be good for him. I wanted him to know I loved him.

But he said, "I can't talk to you, Dave."

"But I need to tell you something."

"I just… I can't. I have to grab these cookies and get back to rehearsal."

"But I—"

"No. I'm sorry."

A couple of students were hovering over my table. I began to worry for my possessions. "Well," I said. "You look great. Even dressed as a farmer."

"You look… well. You look good too. But I really have to—"

"Order for Noel!" the counter guy called out.

"I understand," I said. "I'll be right back. I have something to tell you. Please don't go anywhere."

But by the time I got back to my table to rescue my stuff from curious onlookers, he was gone.

CHAPTER 22

My INSPIRATION came during Student Activity Week, when all of the on-campus clubs and organizations had tables in the Mac and tried to recruit new members. I'd walked by the Queer Student Union's rainbow-flag-bedecked table, and suddenly I had an idea.

Of course, I couldn't just make myself stop and talk to them. I'd slowed down near their table and then saw all of the other students crammed into the Mac and started to panic. I kept walking. I chastised myself on the way out of the building for not being as over myself as I thought I was, but still, a seed had been planted.

That night I found the pamphlet Fred had given me with information about the QSU. It had been awkwardly folded and stuffed into the spiral notebook I'd used to take notes in my English classes the previous semester. I assumed the meeting times on the pamphlet were out of date, but there was a URL on the front. The website had their meeting schedule for the new semester posted, thankfully.

I didn't know if I would run into Noel there. It could be he still didn't go to many meetings, even though they had a new president, according to the website. I figured if he did go, I'd be able to talk to him frankly. If he didn't, though, I still could get some support. I loved my friends, but it was becoming increasingly clear that even though I was out now, they still didn't really understand what I was going through. They didn't get how hard it was to come to terms with this part of me, how hard it was some days to just be open and honest and not shut down and retreat back into myself. Some days were fine, but some were still a great struggle, and I didn't have anyone I could relate to who understood that.

I went to a meeting the first week of October. It was held in a classroom in Dickenson Hall, down the hall from the Women's Studies Department's offices, and someone had moved the desks around so they formed a circle. A guy with a bleach-blond faux-hawk and onyx stud earrings in both ears greeted me at the door and gave me a look like I had walked into the wrong meeting. I touched my Sox cap self-consciously.

"Uh, this is the Queer Student Union?" he said in a nasally voice.

"I know," I said. "I'm a queer student. Can I join the union?"

He looked so deeply skeptical of me, I worried he would start shouting, "Narc!" but he just stepped out of the way and gestured toward the circle of desks.

If nothing else, I was a poster child for there being more than one way to be gay. Maybe I liked sports and didn't get fashion and wore my Red Sox cap every day because I needed it like some kids needed a ratty blue security blanket, and maybe some of these kids had piercings and tattoos or unblemished, unmarked skin, but we were all the same in a way, even the guy wearing a skirt, even the girl with her head shaved, even the—okay, yes—smoking-hot blond guy in a tight T-shirt and jeans. We all had something in common. We were united in our difference.

Noel wasn't there, but it almost didn't matter, because I wanted to get to know these kids, to figure out how we could relate to each other, how I fit in to the campus social hierarchy now that I wasn't pretending to be something I wasn't. I took a seat at the desk next to the hot blond and smiled at him. He smiled back and winked at me. My heart fluttered, but I made myself focus on everyone else. The girl on my other side was pretty, with long brown hair held back from her face with a headband, wearing a polka-dot dress. She shook my hand and introduced herself as Lila.

"You're new. Are you a freshman?" she asked.

"Senior," I said, "but I've never, uh, well. Didn't have the guts to come to one of these meetings before, really. But this semester, I want to change all that."

She smiled. "Welcome!"

I caught movement by the door in my peripheral vision, and I looked up.

Noel.

He was still so beautiful to me, in his crisp clothes, with his hair just so. There was an ache in my chest as I gazed at him. I still wanted him. I still loved him.

He saw me and glanced at me warily as he shook hands with the faux-hawk guy at the door. When that guy gestured for Noel to take a seat, he sat on the other side of the room from me and kept shooting me inscrutable looks.

Lila stood then and walked to the middle of the circle. "Let's get started," she said. The faux-hawk guy left his post at the door and joined the circle. Lila grinned. "I'm Lila. I'm the president of the QSU this semester. That's Seth, our vice president." She pointed to the faux-hawk guy, who waved. She introduced the other two officers, who were already seated in the circle. Then she clapped her hands. "We've got a lot to do this semester and a lot to get to in this meeting. I want to focus on planning for the Rainbow Ball in December. But first, I see a lot of new people here, and I thought it would be good to go around the circle and let the new people introduce themselves and say why they came here today."

A short kid who looked like he hadn't made it all the way through puberty yet was the first to speak. He introduced himself as Chris and said he was a freshman theater major who wanted to find other gay kids, since he'd been the only one at his high school. The next new person was a girl named Kelly who told us she'd just started dating a girl for the first time and she wanted help coming out to her parents. Lila agreed to talk to her at the end of the meeting.

And then Lila gestured to me.

"Uh, hi," I said, looking around the room. All eyes were on me: Lila's, Seth's, Noel's, everyone's. "I'm Dave. I'm here because, well...." I looked at Noel, who stared back, his face still unreadable. I took a deep breath. "So basically what happened is I met this really great guy last semester. And then I read Jerry Grossworth's *In the Wind*?" A few people nodded in recognition. "And I figured out a few things about myself that I guess I knew all along but hadn't really acknowledged. So I went out with this guy and it was so great. I... I fell in love with him." Noel jerked in his chair, but I looked away from him because I couldn't have him in my line of sight now. I had to focus on myself for a minute. "So, he dumped me at the end of the summer." There were sympathetic moans around the room. "I mean, he had good reasons. Very good reasons. I completely understand why he did. But I was just... I was devastated, you know? And I was totally in the closet, so I didn't feel like I could talk to anyone about what happened. I especially didn't because I'd been lying and sneaking around and pushing everyone away. I mean, I was in the closet and that was why the relationship fell apart, and that whole situation, the way it ended, well, it just sucked all around. And then I was alone. Totally, completely alone. It was... that was maybe the hardest thing I've ever had to deal with."

The hot blond guy reached over and patted my back gently, which I appreciated, but I had to get back on path.

I said, "Long story short, some people in my life kind of guessed what was going on and called me on my bullshit. Since then, I've started to come out to my friends and family, and that has been so fucking terrifying, but I did it. I'm doing it. My immediate family and my close friends all know now, and it's been weird, but it feels good. I want to... well, I'm here because I want to be honest. No more lying. And except for my ex-boyfriend, I've never really known any other queer people before, and I wanted to meet them."

"That's really great, Dave," Lila said with an enthusiastic smile. There was a brief round of applause. My heart soared for a moment.

Then she moved on to the next new person.

I spent the next forty-five minutes listening to the other members plan the Rainbow Ball, a semiformal dance for LGBT students that they held every winter as counterprogramming to the prom-like dances each residential area on campus had once a semester. I'd been to a couple of those in the past and they had always seemed pretty queer-friendly to me, but then, I'd always had female dates, so I probably hadn't looked too closely. I supposed there was something to be said for events especially made for the LGBT students so they would have somewhere to go to be themselves without worrying about judgment from others. By Lila's calculations, the QSU had a few hundred members—only about twenty of which showed up for any given meeting—and she wanted them all to feel welcome on the WMU campus.

Through all of this, Noel mostly avoided me and didn't make eye contact.

But, fine, I could be friends with these people. I let Lila volunteer me for a few tasks, I learned the hot blond's name was Peter, and I did feel genuinely welcomed by this community. It was nice to just let go of my insecurities and be myself and be accepted.

When the meeting wrapped, I figured I'd just walk back to my car and drive home. I said good-bye to my new friends and then started to walk down the hall.

"Dave!"

I turned and Noel was walking toward me.

"Was all that true?" he asked. "At the beginning of the meeting, what you said. Was that true? You've started coming out?" His face was open, which gave me some hope. He looked at me, his eyes wide with expectation.

"Yeah. Joe knows, and Kareem, and a few of my other friends. And my parents."

"How did... how did that go?"

I didn't know why he was suddenly talking to me. He was breathless, apparently having some trouble taking in air. I was too. Because here he was standing before me, just as gorgeous as ever. His light blond hair fell softly over his forehead, his skin was flushed, his blue eyes seemed to glow. He wore a red-and-white seersucker shirt that was tugged tight over his shoulders and tucked into a pair of well-fitted khakis. I wanted to touch him, but I didn't dare.

"It was okay," I said. "Better than I expected. I understand now why what I was doing was so destructive, how I was pushing everyone away." I let out a breath. "Now, before you tell me you told me so—"

"No, I won't. I get how hard it is, even if you do have accepting parents."

He was speaking to me, leaning toward me, and I knew I had an opportunity. I took a deep breath, intending to tell him everything. I said, "I get it too. I understand now. That's what I wanted to tell you that day I ran into you at the Mac." I paused to see if he'd react to that, but his face gave away nothing. "I wasn't really honest with anyone. Including you. I get why that was poisonous for me and for everyone else. You thought I was just going through a phase, or you felt like I was treating you like a whim, but what I should have told you was that you meant a lot to me and it sucked when you left me. It hurt so much. I should have told you how I felt, but I was afraid." I took a step back and stood up straight. "I'm not afraid anymore." The erratic nature of my pulse belied that, though. "Well, no, that's a lie too. I'm terrified of everything. I'm terrified of the future. I was terrified of coming here today. But I won't let that fear rule me anymore. I want to be totally honest from now on."

He bit his lip. "You said in there... you said you fell in love."

A cold sweat broke out over my whole body. I didn't deserve this man... yet. But I wanted to. I wanted to be worthy of his love. If he would take me back, I vowed right then, I would work to make myself everything he wanted and needed and deserved. Because Noel was so special and he deserved the goddamned moon, but instead he'd gotten shit on most of his life. I knew I couldn't keep the demons of the world at bay, I couldn't make his parents take him back, but I could be there for him in whatever way he needed.

"I did fall in love," I said. "God, Noel, I still love you. And I should have told you that. I should have sucked it up and told everyone the truth and spared us all a lot of pain. Because I was hurt and I know I hurt you, and that just sucks because you don't deserve it. You're so amazing, you deserved much better than what I gave you. And I was a coward, but I won't be anymore."

"So what are you saying?"

I sighed. "Well, for one thing, I want you back in my life."

"Really? Because I kind of thought you and Peter had a vibe."

"He's a troll compared to you."

Noel coughed up a laugh. We both knew that was a filthy lie, but he nodded. "Did you come out for me? So that I'd take you back?"

"No," I said, which was mostly true. "I came out for me. I couldn't keep living the way I was. In some ways this is really hard. Some of my friends are walking around me like I'm surrounded by eggshells. My dad's been kind of wiggy about it. Joe keeps putting his foot in his mouth around me, and I think he's having trouble figuring out how to act now, even though I'm still the same guy I've always been. And, you know, it's scary. All of this is so scary. But it's good too, because I'm not afraid of being discovered anymore. And I'm being honest. And I like it."

"Yeah," he said and nodded.

"Look, I know I'm probably not your ideal guy. I have all these interests you don't share and I can barely dress myself and my mom says my Red Sox cap is starting to smell kind of weird, which I don't think is true. But I really do think if you...." I wasn't sure what to say here, so I trailed off. I wanted something pithy and perfect but couldn't quite figure out the correct thing. Then I thought of Joe and how he'd taken Preston's speech from *Can't Hardly Wait* to his sister's wedding. So I said, "Maybe there's a reason all this happened. I want to find out what that reason is. I wasn't ready for it before, but I'm ready for it now. Ready for this. For you. Finally." I took a deep breath. "But I get it if you don't want to—"

He kissed me. Just lunged forward, grabbed my face, and laid one on me, hot and fast, and how could I resist that? I kissed him back. I kissed him because I loved him, because he should have been with me, because no other person in the world made me feel the way he did or could have made me rethink my life the way I had.

When he pulled back, I said, "I love you. Please give me another chance."

There were tears in his eyes. He nodded. "I love you too," he whispered. "I didn't want to break up, but I had to, and now you—"

"I know." My chest felt like it would burst. He loved me too!

He hugged me tight. I hugged him back. Because I could do that now. I could stand in the middle of a corridor of a classroom building in the early evening, when classes were still going on, and I could hold him, and not even in that straight-dude way with all the back patting, but just hold him because we loved each other.

I couldn't have said how long we stood that way. I didn't care.

EPILOGUE

WE'D ONLY been in the new apartment about three weeks, and I was still getting used to it. It kind of smelled like fresh paint and floor varnish. I was afraid to walk across the threshold lest I scuff the floors with my shoes and ruin how shiny it was.

As I came in from work, I hung my keys on the little hook thing Joe had made for us as a housewarming gift.

Noel walked out of the kitchen. "Oh, good, you're home. There's mail for you."

"Okay."

He handed me a thick envelope. I recognized the handwriting as Joe's clunky script; he'd addressed it to me and Noel.

"You could have opened it," I said.

"I know, but I thought you would want to."

So I did. And, as I suspected, it was an invitation to Joe and Vanessa's wedding, three months hence. It was going to be held at a fancy house in Newport, Rhode Island, but I had known that for months, ever since Joe had asked me to be his best man. Really, the invitation was a formality, but it was nice that he'd invited both me and Noel instead of me and a plus one. Given Noel and I had been together for two years and had just gotten the apartment together in the Dorchester neighborhood of Boston, I guessed we were considered a real couple now.

The apartment was not the most glamorous place—we were in a section of town still considered "up-and-coming," though there was a flourishing gay community in the blocks around our apartment—but it was home and I liked it. Noel had gotten into Boston University for grad school, and the commute was a little bit of a hike, but not terrible. For now I was working as an editorial assistant at a publishing company in Back Bay, but I wasn't loving it the way I expected to. I really hated it, actually. Mostly I did admin work, which I didn't hate, but the constant threat of layoffs hung over us all the time because business wasn't so hot. Probably more school was in my future as I worked out what I'd do next.

"Also," Noel said, "your mom called. She invited us over for dinner Sunday."

"Okay."

He grinned. "We had a nice chat about you. She thinks I'm a good influence on your life."

"She said that?"

He shrugged. "We also talked about clothes. She's thinking about changing the uniforms at the restaurant and asked for my input."

"Oof."

He laughed and put an arm around me. "She said I'm the best-dressed person she knows, so clearly I am a man of refined taste. Thus she's bringing me on as a consultant for the redesign."

"I don't get what's wrong with the polo shirts."

He just made a soft noise. I loved that he got along so well with my parents. My mother had been exceptionally sympathetic about his parents having thrown him out, so she'd gone about trying to become his second mother. I thought she was overbearing, but Noel seemed to eat it up. His own parents had lately been making tentative overtures, but they clearly wanted nothing to do with *me*, and Noel wasn't willing to compromise on that. "We're a couple now," I'd overheard him tell his mother on the phone the week before. "You take us both or you leave us alone."

I leaned on him now. He smelled so fucking good. I couldn't keep myself from inhaling deeply. It didn't escape my notice he was wearing a T-shirt made of exceptionally soft material. It made me want to touch him all over. I put my arms around him and hugged him tight. I leaned my head on his shoulder.

He kissed the top of my head. "So. Dinner with your parents Sunday?"

"Sure." I didn't even care. I just wanted to hold my boyfriend, who was warm and comfortable and home.

He laughed softly, and his laughter vibrated against me. "Hi," he said.

"Hi," I said into his neck.

"Welcome home."

"Yeah."

He put his arms around me more firmly and hugged me back. "The things you ordered came in the mail today too. The new curtains and stuff. The box is in the living room. We could put them up, or... or we could just stand here hugging."

"Mmm."

"I have a guess for which you'd prefer."

It was still new, our living together. I'd gotten a shitty apartment in Allston with Joe after we'd graduated. Joe was doing IT and AV at a fancy hotel, which actually did pay pretty well, but my publishing salary had only been able to pay for half of a crappy apartment, not half of a decent one. We kind of knew it was temporary, anyway; he wanted to move in with Vanessa, and I was just biding time until Noel graduated from WMU.

It had sucked being away from Noel most of that year, to put it mildly. I had wanted to stay in my and Joe's old apartment, but I couldn't get a job in Western Mass. So I'd moved to Boston, where there were a few jobs, anyway, and that put an hour and a half—or more, a lot of the time—of driving between us. We'd still seen each other every other weekend or so; we alternated me driving out there and him taking the bus out to Boston. When Noel graduated, we found this place, and Noel had been thrilled because it was so much nicer than the place he'd been renting in South Hadley.

I was thrilled because it was ours.

"I love you," I said.

"I love you more," he replied, leaning his head on mine. "You hungry? I could make dinner."

"In a minute. Let me just...."

And I held him. I couldn't seem to let go. I didn't want to ever again.

KATE McMURRAY is an award-winning romance author and fan. When she's not writing, she works as a nonfiction editor, dabbles in various crafts, and is maybe a tiny bit obsessed with baseball. She is active in RWA and has served as president of Rainbow Romance Writers and on the board of RWANYC. She lives in Brooklyn, NY.

Website: www.katemcmurray.com
Twitter: @katemcmwriter
Facebook: www.facebook.com/katemcmurraywriter

THE
BOY
NEXT
DOOR

KATE McMURRAY

Life is full of surprises and, with luck, second chances.

After his father's death, Lowell leaves the big city to help his sick mother in the conservative small town where he grew up. He's shocked to find himself living next to none other than his childhood friend Jase. Lowell always had a crush on Jase, and the man has only gotten more attractive with age. Unfortunately Jase is straight, now divorced, and raising his six-year-old daughter. It's nice to reconnect, but Lowell doesn't see a chance for anything beyond friendship.

Until a night out together changes everything.

Jase can't fight his growing feelings for Lowell, and he doesn't want to give up the happy future they could have. But his ex-wife issues an ultimatum: he must keep his homosexuality secret or she'll revoke his custody of their daughter, Layla. Now Jase faces an impossible choice: Lowell and the love he's always wanted, or his daughter.

www.dreamspinnerpress.com

KATE McMURRAY
DEVIN DECEMBER

A freak blizzard strands flight attendant Andy Weston at LaGuardia Airport on Thanksgiving. Tabloid reports about Hollywood It couple Devin Delaney and Cristina Marino breaking up in spectacular fashion keep Andy sane. And then Devin Delaney himself turns up at the gate Andy is working. Against all odds—and because there's nothing else to do—Andy and Devin begin to talk, immediately connect, and, after Devin confesses the real reason he broke up with Cristina, have a magical night together snowed in at the airport. But the magic ends when Devin boards his flight home the next morning, and Andy assumes it's over.

Then Devin turns up on his doorstep. Andy is game for a clandestine affair at first—who could turn down one of the hottest men on the planet? But he soon grows tired of being shoved in Devin's closet. As Christmas approaches, it's clear that this will never work unless Devin is willing to make some big changes. Devin has a holiday surprise in store—but will it be enough?

www.dreamspinnerpress.com

DREAMSPUN DESIRES

THE GREEK TYCOON'S
GREEN CARD GROOM

Kate McMurray

*Marriage gets less
convenient when love
is involved.*

Marriage gets less convenient when love is involved.

It started simple: Ondrej Kovac marries Archie Katsaros so Ondrej can stay in the US, away from his judgmental family in eastern Europe. Archie marries Ondrej in exchange for the money to bail out his failing company. It's a fraud neither man is convinced he can pull off.

But as Archie introduces Ondrej to New York society and Ondrej proves his skill in the office, they start to discover a connection between them. Can they overcome the rocky foundation their relationship was built on, meddling immigration agents, gossip columnists determined to out their deception, and an aggressive executive set on selling Archie's company out from under him? Only if they can prove to each other their love is worth fighting for.

www.dreamspinnerpress.com

KATE McMURRAY

OUT
IN THE
FIELD

Matt Blanco is a legend on the Brooklyn Eagles, but time and injuries have taken their toll. With his career nearing its end, he's almost made it to retirement without anyone learning his biggest secret: he's gay in a profession not particularly known for its tolerance.

Iggy Rodriquez is the hot new rookie in town, landing a position in the starting lineup of the team of his dreams and playing alongside his idol, Matt Blanco. Iggy doesn't think it can get any better, until an unexpected encounter in the locker room with Matt proves him wrong.

A relationship—and everything it could reveal—has never been in the cards for Matt, but Iggy has him rethinking his priorities. They fall hard for each other, struggling to make it through trades, endorsement deals, and the threat of retirement. Ultimately they will be faced with a choice: love or baseball?

www.dreamspinnerpress.com

The
WINDUP

KATE McMURRAY

THE RAINBOW LEAGUE

The Rainbow League: Book One

Ian ran screaming from New York City upon graduating from high school. A job offer too good to turn down has brought him back, but he plans to leave as soon as the job is up. In the meantime he lets an old friend talk him into joining the Rainbow League, New York's LGBT amateur baseball league. Baseball turns out to be a great outlet for his anxiety, and not only because sexy teammate Ty has caught his eye.

Ty is like a duck on a pond—calm and laid-back on the surface, a churning mess underneath. In Ian, he's found someone with whom he feels comfortable enough to share some of what's going on beneath the surface. The only catch is that Ian is dead set on leaving the city as soon as he can. Ty works up a plan to convince Ian that New York is, in fact, the greatest city in the world. But when Ian receives an offer for a job overseas, Ty needs a new plan: convince Ian that home is where Ty is.

www.dreamspinnerpress.com